ALSO BY JOSEPHINE CAMERON

Maybe a Mermaid

A DOG-FRIENDLY town

JOSEPHINE CAMERON

FARRAR STRAUS GIROUX
NEW YORK

Farrar Straus Giroux Books for Young Readers
An imprint of Macmillan Publishing Group, LLC
120 Broadway, New York, NY 10271
Copyright © 2020 by Josephine Cameron

Printed in the United States of America by LSC Communications,
Harrisonburg, Virginia

Designed by Cassie Gonzales
First edition, 2020
1   3   5   7   9   10   8   6   4   2

mackids.com

Library of Congress Cataloging-in-Publication Data

Names: Cameron, Josephine, author.
Title: A dog-friendly town / Josephine Cameron.
Description: First edition. | New York: Farrar Straus Giroux, 2020. |
    Audience: Ages 8–12. | Summary: As his family's dog-friendly
    bed-and-breakfast establishment in dog-friendly Carmelito,
    California, welcomes celebrity dog Sir Bentley, twelve-year-old
    Epic McDade and his younger siblings investigate the
    disappearance of a $500,000 dog collar.
Identifiers: LCCN 2019035876 | ISBN 9780374306441 (hardback)
Subjects: CYAC: Dogs—Fiction. | Brothers and sisters—Fiction. |
    Bed and breakfast accommodations—Fiction. | Mystery and
    detective stories. | California—Fiction.
Classification: LCC PZ7.1.C327 Do 2020 | DDC [Fic]—dc23
LC record available at https://lccn.loc.gov/2019035876

Our books may be purchased for promotional, educational, or business
use. Please contact your local bookseller or the Macmillan Corporate
and Premium Sales Department at (800) 221-7945 ext. 5442 or by email
at MacmillanSpecialMarkets@macmillan.com.

For Joey & Jim, who gave me the brain spark

With Grandma Gwen, Anna, Kathy, Ashley, and Bentley
always in our thoughts —J.C.

THE PROPRIETORS

Elly and Marc McDade (Mom and Dad)

"A DIAMOND IN THE RUFF! CARMELITO, CALIFORNIA'S PREMIERE BED AND BREAKFAST FOR DOGS AND THEIR HUMANS."
—WOOF MAGAZINE

Rondo McDade, age 9, Epic McDade, age 12, Elvis McDade, age 8

THE FRIENDS

Declan and Frank

Miyon and Layne

THE GUESTS

Clive, Nicole, and Pico Boone

ROOM 1

Thomas Scott, Madeleine Devine,
and Sir Bentley

ROOMS 2&3

Asha Dillon

ROOM 4

Delphi Jones, Melissa Dubois, and Morrissey

ROOM 5

A DOG-FRIENDLY town

WEDNESDAY

1:30 A.M.

THE CRIME

Madeleine Devine's scream was loud enough to wake my younger brother, Rondo, and that's saying something. I've tried every trick in the book—flicking his ear, shaking his bunk, dripping cold water on his face—and I've never seen Rondo get out of bed that fast.

For a fourth grader, my brother attracts trouble on a professional level. I'm sure Madeleine's scream triggered his curiosity and sucked him out of bed with the force field of a rare-earth magnet. Which meant I was going to have to do the responsible-older-brother thing and find a way to drag him back. With all five rooms of the Perro del Mar Bed and Breakfast occupied, a celebrity in Room 3, and now one of our guests having a meltdown in the middle of the night, the last thing Mom and Dad needed was Rondo roaming the halls like a magnetized electron on the loose.

I pulled the warm blankets up to my chin and calculated how long I could wait for him to come back on his own.

Maybe he was in the bathroom. I could close my eyes for another ninety seconds at least.

I'd barely let them shut when my sister, Elvis, rolled out of the bottom bunk, padded across the room, and aimed her morning breath straight into my nostrils.

"Epic, are you awake? Is this a dream?"

I kept my eyes closed and wished we *were* stuck in one of my sister's legendary nightmares. But Madeleine was still screaming. And the barking dogs and slamming doors in the guest wing were a dead giveaway that this was real life. Elvis's nightmares are usually set underwater or on some alien planet. Never at home at the Perro del Mar.

"This is exactly like an episode of *Bentley Knows*." She shook my shoulder. "If there's a crime happening right now, I bet Sir Bentley will solve it. Wouldn't that be exciting? We should go downstairs so we can watch. Do you think? Or should we wait? How long does detectiving take? Epic, are you dead?"

My sister was breathing fast and talking nonsense. She was probably still half asleep. I held up two fingers—the Sunny Day Academy signal to take a deep breath and chill out.

"There's no crime, El. Give me a minute," I said. "I'm waiting for Rondo. Thirty more seconds."

I forced my own breath to slow and tried not to focus on worst-case scenarios. A guest screaming in the middle of the night didn't have to mean murder. It could be a spider in one of their beds. Or a stubbed toe. Suddenly, the screams stopped. It sounded like the barking was moving downstairs.

Elvis started with the fast breathing again. "Why are we waiting for Rondo? Where is he? On *Bentley Knows* . . ."

I put my feet on the floor.

"Come on. You've never even seen a full episode of that show." I handed her a pair of sandals, grabbed the pocket flashlight I'd made out of old Christmas lights, and pulled my messenger bag over my shoulder.

We tried Mom and Dad's room first, but no one was there, so we headed for the stairs. Near the front entrance of the Perro del Mar, there's a wide, brightly lit staircase in the lobby. It has a banister Mom made from scratch out of antique iron fence posts, and an upcycled champagne-bottle chandelier hangs overhead. But in the back of the house, the section where none of the guests ever go, the family stairwell is narrow and dark. A dim bulb at the bottom lets off a ghosty glow, and one of the steps has such a bad creak, Elvis won't touch it. Ever.

"Don't step on the Ghost Stair," she whispered, grabbing my hand in a death grip as she stepped over the board that always creaked. Even though her thumb was still soggy and wet from sucking it all night, I managed to hold on and not gag.

"Don't worry, El," I said. "Deep breaths. Everything's going to be okay."

I tried to say it like I knew it was true, and when we got

to the lobby, things *were* strangely calm. I don't know what I expected, but aside from the fact that all the guests were in their pajamas, life at the Perro del Mar seemed almost normal.

The lights were on, and Dad was grinding coffee in the kitchen.

Guests were scattered around the lobby, lounging on the furniture, tapping on their phones. The only one who paid any attention when Elvis and I walked into the room was Pico, the Italian greyhound from Room 1. He was wearing flannel polka-dot pajamas and shivering from nerves or cold. Probably both. Pico locked eyes with me and gave a shiver of relief. Whatever was going on, he obviously thought *I* was going to fix it.

Like I said: normal.

Except that everyone else in Carmelito, California, was asleep, and Mom was on the phone with the police.

"No, I have no idea who stole it," she said. "I don't know anyone who would do such a thing . . . The value?"

Mom turned toward Madeleine Devine.

"I'd guess it's worth at least . . ." Madeleine's screamed-out voice was raspy, and she cleared her throat. Everyone in the lobby leaned in to hear. "Half a million, maybe?"

Mom was so shocked she almost dropped the phone. "Half a million," she said into the receiver. "No, Luis, I'm not joking. Someone stole a dog collar worth half a million dollars."

Elvis tugged her hand from mine and stuck her thumb back in her mouth.

"We're going to be on the news for sure," she mumbled. Her eyes were fixed on our celebrity guest. Like any minute now, the *Bentley Knows* theme music would flood the room and the culprit would be revealed. She leaned forward on her toes, but Sir Bentley slouched in the corner, droopy-eyed, and yawned.

"Psst, Epic!"

Mom held her hand over the phone and shook her head at me, waving toward the family stairs. I knew she wanted me to get Elvis out of the way and back to bed, but I had bigger problems.

I kept scanning the lobby, hoping I'd missed something. But no matter how many times I looked, I couldn't find my brother. And now I couldn't keep the worst-case scenarios out of my brain. Madeleine hadn't screamed because of a spider. She hadn't stubbed her toe. An *actual* criminal had been in our house. Stealing things.

A half-a-million-dollar dog collar was missing.

And so was Rondo.

SUNDAY

6:07 A.M.
(THREE DAYS EARLIER)

CANINE COMFORT
GUARANTEE

Mrs. Boone cracked the door of Room 1 and poked her head out into the hall, looking like she'd swallowed a cockroach. Scrunched eyes. Puckered lips. Her hair was piled into a silk sleeping scarf knotted at her forehead, and a mass of tiny black curls sprouted out the top like a volcano about to blow.

At her ankles, a small, wet dog nose poked through the barely open door and sniffed frantically in my direction.

"Young man, Pico's been waiting an eternity!"

Seven minutes late isn't the tiniest fraction of an eternity. But I didn't mention that to Mrs. Boone. If you calculate the time in dog years, it's more like forty-nine minutes. And with the Boones' dog, Pico, you have to adjust for three more factors: 1) his internal clock is calibrated to the nanosecond; 2) he worries about everything; and 3) he counts on me.

Free dog walking is part of the Perro del Mar Bed and Breakfast's Canine Comfort Guarantee, and while most guests come for a weekend, the Boones had arrived for last June's Puppy Picnic and liked it so much they never left. Which meant I'd shown up for Pico every morning at 6:00 A.M. sharp for a year straight. Mom is our official B&B dog walker, but Pico refuses to go out with anyone but me.

"Sorry," I said. "Mom needed me to bring *them*."

I nodded in the direction of Rondo and Elvis, who were both leaning on the hallway wall like it was the only thing holding them up. El hadn't changed out of her rainbow pajamas, and she had her cheek pressed up against the silver wallpaper. Eyes closed, thumb in her mouth. Rondo, who'd taken a snail-paced seven and a half minutes to get out of bed and then refused to put his book down long enough to brush his teeth, had his nose in a paperback called *The Right Way to Do Wrong: An Exposé of Successful Criminals* by Harry Houdini. I don't know where he finds this stuff.

Pico used his head to wriggle the door open another centimeter, but Mrs. Boone used her toe to block him.

"You're usually so reliable, Epic. I hope this isn't going to become a habit. Is everything okay?"

I winced. I'd barely slept. We'd gotten home at nine from the sixth-grade graduation "celebration," and no matter how hard I tried, I couldn't turn off my brain. Even at three in the morning, when I was dead tired, my synapses kept firing, running through impossible next-year scenarios. In her graduation speech, the head of school told us leaving Sunny Day Academy was a privilege. She called it an "initiation into the next evolution of the soul" and said we were rocketing toward new adventures, challenges, and world-changing responsibilities.

Everyone, including my best friend, Declan, had cheered. Like we were heroic astronauts heading for Mars instead of a tiny class of five kids who were getting kicked over to a new school because Sunny Day ended after sixth grade.

I didn't get why everyone was so happy. Sunny Day wasn't like other schools. It was an Expeditionary Learning school, which meant we didn't have tests, grades, or textbooks. We went to the beach to learn about tides. Made robots to learn about circuits. Put on plays to learn about Shakespeare. What if I didn't *want* to rocket away? What if I didn't want to evolve?

As if he could read my mind, Pico gave a frustrated whimper from behind the door. He didn't even know the worst of it. Carmelito Middle School started a whole hour earlier than Sunny Day. Which, come September, was going to put a huge seventh-grade-sized wrench in my Pico-walking schedule.

But I didn't explain any of that to Mrs. Boone.

"We've got to be back by seven to help Dad with breakfast," I said to her. "So Mom can finish building a new dog bed for Room 2 and fix the toilet in Room 3."

My sister jerked like she'd been hit with an electric shock. Her eyes popped open, and her thumb dropped out of her mouth.

"Holy guacamole!" She smacked her hand to her forehead. "SIR BENTLEY'S checking in today!"

"What?" Mrs. Boone looked at me for confirmation.

I nodded. "Last-minute change to the guest list. Mom got a call last night."

Elvis blinked bright-blue cartoon-saucer eyes at us. "He's coming for the Puppy Picnic. And he's staying for the whole week! With his *entourage!*"

Mrs. Boone clapped her hands in front of her face like a five-year-old who'd won a pony ride. "Clive! Wake up! Epic has news!" Mrs. Boone let the door swing open, and she disappeared into the suite.

The second the door opened wider than a crack, Pico ran at me full speed, his skinny, white-tipped tail flopping out the back of a yellow jumpsuit. He looked like a tiny banana with legs. Pico's not one of the froofy, weird-hairdo dogs some of the guests bring in. He's an Italian greyhound. Or as the Boones would say, an IG, or an Iggy. It means he looks exactly like a regular greyhound that shrunk in the wash. He's got a narrow face and pointed ears that stick out like propellers when he's happy. Which, at the moment, he definitely wasn't.

I knelt down and he hurled himself into my arms, breathing hard and shaking from his ears to his toes. Not excited shaking. Panic shaking.

Elvis tried to sweet-talk him. "Whasamatter, wittle buddy? Donchu worry . . ."

Pico shuddered at the sound of her voice and buried his head in my armpit.

Rondo lowered his paperback and pushed his messy, long blond hair away from his face. "Dude." He frowned. "You should try harder to be on time. That dog totally thought you were dead."

I daggered him with my eyes and pulled a Brushbot out of my messenger bag. It was nothing but a toothbrush head I'd glued to an AA battery and a three-volt motor, but Pico loves robots. The minute I connected the wires and set it spinning on the floor of the hallway, his muscles relaxed. He settled right down, staring at the bot like he'd been hypnotized.

"It's okay, Pico." I held him close but not too tight, so he could feel safe, not suffocated. "I'm here now. And Dec and I have a plan. You're going to be fine."

When Mrs. Boone reappeared at the doorway, her mood had completely changed. She was all giggles and frantic movement. She waved her arms at us.

"Well, what are you waiting for? Come in and tell Clive!"

THE BOONES

The week of the Puppy Picnic is always busy, but this year, Carmelito was getting an award: America's #1 Dog-Friendly Town. Which made sense. Carmelito's a great town. We have canine water fountains, a leash-free beach, and three dog parks. And the Perro del Mar was picked to be one of two "Official DFT" hotels for the weeklong celebration. Also an obvious choice. The Perro is small, but where else can you get organic, gluten-free puppy pancakes and custom-made dog beds?

Mom and Dad almost never get worked up about Perro stuff, because our mission is to be "an oasis of peace in the world." But last night, when we got home from Sunny Day's graduation party, Mom had seven voice mails. The three rooms that had originally been reserved for the DFT award committee were suddenly being assigned to a "celebrity host" and his "entourage." Sir Bentley needed organic linens, a paleo diet, 24-7 air-conditioning, and a whole bunch of other things Mom wrote down on a list. When she asked me for help, Mom's voice almost sounded panicky.

I never mind helping with Rondo and El. They follow me everywhere anyway. But we only had seventy-one days of summer vacation before Mom had to take over Pico duties. I wanted to make sure he was prepared, and my siblings aren't exactly the best people to have around when you want to follow a plan.

After Mrs. Boone invited us in, Elvis hopped all over the suite, touching everything in sight. Rondo parked himself on the floor, legs crisscross, eyes glued to a flat-screen TV on mute. Mr. Boone sat next to him in rumpled pajamas, flipping channels. Clive Boone was over six feet tall, and next to my brother, he looked like a giant. An exhausted giant. A haze of white beard-stubble stood out on his brown face and the dark circles under his eyes were puffed out even more than usual.

The Boones were usually organized, but today, all the closets in their suite had apparently exploded. There were two open suitcases on the floor. Which wasn't that strange. Even though they essentially lived at the Perro, the Boones still owned a house in Los Angeles. It had to cost a ton, but the Boones never seemed worried about money. Every few weeks, one of them would go check in on the house and "take care of the finances." Dad liked to joke that they had to visit the vault and melt down another gold bar to pay for all of Pico's pampering.

What *was* strange was that the couch and armchairs were covered in Iggy-sized T-shirts, bodysuits, booties, and head-gear. All laid out in matching outfits—a Hawaiian shirt paired with yellow doggy sunglasses; a color-coordinated sequined cap, sweater, and booties; a white clip-on shirt collar and power tie. The coffee table and kitchen counters were covered in paper—photos, Post-its, and clippings from celebrity magazines.

"Look! It's Sir Bentley!" Elvis dried her thumb on her pajamas and reached for a scrapbook open to a page filled with Mrs. Boone's scrawled handwriting.

Mrs. Boone flew to her side. She put on a stiff smile and closed the book, covering it with a stack of newspapers. The top one had a front-page article about the Puppy Picnic.

"That book is *private*, dear," she said, drawing the words out slowly like my sister was four, not eight. People tend to do that with Elvis. Partly because she's small for her age, and partly because she still likes to put on a baby-talk voice. The thumb-sucking definitely doesn't help.

"Anyway." Elvis rolled her eyes. "Sir Bentley's people told Mom there's going to be a surprise visitor at Yappy Hour!"

Mrs. Boone was pulling a cotton cap over Pico's head. Even though it was June. In California. But she froze in place and waited for Elvis to spill the beans.

"Who?"

"I can't tell you." Elvis whispered mysteriously, like she was purposely holding back the answer.

"She doesn't know," I said. "Nobody knows."

El glared at me. Mrs. Boone looked like she was going to pass out from the suspense.

"I'll find out," Mr. Boone said, still flipping channels. "The DFT award is a game changer, you know. If this week goes well, your parents will be swimming in reservations for life." He stopped at a station that was playing an episode of *Bentley Knows*.

My sister squealed and flung herself onto the floor next to Rondo, her head about five inches away from the TV. Even Pico turned to watch. They were all mesmerized.

"Rondo. El," I said. "Dec's waiting outside."

"One sec." Rondo didn't take his eyes off the television. "This guy's a genius."

On screen, a Saint Bernard bounded into a burning building and came back out holding a bundled blanket in his mouth. A sobbing mother retrieved her baby from the bundle while the Saint Bernard's droopy dog eyes practically filled with tears of joy at the reunion.

"Classic episode," Mr. Boone said. "Exceptional animal acting."

He unmuted the TV, and the cheesy theme music to *Bentley Knows* kicked in while the actress showered the dog and the baby with kisses. "How did you *know*, Bentley?" the TV mom sobbed. "How did you find my baby?"

"Because he *is* a genius," Elvis murmured, starry-eyed. She'd probably seen three scenes of *Bentley Knows* in her whole life, but the wall next to her bed was covered with pictures of the slobbery Saint Bernard hero of the show.

The very same Sir Bentley who was checking in to the Perro del Mar this afternoon.

"Not fourteen, fifteen!" Rondo blurted. Pico flinched, and I picked him up. His heartbeat thumped against my chest. "They're not counting the house in Malibu!"

We all stared at Rondo. His hair fell in his face as he shook his Harry Houdini paperback at the TV. I had no idea what he was talking about until I realized he wasn't actually watching the show. His eyes were on the news ticker scrolling across the bottom of the screen:

HOLLYWOOD HEIST . . . EARLY SATURDAY, SILK BANDIT STRUCK FOURTEENTH HOUSE THIS MONTH . . . ESTIMATED $20 MILLION IN LOOT . . . LATEST VICTIM: TEEN ACTRESS CHLOE COSMO . . . LOS ANGELES POLICE DEPARTMENT FOILED AGAIN . . .

"Seriously, Rondo?" I'd had enough. I grabbed Pico's doggy water bottle, organic pup-pup treats, and slightly damp octopus chew toy, then hoisted my messenger bag on my shoulder, and headed for the door.

"Come or stay," I said. "Your choice."

CARMELITO RUNS WITH THE BIG DOGS
posted by @pooperscooper1

Ever been to Carmelito, California? A mere four hours in standstill traffic up the coast from Los Angeles? Me neither. But Dog Elegance™ has! The swanky folks at everyone's favorite doggy lifestyle corporation have given the place their top honor: America's #1 Dog-Friendly Town!

Which means everydog who's anydog will be heading to Carmelito for the 10th annual Dog Elegance™ Award Ceremony this Friday, June 25. The ceremony coincides with Carmelito's annual Puppy Picnic (awww!), but you can bet your canine booties that Dog Elegance™ will put their own stamp on the shindig.

In fact, sources tell us that DE plans to pull out *all* the stops for this 10-year anniversary of America's #1 DFT. We expect surprise makeovers for several of Carmelito's quaint dog-friendly events. To start, we're keeping an eye on the weekly Yappy Hour at the Perro del Mar B&B. And later, we'll stop by the Moondoggie Inn . . . We've got a hunch there's going to be a treat that'll be *doggone* unforgettable.

DE headquarters is keeping the deets on the down-low, but there will be celebrity drop-ins, giveaways, and pop-up concerts all week long. You can trust your newshounds at the Hollywood Dog Dish to get you the poop-scoop. Here's what we can confirm so far . . .

Celebrity host(s) #1: Pendleton Triplets! Yes, it's true. Reliable sources have leaked the news that those labradoodle cuties are wrapping their latest film in Tokyo and flying straight to the Golden State to find out if Carmelito lives up to the hype. They'll be dogging around town all week, bringing a massive dose of *adorable* to the festivities and cohosting the award ceremony on Friday.

Celebrity host #2: Dog Elegance™ has been left in the lurch on this one. Their original A-list pick, Trixie (from the sobfest documentary *Dogs of War*), recently hightailed it to Syria to help with emergency relief efforts. Thank you for your service, Trixie, but at this late hour DE's going to have to sit up and beg for a replacement. Our money's on Chippy Chihuahua or that made-for-TV slobber-dog Bentley. (Sorry, I can't call him "Sir." Filming in England doesn't make you royalty, pal. Also: Why is *Bentley Knows* still a show? It jumped the shark three years ago. Literally. Remember episode 62? Someone thought it was a good idea to have that dog jump a Jet Ski over an entire *school* of sharks. *rolls eyes*)

That's all the poop we've got time to scoop. Even as we type, we're sniffing up several smelly trails. Little Carmelito isn't going to know what hit it!

#dogfriendlytown #poopscoop #carmelitoforthewin

Sponsored by: Dog Elegance™, Paws for Peace, Poochie Playpens

VOMIT COMET

My friend Declan tried to drag his front tire onto the Perro's bike rack, but Elvis got in the way, pulling Dec's dog, Frank, out of his bike basket and cooing at him.

"Why are they awake?" Dec asked. "Are they coming, too?"

"Of course we're coming—*muah, muah*—aren't we coming, wittle cutie sweetie? *Muah, muah, muah.*"

Elvis made kissy-faces as Frank shook his bizzaro-ears and tried to scramble out of her grip.

Dec's dog is possibly the strangest mutt in California. The vet thinks he's some kind of chihuahua-husky mix. He's barely the size of a football and has one small white ear. The other ear is black and so hairy it looks bigger than his head. Frank's body is white, but he's got a raccoon mask around his eyes and a long, feathery black tail. It's like he was created by a toddler playing with one of those mix-and-match board books. Dec's had him since second grade, and they're the perfect pair—super smart and as weird as it gets.

"Yeah, sorry," I said.

Dec shrugged. "I've just never seen them out this early. Except for surfing." He's known Rondo and El since they were babies, so he's used to them hanging around.

"Did you bring the map?" I asked.

"Better. I digitized it." Declan pulled a smartphone out of his pocket.

"No. *Way!*" Rondo closed his book. "Do you have apps on that?"

I watched Rondo and Elvis crowd around Dec, but my brain couldn't compute what was happening. All the families at Sunny Day Academy had agreed on one thing: no devices. None. We'd never had computers or tablets—not even MP3 players.

"Where'd you get it?" Elvis asked.

Dec wagged his bushy eyebrows like he'd won the lottery. In space.

"Flo thinks we should start mainstreaming," he said. "So we'll fit in at the new school."

"*What?*" This wasn't your average parent policy shift, this was a full-scale, 360-degree, aliens-stole-my-body change in worldview. Dec's mom, Flo, was the one who'd *started* the no-device campaign.

"It's fun." Dec grinned. "I stayed up until midnight reading celebrity gossip blogs. That's a thing."

"Why?"

"I want to be conversant with our peers. Don't you? Also, I'm going to learn how to play soccer. Want to join me?"

I stared at him. Was he serious? Mainstreaming? Dec and I had been the first class of kindergartners at Sunny Day Academy—all two of us. Flo had painted the mural in the Great Room—BE THE CHANGE YOU WANT TO SEE IN THE WORLD— and Mom picked our mascot, the Sunny Day Changemaker, and our motto: "Follow Your Curiosity." That was the whole point. To do things differently. Not to change yourself to fit in at a school you don't even want to go to.

"Show me the map," I said.

Every time we worked on a project together, Dec and I had at least one mind-meld moment. For the Pico Project, it was when we'd both blurted "Vomit Comet!" at the exact same time. The Vomit Comet is an airplane that astronauts-in-training use to acclimate to zero gravity. The plane flies in a parabolic pattern, racing up and down like a roller coaster, causing the atmosphere inside the plane to drop close to zero gravity for twenty-five seconds at a time. It allows the astronauts to get used to weightlessness gradually. Twenty-five seconds seemed like something Pico could handle.

Dec and I had mapped out our usual dog-walking route and marked the places and times where we would swap leashes. The first day, we were scheduled to swap once, Dec holding Pico's leash for twenty-five seconds when we got to the Moondoggie Inn. The second day, we'd increase to two swaps: at the Moondoggie and then again at Paradiso Park. Once we worked up to the full sixty minutes, scheduled for August 1, we'd add Mom into the mix.

It was a solid plan. Except I was a little worried that we were underestimating the "vomit" part of the equation. I'd read that so many people get sick during the parabolic flights that NASA probably cleaned a total of 285 gallons of vomit out of the original KC-135 airplane. I wasn't sure what the Pico-equivalent reaction to change was going to be, but I seriously hoped it wasn't puke.

We headed toward the beach. Dec scrolled on his new phone while Elvis avoided sidewalk cracks and "accidentally" bumped into Rondo on every third step. Rondo grunted at her, reading while he walked. Even with all the extra commotion, Pico seemed all right. Most shops on Main Street don't open until nine, which means all the things that freak him out—cars, crowds, fast-walking ladies in high heels—don't exist. And the fog that collects over the ocean at night makes every morning feel quiet and soft around the edges. At the corner of Ocean Drive, Pico and Frank paused to drink from a canine water fountain, and I squinted across the street at Carmelito Beach. Through the haze, I could see a handful of surfers lined up, trading waves.

"There she is." I pointed to a surfer in a bright green swimsuit who was cutting up the waves like a pro. Dec and I had been watching her for weeks. She looked like she might be our age, but we hadn't seen her anywhere but the beach. She'd shown up around May and had surfed every morning since, rain or shine.

The girl cut to the right, flipped her board, and wiped out

spectacularly. Rondo whistled through his teeth, impressed. Pico tugged at his leash and started to cross the street, but before we hit the curb, Elvis held out her arms like a traffic cop and stared across the street at the windows of the Moon-doggie Inn.

"Wait. Stop!" she said. "We NEED to do something like that!"

The Moondoggie is usually decorated with old-school surfboards and posters from 1960s movies like *Gidget Goes Hawaiian* and *Beach Blanket Bingo*. But all of that had disappeared overnight. Now the front of the inn was plastered with movie posters starring the Pendleton Triplets. Cheesy glamor shots of three blonde dogs in fancy dresses.

THREE WISHES: dogs in sparkly, fairy-godmother getups.

TRIPLE WEDDING: dogs dressed as brides.

THIRD TIME'S A CHARM: princess dogs standing in front of the Eiffel Tower.

Above the door, a handwritten, glittery sign read WELCOME PENDLETON TRIPLETS! WE LUUUUUV YOU!!!

Rondo made a face. "Labradoodles aren't even real dogs. They're a science experiment."

"We need to do something—*hic*—to welcome Sir Bentley. Look!" Elvis said, pointing at herself as she hiccuped again.

Rondo rolled his eyes. Our sister thinks all her best ideas come with hiccups.

"Idea Hiccups!" Elvis said. "We have to do it! I could make

a sign. We could—*hic*—get balloons. And those—*hic*—party-blower things."

"Mom would rather stick a fork in her eye," Rondo said.

"He's right," Dec said. "Your mom thinks balloons are toxic."

"Ep—*hic*," El pleaded as we crossed the street.

The second his foot hit the sidewalk in front of the Moon-doggie, Dec's phone dinged.

"Swap time," he said. "Check it out. I can set the timer on my app."

Rondo and El crowded him again, and Pico jerked his head in my direction. His ears went into high alert.

"It's okay, Pico," I said. "It's twenty-five seconds. You can do it!"

It was our first swap, so I should have been paying extra attention. I should have been thinking about those 285 gallons of vomit, but as Dec reached for Pico's leash and held out Frank's to me, I saw an epic wave out of the corner of my eye and a flash of green rising to meet the challenge. I turned my head to get one more look at the surfers when a loud voice boomed out of nowhere through the haze.

"HEY, HEY, HEY, IT'S THE MIGHTY McDADES!"

I flinched.

Elvis screamed.

Frank started barking like he was a hundred-pound pit bull on the attack.

Italian greyhounds might only weigh as much as a bowl-ing ball, but they're still greyhounds. They can run twenty-five miles an hour. I dove for the leash, but Pico took off like he'd heard the starter gun at a racetrack. He tore down Ocean Drive, curved up toward Paradiso Parkway, and vanished into the mist.

FARMERS' MARKET

"Sorry, dudes. I didn't mean to . . ."

I knew who it was before I saw the dopey grin and dripping wet board shorts.

Brody Delgado inherited the Moondoggie Inn when I was in fifth grade, and he's one of the most annoying people I know. He's constantly giving us nicknames, hanging around the Perro del Mar, asking Mom and Dad how to do stuff like taxes and reservation policies, and then stealing all our ideas. If it were up to me, he'd be banned from the premises, but his grandpa helped out Mom and Dad when they were new to Carmelito, so now we're supposed to be nice to him because of paying it forward.

Brody set down his surfboard and looked at us like we should say something to make him feel better. Like, *No problem, dude, Pico needed to go for a run anyway!*

Instead, we booked it down Ocean Drive, yelling our heads off.

Pico was long gone. Probably having a panic attack in

some stranger's yard halfway across town. *If* he'd made it across Paradiso Parkway without getting flattened. Running up Ocean Drive is like running up a four-block bridge from calm to chaos. It starts at the beach—all fog, sand, and waves—then curves back through town and ends at the busiest street in Carmelito. Even when the rest of town is sleepy and deserted, Paradiso Parkway is packed with cars and semis bypassing the highway on their way up north to San Francisco or south to Los Angeles.

We caught our breath at the crosswalk and scanned the road for a dog dressed like a squashed banana.

"He's not here, so he's not dead," Elvis said. "That's good."

"Not dead *here*," Rondo corrected her. "He could still be dead somewhere else."

"Thanks a lot," I said.

We waited for Dec to catch up with us. He had Frank tucked under his arm.

"I swear you guys have a cheetah gene in your family," he wheezed.

The white WALK sign blinked at us and we crossed the road to Paradiso Park, stopping near the gazebo to scan for Pico. Vendors were setting up tents, getting ready for Carmelito's daily farmers' market. The park was usually dead this early in the morning, but today, there were a handful of tourists and dogs wandering around taking selfies and trying to buy things from shop owners who hadn't set up their booths yet.

A man with a camera was filming while two guys stood on ladders hanging a banner above their heads.

DOG ELEGANCE™ PRESENTS
CARMELITO: AMERICA'S #1 DOG-FRIENDLY TOWN
AWARD CEREMONY: FRIDAY 12:00 P.M.

I couldn't see Pico anywhere. My hands shook as I rummaged around in my bag. We'd hit up the obvious booths first. Pico knows the farmers' market free-food circuit by heart. Richardson Farm has a bowl of complimentary vegan dog treats, Carmelito Creamery gives away frozen yogurt Pup-Pop samples, and Barker Bisson always slips Pico a few of his favorite Barker Bacon Bits. But Barker hadn't seen Pico today. No one had.

"We've got to get inside Pico's head," Rondo said, tapping his Houdini book. "Think like an Iggy."

Elvis got down on her hands and knees and crawled around on the grass.

"I'm Pico," she said in a high, raspy voice. "I wants a woofy hug."

"Hold on," I said. I'd found what I was looking for underneath all Pico's stuff in my bag.

"Screambot." Dec nodded. "Good call."

Pico had a love/hate relationship with Screambot. It was the battery pack from an electric pencil sharpener connected to the guts of a remote control car Grandpa had sent Elvis for her birthday last year. The car was cool, except it had a button you could press that made the sound of tires screeching. It started low and got higher and louder, and Elvis pressed the button so much that Mom threw the whole thing away.

I'd salvaged it, cut out the sound elements, and pieced the wires back together so Elvis could still drive the car around. Then I connected the audio components to the pencil sharpener and turned it into a monster bot that screams. Every time I pressed the button, Pico would raise his head and howl like he was scared out of his mind. But when the screeching sound faded, he'd wag his tail and nudge my hand until I hit it again. Pico could sit on the beach and play Screambot for hours.

I pressed the button. The monster screeched.

"It's not very loud," Rondo said. "We need something to amplify it with."

"Pico's got good ears," I said hopefully.

Elvis crawled over to Barker Bisson's tent and came back with a copy of the *Carmelito Cryer* from Barker's free newspaper stack.

"Here. Megaphone."

She rolled it into a cone shape, and we held it up to the Screambot's speaker. I pressed the button again. Amplified by the cone, the sound was at least twice as loud.

From the far end of the farmers' market, around the corner from the food tents, we heard a howl. Then another. A few of the tourist dogs joined in, and then Barker's German shepherd started to bark. I felt bad for setting off a howl chain, but it was worth it. We knew exactly where Pico was. I started jogging toward the booth for Martinez Antiques.

I should have thought of it to begin with: Mr. Martinez knows I like to tinker, so he lets me salvage parts from old junk he can't sell. Motors, batteries, old pieces of metal. Anything I can use for my projects. And every morning, while I scavenge his junk box for supplies, Pico gets a free three-minute doggy massage from Declan's mom at Flo's Floral Essences in the next booth over.

Elvis had been right. After getting scared out of his wits and dragging his leash across Paradiso Parkway, Pico was wasn't going to care about bacon treats. He was going to need a hug.

DELPHI

As we got close to Flo's booth, I caught a glimpse of a yellow banana in the arms of a woman with a short black Mohawk. She wasn't old. Maybe college age. She stood in front of Flo's Floral Essences, rubbing Pico's ear exactly the way he liked. Declan's mom, in her usual long, floral dress and thick brown braids, was chatting her up.

"Epic, look who we found! Or who our new friend . . . ?" Flo motioned to the stranger holding Pico.

The woman smiled. "Delphi," she said.

"Look who Delphi found!"

My knees felt wobbly. Partly from all the running, but mostly from relief. I'd been keeping it together okay while we were searching for Pico, but now that we'd found him, I had a lump in my throat the size of an avocado. I was so glad he was safe.

Pico didn't leap out of her arms and shake with relief like I expected him to. I hoped it was because he was too exhausted to move. Not because I'd betrayed his trust. I'd handed his leash over to someone he didn't want to walk with. And then I'd let go.

"I caught him racing across the lawn like a bullet train," Delphi said. "I love Iggys!"

Elvis threw her arms around the woman's waist. Which, honestly, I kind of felt like doing, too.

"You're our hero!" El yelled. "And I *love* your tattoos!"

A giant, full-color dragon snaked and twisted all the way up one of Delphi's arms and down the other. The way she held Pico, it looked like the dragon was circling him with its green-and-blue tail and massaging Pico's ear with its fire-breathing mouth.

"Nice jewels," Rondo said.

At first I didn't know what he was talking about. Delphi wasn't wearing any flashy jewelry. But then I saw that hidden inside of the dragon, her bronze arms and neck were completely covered with brightly colored jewels. The closer I looked, the more jewels I saw. It was like a seek-and-find puzzle. Even the dragon's eyes were shaped like blue diamonds. The tattoo artist had shaded them to look like the angles were glinting in the light.

Elvis started doing jumping jacks while Delphi posed for Dec's photo. "Are you here for the Puppy Picnic, Delphi?" she asked. "We're America's number one dog-friendly town. Did you know that? Sir Bentley's coming to stay at the Perro del Mar!"

Flo gasped and started peppering El with questions.

Which was exactly what my sister was angling for. But Delphi didn't seem to notice or care about Elvis's big announcement. She shifted Pico in her arms to type something into her phone, then handed him to me.

"I gotta run. Can I get a picture of Pico, though?"

I nodded. "Thanks for catching him."

Delphi pulled a heavy-duty camera out of her backpack and snapped a few shots. "Iggys don't run into your arms every day. I think it was a sign," she said.

"What kind of a sign?" Rondo asked.

"I had a hunch my girlfriend and I should come to Carmelito, and the universe is telling me that it's going to pay off. Big-time," she said. "Always follow your curiosity. Right, Pico?"

Flo and Elvis stopped talking. We all stared at Delphi.

"What?"

"That's our school motto," I said. "Follow Your Curiosity."

"Huh." Delphi tucked her camera back in her bag and gave Pico's ear a tug. "Sounds like another sign to me. Hold on to him now, okay?"

"I will," I said.

Delphi ran off to join a woman in a long skirt with a bulldog at her side, and Rondo started in on a rant about how the probability of random coincidence is much higher than people think.

"Sure, there are a lot of people and dogs in the world, but if you look at the specifics—we're in a dog-friendly park in

America's Number One Dog-Friendly Town—mathematically, that's going to increase your odds. Then if you calculate the number of Italian greyhounds in relation to . . ."

Dec scrolled on his phone while Rondo talked, and I only half listened, holding Pico tight. I felt awful about letting him go. Sign or no sign, if Delphi hadn't caught him, who knows where he would have ended up. He could have gotten squashed. Or kidnapped. It was my responsibility to take good care of him, and I'd let him down. I wasn't looking forward to telling the Boones. Or Mom and Dad. I was supposed to be the one they could count on. The one Pico could count on, too.

"I'm sorry, pal," I whispered. Pico shivered in his cotton cap and banana jumpsuit. "You're safe now. I promise."

I wondered if Dec and I should scrap the whole Pico Project. On the one hand, our teachers at Sunny Day taught us that every good scientific breakthrough starts with failed results. You can't give up based on one bad outcome. On the other, Pico had suffered because of our experiment. That wasn't an outcome I wanted to replicate.

Flo clucked her tongue, laid her hand on Pico's head, and unscrewed a bottle of white chestnut oil.

"His aura's shattered, poor thing. Let's get him on the massage table. I'll fix him right up."

COCOON OF SERENITY

When guests check in to the Perro del Mar, everyone but Mom is supposed to stay scarce. Check-in is at four, so around three thirty, Dad puts Doris Day ballads on the record player and Mom spritzes Flo's Blissful Surrender floral essence blend all over the lobby. The Perro isn't just a hotel. When guests walk into our space, they get to see how life *could* be: unplugged, upcycled, organic, and free-range. Our job is to make them feel like they've entered a Cocoon of Serenity that they can take with them anywhere they go.

So it didn't matter that we spent the whole day changing sheets and fluffing pillows like our life depended on it. Or that Elvis spilled a whole vase of flowers down the stairs at the exact moment Rondo and I were carrying up the towels and we had to run the laundry all over again and put a fan on the stairs to dry the rug. Or that some guest left a dog leash under the bed in Room 4 and Mom accidentally vacuumed it up, which meant I had to take apart the vacuum and put it back together again while Dad stood in the garden swearing at the squirrel who'd put bite marks in all the perfect strawberries he'd planned to use for Yappy Hour margaritas.

Finally, after everything was cleaned up and ready to go, Mom got a brain spark about adding some feet from an old claw-foot tub to the custom dog bed she'd built that morning for Sir Bentley's room. So we all rushed up to Room 2 and worked together to lift the bed, which had to weigh two hundred pounds, and Mom smashed her thumb so hard her fingernail turned black and bloody, and Rondo had to run to the bathroom and puke because it was so gross.

But the minute Doris Day started singing, Dad disappeared into the kitchen.

Rondo, Elvis, and I went upstairs to our room.

Mom took her place behind the front desk with a cup of ice for her thumb.

And the Perro del Mar metamorphosed—from a noisy, chaotic mess into a bliss-scented, silver-wallpapered cocoon.

Rondo punched his blue beanbag into optimal sitting shape and flopped onto it. "Bro," he said to me. "Let it go."

Even Elvis agreed. She spread out her watercolor pencils in rainbow order and gave a hopeful shrug. "Everyone's okay. Right?"

Things had been so busy getting the Perro del Mar ready

for Sir Bentley that I never had a chance to tell the Boones or Mom and Dad that I almost lost Pico.

"Not telling is basically lying," I said.

"Let's recap," Rondo said. "You briefly lost a dog and then found him again. Pico's fine. The end. Plus, they had *this* at Martinez Antiques. Pretty sure everything turned out great." He held up an antique book called *Our Rival, the Rascal*. "Houdini says it's the greatest book on criminal behavior ever written."

"You owe me five dollars for that," I said.

Rondo reached over and took another ancient book off his shelf and shook it. *The Complete Sherlock Holmes* made a rattling sound. He'd spent all winter break hollowing it out with an X-Acto knife and gluing all but the first several page edges together. He opened the book, took out the small box that he kept inside his "safe," and counted out the five dollars he owed me. All pennies and nickels.

I rolled my eyes. "I'll wait for real money."

"Suit yourself." Rondo scooped the coins back into *Sherlock Holmes* and cracked open his new book.

Elvis was drawing a wispy pink heart around the Sir Bentley sketch she'd been working on all week, so I sat at my desk and started to tinker with the Beast, a creature I'd been building since kindergarten. It had metal ears that moved, LED lights for eyes, and a red tongue I scavenged from an old alarm clock. I wasn't inspired, though. My eyes kept focusing on a graduation card that was propped up against my project lamp. On the front, there were two dogs in graduation caps stuck behind a fence. TIME TO BREAK OUT! it said. My grandma had written *Epic* and *Declan* on each of the dog's collars, and when you opened the card, it played music: "Who let the dogs out? Woof! Woof! Woof! Woof!"

Which was funny, except I didn't want to break out of Sunny Day, and the song reminded me of Pico racing down Ocean Drive. Maybe it didn't seem like a big deal to Rondo, but Pico was almost roadkill because of me.

I ripped the back of the card in half and pulled out the insides: a square circuit board with a metal clip and a flat, round speaker. There was a plastic tab that kept the clip from touching the metal on the circuit board. When I pulled the plastic tab out of the way, electricity flowed through the circuit, and the song played. When I pushed the plastic tab back under the clip, the circuit was broken, and the song stopped.

I hot-glued the graduation-card components to the bottom of the Beast's red alarm clock tongue so that when I pulled the tab, the song burst straight out of the Beast's mouth: "Who let the dogs out? Woof! Woof! Woof! Woof!"

"That'd make a good burglar alarm," Rondo said, looking up from his book.

"I guess," I said. "You could rig it so the tab gets pulled when a door opens . . ."

Elvis dropped her pencil, rushed over to her dresser, and grabbed a card with a bunch of dogs barking out the tune to

"Happy Birthday." My grandparents definitely had a theme. She handed it over to me.

"Test it on my drawer."

Elvis has a drawer that's "Top Secret"—at least according to the signs and stickers attached to the surface. In reality, everyone knows what's in there: her diary, dozens of Sir Bentley drawings, and a picture of El hugging our old dog, Yoda. Rondo and I figured out we didn't even need to take the card apart. We taped it inside the dresser, so when we opened the drawer, the card opened, too, and played the song. Elvis kept opening the drawer and resetting the alarm long after we'd finished the build-out.

"You're going to wear out the battery," I said.

"I like to see that it works."

On her seventeenth open, the barking birthday song was echoed by another woof. One that sounded like it was coming from downstairs.

"He's here!" Elvis grinned like it was her birthday, the Fourth of July, and the first day of school all wrapped up in one. Before I could stop her, she grabbed her latest Sir Bentley drawing and took off for the hall.

SIR BENTLEY

I managed to grab Elvis by the back of her shirt before she could bolt down the family stairs.

"One peek," I said. "But only if you promise to be quiet. And we come straight back upstairs."

We tiptoed down, pausing halfway to step over the Ghost Stair so the creak wouldn't give us away. Elvis almost lost her balance and took a nosedive, but I caught her by the arm. Her Sir Bentley drawing crinkled loudly. I took it, rolled it into a scroll, and handed it back to her with my finger to my lips.

We made it to the bottom step, for all the good it did us. We couldn't see a thing. On our right was the swinging door to the kitchen. Straight ahead of us, we had a stellar view of the dining room, where absolutely nothing was happening. The front desk was to our left behind the wall Elvis was leaning on.

"I think the paparazzi are confused." A loud, high-pitched

voice drifted into the stairwell. "They're all at the hotel down the street."

"They probably got a bad tip," a man's voice said.

"Asha, check social media." The first voice rose higher. "See if we have any mentions."

The Doris Day music wasn't working. This woman didn't sound relaxed at all.

"I can't *see*," Elvis whispered.

I shushed her, but Rondo pulled a tin of mints out of his back pocket. *Mints?* Did he think she cared about bad breath right now?

Burglar trick, he mouthed.

Inside the tin were a bunch of small objects. Rondo took out a mirror the size of a credit card and faced it toward the lobby. He held the mirror at arm's length, and I could see the back of Mom's head. He tilted it to the left, and I saw a tall, fake-blond woman wearing sunglasses so big, they covered half her face. He panned lower and a furry brown tail with a white tip came into view. Elvis let out a squeal.

I gave her a warning look, but it was too late. The kitchen door swung open to our right. We froze, ready for trouble, but Dad didn't even glance in our direction. He fiddled with his mustache and walked right past us into the lobby.

Rondo elbowed me. Dad *never* greeted the guests. He also never wore a button-down shirt and his best porkpie hat.

"I'm Marc," Dad said. "Welcome to the Perro del Mar!"

"His hat is blocking everything," Elvis hissed.

"Do you want to go upstairs?" I whispered as threateningly as I could.

Elvis suddenly quit fidgeting with her drawing and went perfectly still. A giant, slobbery Saint Bernard sniffed his way into our line of sight and paused halfway between the dining room and the stairwell. His brown fur was so shiny and smooth it flowed around him like he was in a shampoo commercial. His collar sparkled in the light. He tilted his head and gazed up at us with the same sad, wise brown eyes that had made the mother at the burning building cry on *Bentley Knows*.

Elvis let out a sound halfway between a snort and a squawk, and the next thing I knew, she was out in the lobby with her arms around her fluffy hero, crushing her rolled-up drawing between them.

Rondo shrugged and hopped off the stairs to join her.

"You guys!" I said. But I had to admit—I kind of wanted to meet him, too.

MADELEINE DEVINE

I set foot in the lobby at the exact moment the Boones came down the guest staircase on the other side of the room.

"Look, Pico," Mr. Boone said loudly. "It's your favorite detective doggo, Sir Bentley!"

Pico was all decked out in a fancy white shirt collar and red Pico-sized tie. He took one look at the giant bear of a dog in his lobby, shivered, and buried his nose in Mr. Boone's neck. I knew it—he was *still* stressed out from the great Brody escapade. I tried to wipe the guilty expression off my face.

Mom gave an embarrassed laugh and stuck her thumb in the cup of ice. "Well, Madeleine . . . er . . . Ms. Devine, you might as well meet . . . everybody!"

Sir Bentley's entourage looked like they'd stepped right out of Hollywood. Madeleine Devine wore gigantic dangly earrings, three necklaces, and a jeweled bracelet as thick as the armored cuffs Roman soldiers used to wear into battle. The man standing next to her was short and skinny in a pinstripe vest, octagonal glasses, and a sunburn on his nose and cheeks. He couldn't take his eyes off Mom's champagne-bottle chandelier. The third guest was a supermodel-tall woman in a black dress and spiky heels. Her hair exploded in a loose Afro around her head, and her lips were painted with dark red lipstick.

"Hello, everyone," she said in a deep, honey voice. "I'm Bentley's stylist, Asha."

As if to prove it, she clacked her heels toward Sir Bentley and pulled a gigantic handkerchief out of a secret pocket in her dress. She sopped up a long string of drool that was hanging from his face and smoothed the fur that had been roughed out of place by Elvis's hug. Asha nudged my sister until there was an arm's length of space between Elvis and the dog.

"That's better. Beauty first, sweetie," she cooed.

The minute the stylist turned her back, El reached over and messed up the fur on Sir Bentley's head, making it poke up like a punk rocker.

Madeleine shook hands formally with everyone, even me, Rondo, and Elvis. Her icy fingers were loaded with rings, and she squeezed my hand hard enough to make the knuckles crack.

"Did you say *Epic*?"

"You should have seen the day he was born." Dad ruffled my hair. "The surf was—"

"Epic." Madeleine interrupted without cracking a smile.

"Right on!" Dad grinned. "This is his brother, Elrond . . ."

My brother examined his shoes while Mom explained

about her favorite character in *The Lord of the Rings*. Rondo does not love being named after an elf.

"And our youngest, Elvis."

People who are weirded out by names usually react the strongest to my sister's. But before anyone could comment, Elvis threw out her arms and broke into a full impression of Dad's favorite oldies musician, Elvis Presley.

"You ain't nothin' but a hound dog! Cryin' all the time!"

Elvis sang in a low voice, using her scrolled drawing as a microphone, and shook her hips like Elvis—or as Dad called him, the King. She was so hopped up on Sir Bentley excitement, she threw in extra rubber legs and windmilled her right arm before sliding to her knees at Madeleine's feet. With a bow of her head, she presented Madeleine with the scroll.

Sir Bentley wagged his tail and flopped to the ground next to my sister. Madeleine Devine unrolled the drawing, and her shoulders relaxed. She finally looked like she'd entered a Cocoon of Serenity.

"Asha, are you getting this?" she asked happily.

"Yes, ma'am," Asha said, pointing her phone at my sister.

"She likes you," Madeleine said to Elvis. "A fellow performer."

My sister glanced doubtfully at Asha. "*She's* a performer?"

Madeleine winked. "Keep a secret?"

Elvis nodded, and everyone in the room leaned in.

"Sir Bentley's a girl."

My sister put her hands to her head and made a *pow* gesture like her mind had been blown. All the adults laughed except Mrs. Boone. She'd been standing by the stairs crossing and uncrossing her arms impatiently during the introductions. Now she worked her way into the middle of the room.

"Clive and I are such big fans," she said, trying to squeeze herself into the space between Elvis, Madeleine, and Sir Bentley. "We've been studying Sir Bentley's work, and we'd love to talk to you about our— Oh my! Those diamonds are stunning!"

Madeleine Devine held up her chin and touched a necklace.

"Thomas gave me this," she said. "Isn't it fabulous?"

"I meant the dog," Mrs. Boone lifted her glasses from the string around her neck and peered at Sir Bentley.

"Oh, that." Madeleine stroked back the fur on Bentley's neck to show off a giant, jewel-encrusted collar.

Dad whistled through his teeth.

"My beau is no fool." Madeleine said. "He knows he's got to woo us both."

Rondo elbowed his way in to get a better view of the jewels.

"Who's your beau?" Elvis asked. "The king of England?"

Madeleine shot an adoring look at the skinny man who was still gazing up at Mom's chandelier.

"He's sort of a king," she said. "Aren't you, honey? Don't you want to introduce yourself? Thomas?"

The man turned his head. He looked surprised to see everyone.

"Thomas Scott," he said. "CEO. Chow Chow Enterprises."

"Chow Chow? Is that in the canine space? Entertainment?" Mr. Boone asked, but Thomas didn't seem to hear him.

"Who's the artist? It's . . . incredible!" He waved his hand around the room at Mom's champagne chandelier, iron-fence banister, and metal-pipe furniture.

"I . . . me . . . I guess." Mom blushed.

"Elly makes all the furniture at the Perro," Dad said proudly.

"*Absolutely* stunning." Thomas put his hand on his heart and actually got tears in his eyes. "A commentary on waste and overconsumption?"

I grinned. That was *exactly* what Mom was going for with her projects, but no one ever noticed. Her blush got deeper, but she was beaming.

"Is it comfortable, though?" Mrs. Boone was still eyeing the dog collar suspiciously. "She doesn't sleep in it, does she? You have to be careful not to abrade the skin. Dogs are very sensitive."

Thomas Scott stepped forward, took Mrs. Boone's hand, and brought it to his lips like an old-fashioned movie star. Rondo made a gagging sound, and I thought Mrs. Boone might pop Thomas in the nose, but instead she gave a surprised giggle as she withdrew her hand.

"A true dog lover. *Enchanté.* I assure you it's made with

the softest Italian leather. Now, Elly." He reached for Mom's hand, and there was an awkward moment when he saw her bloody thumb and decided to go for an air-kiss instead. "What else can you show me?"

"There's a brand-new installation in Madeleine's room," Mom said. "We didn't have a dog bed large enough for Bentley, so I created—"

"*My* room?" Madeleine interrupted. "Why is there a dog bed installed in *my* room?"

"I assumed . . ."

"You don't expect Sir Bentley to *share a room*, do you?"

I watched Mom try to keep her smile in place.

"Of course . . . typically . . . we don't allow our canine guests to stay unaccompanied. I'm sure you understand."

"Typically?" Madeleine obviously *didn't* understand. "We have three rooms reserved, and we should be able to use them how we like."

"We try to maintain—" Mom started firmly, but Thomas pulled Madeleine to the side and put his arm around her waist.

"Babe, *we* know Sir Bentley's not typical. She's a celebrity. *Everyone* changes the rules for celebrities, but maybe it's different here." Thomas lowered his voice a little, but not enough so we couldn't hear. "We don't have to stay, but I *would* like to see that dog bed. Don't you think we should send a photo to Calla Wilkins? I owe her an email anyway."

We all stared at Mom. She had a whole shelf of books about furniture design by Calla Wilkins. It'd be like if someone offered to show your invention to Thomas Edison.

"Mom," I whispered. "Couldn't we let them—"

Dad didn't wait for her to decide. "We'll make an exception," he announced. He gave Mom an excited squeeze and mouthed *Calla Wilkins* at her. "Let's get the luggage upstairs. Wait till you see the headboards Elly designed."

MORRISSEY

It would have been easier to leave the iron-clawed dog bed in Room 2 and move the humans to Room 3, but Madeleine insisted that Sir Bentley needed the backyard view. And since the bed was too massive to fit through the door, Dad and Mr. Boone had to help Mom take it apart and move it in pieces. Thomas filmed the whole thing on his phone, peppering Mom with questions about her materials and techniques. Asha whisked Sir Bentley away into her own room for "celebrity downtime," and Mrs. Boone took Pico out to the garden so he didn't have to get freaked out by the power tools.

Which left me, Rondo, and Elvis to wait in the lobby for our final guests to arrive. Mom's reservation book said *M. E. Dubois: two adults, one bulldog, six nights, paid in full by Dog Elegance Inc.*

"Dog Elegance," Elvis said excitedly. "Do you think it's another famous celebrity?"

"Maybe," I said. Dog Elegance was a huge corporation that

owned everything from pet stores to doggy clothing lines all over the world. Half the stuff in the Boones' suite was branded by Dog Elegance.

"It could be that football player from the Dog Elegance puppy food commercial," Rondo said. "He's so huge he can fit two puppies in one hand."

"How do you even know that?" I asked.

Rondo ignored my question and went back to his book.

Turns out, M. E. Dubois wasn't a football player or a celebrity at all. She was a soft-spoken veterinary student from UCLA who'd volunteered to be an on-call emergency vet for Dog-Friendly Town week. She wore a long, flowy skirt and carried an old-school leather doctor's bag in one hand and the leash to a grumpy-looking bulldog in another.

Her partner had a Mohawk and a dragon tattoo.

"You guys!" Delphi gave us all high fives. "It's another sign! Melissa, I *told* you this is going to be our lucky week."

I was glad it was Delphi and her veterinarian girlfriend checking in and not some famous actor or award judge that my parents would get stressed out about. Maybe I could convince Dad to bring them complimentary room service to thank Delphi for finding Pico. Except I still needed to tell Dad I'd lost him in the first place.

Elvis rubbed the bulldog's ears and showered him with baby talk. "Didchu know your very own Delphi is a hero? Yes she is, she's a wittle sweetie hero."

"You're a vet?" Rondo asked Melissa. "What's the grossest thing you've seen?"

"I study behavioral science, actually." Melissa's pale cheeks pinked up. "I'm researching risk assessment in animals, especially as it pertains to groups."

When she saw the disappointment on my brother's face, she quickly added, "I once saw a worm-infested pig intestine. That was nasty."

Elvis and I gagged, and Rondo grinned.

Delphi patted Melissa's arm proudly. "Mel's super smart, but she can meet you at any level you need."

"What's in there?" Elvis said, pointing to Melissa's leather doctor's bag. "Emergency vet stuff?"

"It's—" Melissa started, and Delphi finished her sentence.

"*Very* important emergency supplies," she said.

We gave them the tour of the dining room, snack bar, and garden patio, then Melissa went to get the rest of their bags while we headed upstairs—or tried to. The bulldog refused to move past the second step.

Delphi bit her lip. "We don't have stairs at our apartment. I don't think Morrissey likes them." She gave the leash an encouraging tug. Mrs. Boone came in from the garden and gasped. "Don't pull on the leash like that! You're terrifying him." She held her hand over Pico's eyes. "Don't look, Pico!"

Delphi and I tried to lift the bulldog, but it was like trying to pick up Elvis when she's in rag doll mode. I swear she can triple her weight with that move.

We froze when Madeleine Devine appeared at the top of the stairs.

"Stop. Stop!" she scolded.

Delphi's face burned. "I . . . we . . . Morrissey's not usually this stubborn."

"He's not stubborn." Madeleine snatched the leash and shooed everyone out of the way. "He's a very short dog with broad hips. Stairs are unnatural to him."

She unraveled a silk scarf from around her neck and wrapped it loosely under Morrissey's belly for support. Then she locked eyes with the bulldog.

"Listen, Morrissey. There's a cozy bed upstairs for you. Staying down here is not an option."

Madeleine pulled a treat out of her pocket, placed it on the step above his nose, then lifted Morrissey's paw gently toward the treat.

She snapped her fingers. "There. It's delicious."

Morrissey sniffed and lifted his bulky body toward the treat.

Mrs. Boone dumped Pico in my arms so she could dig a tiny notebook out of her purse. Pico snuggled in, resting his chin in the crook of my elbow, and I instantly felt better. He wasn't mad at me. He was fine. Maybe Rondo and El were right. If Pico wasn't hurt, why make a big deal out of losing him?

"Would you look at that?" Mrs. Boone was scribbling down

everything that Madeleine said and did. Like someday Pico was going to develop broad hips and short legs and she'd need the instructions to get him up the stairs.

Dad, Mom, Thomas, and Mr. Boone came out of Room 3, and it was like we were watching a rocket launch, the way we all cheered and clapped when Morrissey got to the top of the stairs. Thomas gave Madeleine a big, sloppy kiss, and Elvis threw her arms around the bulldog, praising him like he'd won a gold medal at the Olympics. She hugged Madeleine, then me, and with more enthusiasm than she could contain, she took a flying leap at Delphi. The two of them almost took a header down the stairs.

"Elvis!" Dad looked horrified. *"Personal space!"*

"It's all right." Delphi regained her balance and gave my sister a fist bump for not killing them both. "We're old friends."

Mom frowned. *"How* do you know my kids?"

Delphi didn't skip a beat. She knew exactly how to cover for me.

"Farmers' market," she said. "Epic, let me take a picture of Pico. I love Iggys."

Pico's ears perked up at the sound of his name, and I rubbed one of them while Mom stared me down. My head was all tingly, and my fingers wanted to twitch. Rondo gave me a be-strong-and-let-it-go look, but it was too late.

"I lost Pico," I admitted. "And Delphi found him."

"What?"

Mrs. Boone's cockroach-swallowing pucker was back. She yanked Pico out of my arms.

"He didn't mean to," Elvis protested.

"Clive!" Mrs. Boone wailed. "Epic lost our *baby*!"

MONDAY

4:45 A.M.

DAWN PATROL

"Rise and shine, the surf is fine."

It was still dark outside when Mom and Dad knocked on the door of our bedroom. I opened an eye and slowly let the world come into focus. For the second night in a row, I hadn't slept. Only this time, instead of lying awake thinking about graduation, my brain replayed scenes of Pico racing up Ocean Drive and Mrs. Boone snatching him out of my arms when she learned I'd lost him. Every time I tried not to think about Pico, my brain skipped to Declan scrolling on his cell phone. Reading celebrity blogs. Mainstreaming. It was not the greatest start to the summer.

"Five- to six-foot swells today, and optimal winds!" Dad flipped on the light.

Rondo jerked awake and sat straight up. He checked the clock, then flopped back on his pillow so hard that the springs of the bunk bed rattled. In the bunk below him, Elvis moaned, "Mars is on fire." The sound turned into a sleepy snort.

"Let me hear an okay," Mom said, dropping rash guards on each of our heads.

I rolled over and let my feet dangle off the edge of my bed.

"Okay." My morning voice sounded like a bullfrog.

Some kids I know go to church every week. My family has Dawn Patrol. Every Monday, before breakfast or guest check-out, even before my 6:00 A.M. walk with Pico, we carry our boards down to Carmelito Public Beach to surf. As long as the waves are safe, it's nonnegotiable. Dad could be sick as a dog and the waves flat as pancakes, and he'd still drag his longboard to the beach on Mondays. As tired as I was, it felt good to know that even with a full house and a dog-celebrity entourage, we still had our priorities straight.

Dad's friend Luis was waiting on the sand. Luis meets us every Monday with his Westie terrier, Cookie Monster, who spends the whole morning barking her head off and chasing sandpipers on the leash-free beach. We kicked off our sandals, and the six of us silently waded into the water. That's the rule. Morning surfing is for thinking. Or not thinking. But definitely not talking. Dawn Patrol is time to recharge and let go of the noise. Clear our minds for the week ahead.

Which, if yesterday's check-in was any clue, was going to be intense. It was past Elvis's bedtime before Sir Bentley's crew finally stopped asking Mom and Dad for things—filtered water for Bentley's bowl, herbal tea bags for Madeleine's beauty routine, a sleep mask for Asha, the local newspaper for Thomas Scott. Elvis did everything she could to wind up in Sir Bentley's room, offering blankets and a free doggy massage. She even talked her way into giving a full demonstration of how the faucets work in the bathroom.

It was going to be a long week. But right now, it was Dawn Patrol. I could worry about everything else—including Pico and Dec—later.

Carmelito Beach usually has two sets of waves breaking. I paddled to the smaller set, and my family and Luis headed for the bigger swells, where a handful of other surfers were lining up in the fog. I love Dawn Patrol, but I'm not a huge fan of that second set. First, you have to wait in the lineup, make sure you paddle at the right time, and try not to steal anyone's wave. Then, maybe you're up on your board for thirty seconds before the ocean throws you down, pummels you, and you start the process again. No matter how I calculate it, the whole time/effort/result equation never works out.

On the smaller set, I get the whole world to myself. I'm not in anyone's way, so I can surf whenever I want. Or turn over on my back and watch the sky. I like to imagine the gravitation of the moon, two hundred forty thousand miles away, pulling at the tide right here in Carmelito. Dad says his favorite thing about the ocean is that it reminds you that Earth barely registers as a speck in the cosmos. We're just here to ride the wave.

"Hey, dude, you awake?"

A muscular guy with a dark beard grinned as he paddled past me toward the swells farther out. The girl in the green swimsuit followed behind. Her hair fell into her face as her arms pushed through the water.

I scrambled to sit up on my board. I could practically hear Declan shouting telepathic messages at me: *Say something, stupid!*

"I wasn't sleeping," I blurted. "I mean . . . it maybe looked like I was, but I was watching the cosmos . . . I mean, the universe . . . It's so huge . . . you know . . . uh . . ." *Stop. Talking.* I forced my voice to fade out.

The girl stopped paddling for a second. She pushed a long blue streak of hair out of her face. "Ninety-three billion light-years."

"Huh?"

"The diameter of the observable universe. You're right. It's huge."

The girl smiled. It was an awesome fact. Ninety-three billion light-years. I tried to commit it to memory while forcing my mouth to work up a response. But before I could find anything interesting to say, the girl in the green swimsuit was already long gone, paddling out to join the lineup. I groaned, rolled onto my stomach, and waited for a nice, easy wave to ride.

"Epic!" Elvis yelled when we met back up on the beach. "That was incredible! You crushed it! We all crushed it! We haven't had waves this good since . . . the beginning of TIME."

Being silent for an hour is hard for Elvis. She usually

goes overboard the second the Dawn Patrol cone of silence is lifted. But she was right. We'd crushed it. I had the smaller waves all to myself, and I surfed one after the other, feeling balanced and strong. I even made a couple great bottom turns. But mostly, I rode them out steady and didn't get pummeled. It was a good day.

"Did you see Rondo?" Elvis asked.

Luis let out a belly laugh. "He stole a wave from the new girl!"

I stared at my brother. "You did?"

Rondo grimaced. "It was an accident. I don't want to talk about it."

She was still out there, cutting it up for real. I watched her chuck spray into the air while Dad helped Luis tie his longboard to the top of his police car and Elvis pelted Cookie with kisses through the window. When we finally headed toward home, my sister danced up Main Street like a flamingo on three shots of espresso. Rondo balanced his surfboard on his head and howled every time she bumped into him. Mom grinned at Dad as he gave us all a Dawn Patrol sermon about the three necessities of life: sun, surf, and a creative pursuit.

"I had a brain spark on that last wave," he said. "Quinoa waffles with strawberry compote. Maybe a mint garnish? Or basil? What do you guys think?"

"Mint!" Elvis yelled at the same time Rondo said *basil*.

"I'd try either," I said. Every dish Dad makes is genius.

I'd had a brain spark, too. I could add a tail to the Beast

and use a pull-string to make it wag. I was sure I had an old toy in the closet that I could scavenge the pieces from. Or maybe I could build it from scratch. I could get started after breakfast. Instead of worrying about middle school and losing Pico and Declan getting weird, I'd decided to focus on the one reliably good thing about summer: endless time to build.

"Epic." Mom tugged at my elbow and pulled me a few steps behind everyone else. "I have a family announcement to make, but your dad and I need you to help us get the kids on board."

FAMILY ANNOUNCEMENT

Mom's announcement wasn't as earth-shattering as she'd made it out to be. She was sending my siblings off to art camp.

"Okay?" I didn't see the problem. El was going to love it. Art was her favorite thing next to dogs. Rondo, on the other hand, would hate it with a passion, but he'd survive if he could bring a book.

"It's at the middle school." She was whispering now. "A half-day camp. Four days. Starts today."

"Great."

It was a genius idea. It would keep El and Rondo out of the guests' way, and I could spend time working on the Beast and helping with the garden and Yappy Hour. But Mom looked embarrassed.

"Elvis was all over the guests, and that Devine woman is so . . . overwhelming. I had to get them out of the house." Mom's face got red, and she started to laugh. "I actually called the camp director at *home*. At ten o'clock last night! I tried to get you all into soccer camp so you could be with Declan, but it's full."

"I don't want to play soccer, anyway."

Mom gave me an awkward, toothy smile.

"What?" I asked. There was something she wasn't telling me.

"I might have lied and told them you were in fifth grade. So you could go, too."

"*Fifth* grade?" I was going into seventh. What was I supposed to do? Shrink?

"Why do *I* have to go?"

"It was just an idea. You don't have to go."

Good. It was summer vacation. Getting locked inside the middle school with a bunch of little kids wasn't vacation.

"Go where?" Elvis said. She'd given her surfboard to Dad and hopped on one foot in our direction.

Mom took a breath. "Art camp," she said.

"I love art." Elvis switched feet and took three hops back.

"Great," Mom said. "It starts at nine."

Both of Elvis's feet landed firmly on the pavement. "Today?"

Mom and I stopped walking.

El's eyes welled up with tears. "When *Sir Bentley* is here?"

By the time Dad and Rondo turned back to see what was going on, Elvis was in full meltdown mode, arms crossed, tears splashing down her face.

"Take a breath, El," Dad said. "It's all good."

Elvis glared at him through her tears and turned to Rondo.

"They're making us go to camp. Today."

My sister's no fool. She knew where to find an ally. Rondo set down his board and went off on a tirade about how Sunny Day students have *one* assignment every summer, and that's to live out our school motto: Follow Your Curiosity. Which means hanging out at the beach. Staying up late making robots. Not sitting in a classroom for the best half of the day.

"Art camp?" he asked. "Are we seriously talking about ART CAMP? We can make art at home."

Mom and Dad looked desperately at me.

"See, Epic?" Mom said. "We thought it would be easier if . . ."

I understood what she was getting at. My siblings weren't going to get on board with spending most of the week indoors. For *hours*. Not without a very good reason.

I shifted the surfboard under my arm and lied my face off. "It's my fault, guys," I said. "I want to go. It's at Carmelito Middle School. We can scope out what my life will be like next year."

Rondo stopped talking, and Dad shot me a grateful smile. El looked skeptical.

"You know I'm freaking out about going there," I said.

It was true. I hadn't exactly said it out loud, but they all knew I was dreading it. The chances of me fitting in at

Carmelito Middle School were so low, even Rondo's theories of probability couldn't calculate it. I'd never taken a test in my life. I'd never had a textbook or a locker. Or used a computer. And Declan, apparently, was planning to do whatever it took to fit in. So that left me. Alone.

The idea that art camp could *possibly* change any of that was absurd. But it was the only thing I could come up with that my sister might buy.

Elvis brushed tantrum tears off her cheek. "You *need* us to go with you, don't you?" she asked.

"Sure, dude," Rondo said. He gave me a reassuring nod. "We'll check it out. It won't be that bad."

"But I want mint on my waffles," Elvis said, and went back to hopping on one foot toward home.

"Thanks, Epic," Dad said when El and Rondo were far enough ahead. "We owe you one."

Mom squeezed my shoulder and gave me a schmoopy kiss. "You never let us down."

I tried to remember the feeling I'd had on the ocean. The earth was a speck. Carmelito was a speck. In the scheme of things, middle school was an infinitesimal speck. I took a breath, and we turned down the alley that led to the backyard of the Perro, all set to unlatch the gate, leave our gear on the porch, feed the chickens, and let the calm of Dawn Patrol guide us through our week.

But the entire alley was blocked by a delivery truck. Two

dudes in overalls were hauling squares of black plywood and piling them in our backyard.

"What's all this?" Dad asked.

One of the guys dropped a square near the chicken coop with a thud. "We're here to set up the stage."

Doggone It, We Were Right!
posted by @pooperscooper1

Are we smart or are we smart? As predicted by our crack team of pooper-scoopers, celebrity canines and their humans are flocking to Carmelito for the 10th Anniversary Dog Elegance™ Dog-Friendly Town Awards.

A cuddleworthy movie star trio? Check!

One droopy television detective? Check.

And tonight? A pop-up event with a SURPRISE guest. Your newshounds have dug up more than a few bones that point in the direction of a musically talented pint-sized platinum pup. And, oh-my-mother, is he swoonworthy! Curious? First, we have a soft and cuddly side note . . .

Something's brewing with the Pendleton Triplets. Our sources have spotted guru dog trainer FiFi Khan in meetings with Netflix, Disney, and Lucasfilms. Did you catch that last one? George. Lucas. Films. No one official will confirm our theory that a *Star Wars with Dogs* project is in the works . . . but they won't deny it, either! Come on, a Pendleton Wookiee? Melt my cold, cold heart already.

Meanwhile, back at the ranch, sources have confirmed that you do NOT want to miss the pop-up event at tonight's Yappy Hour at the Perro del Mar B&B. If rumors can be trusted (and we *know* that they can), this sleepy little inn is about to experience the wake-up call of a lifetime. Plus,

there will be tasty treats. Believe it or not, we hear Perro co-owner Marc McDade is a chef worth his salt, AND he's married to the next Calla Wilkins–style home decor genius. Who knew? This dinky Carmelito is full of surprises. And because we at the Dog Dish are devoted to you, our readers, we will post updates as fast as our little fingers can type.

Sound the horn and release the hounds . . . Let the games begin!

#dogfriendlytown #poopscoop #popuppups

Sponsored by: Princess Pupwear, Dog Elegance™, KhanArts Dog-Training School

ART CAMP

From the outside, Carmelito Middle School looks like a brick Kleenex box with windows, so it made sense that everything inside was white. White walls, white ceiling, white doors. The floors were white, too, but there was a yellow line painted down the center of each hall. Bright yellow posters announced KEEP TO YOUR RIGHT. RESPECTFUL STUDENTS STAY IN THEIR LANES.

Rondo immediately moved over into the left lane.

This was my new school. I tried to imagine walking to class on the right side of the hall every day. With four hundred and fifty other kids lined up in their lanes. Dec and I were going to stick out like sore thumbs. Unless he'd already added "stay in the right lane" to his mainstreaming to-do list.

Elvis started walking the line like a tightrope, one foot in front of the other. At a snail's pace.

"El, we're late, remember?" I nudged her off the line. A little harder than I meant to.

"Hey!" Elvis nudged me back. More like shoved.

"Was that a choice for peace or conflict?" Dad asked, but even *his* voice had an edge to it.

We were all cranky. I hadn't been able to walk Pico because Mrs. Boone didn't "feel comfortable" after the farmers' market fiasco. Even though I promised her seven times that I'd never let it happen again. Mom tried to walk him instead, and Pico was so mad he wouldn't budge. Even after Mr. Boone took over, Pico wouldn't go to the bathroom—a recipe for future disaster that the Boones would probably blame me for. Dad was annoyed because Madeleine Devine told him his strawberry compote could use more honey. And *everyone* was annoyed at the sound of the construction in the backyard.

Madeleine wouldn't say much about the stage. She only told us that Dog Elegance wanted to kick off the week in style, and weren't we lucky that they'd chosen the Perro for the first surprise event? At eight forty-five, right in the middle of breakfast, another crew had shown up. A sound guy with a PA system, a landscaper, and a lighting designer—which apparently is a thing.

Elvis was trying to be strong, but she couldn't help putting on a sad-puppy face and muttering, "We're going to miss *everything*," about a thousand times until Madeleine Devine felt so sorry for her she promised to arrange a special Yappy Hour treat for El. Rondo was reading Houdini and kept forgetting to eat his breakfast. By the time he finished shoveling quinoa waffles down his throat, we were running thirty minutes late for the camp nobody wanted to go to.

The door to Classroom 405 was closed. Through a tiny rectangular window, I could see a crowd of kids sitting on a blue rug listening to a ghostly pale middle-aged teacher with frizzy hair. I looked at Rondo. He shrugged. Sunny Day didn't have doors. Or classrooms for that matter. Our exploration spaces were "open concept." Students were expected to come and go all day. I stared at the closed door and wondered if it would be better to knock or to slip in, sit in the back, and pretend we'd been there all along. Better yet, we could turn around and go home.

Instead, Dad flung the door open and announced loudly, "Special delivery: one genuine McDade trio!"

All the kids swiveled their heads to look at us. Elvis popped her thumb in her mouth.

"Class starts at nine, Mr. McDade," the teacher said, rushing toward us. "Also . . ." She shook her head as she sized us up. "There seems to be a misunderstanding. This program is for third through fifth grade."

I tried to slouch my shoulders, and Dad opened his mouth to explain, but the teacher interrupted. "The curriculum will be too advanced for her."

Elvis kept sucking her thumb, but Rondo leaned forward, his chin jutted out in his trademark ready-to-make-a-scene pose.

"It's okay. She's going into third grade in the fall," I said quickly, and gave Rondo a warning look.

"She's also smarter than most sixth graders," he said, staring the teacher down.

It bugged me that we were absolutely, 100 percent lying about *my* age, but all the teacher could see was Elvis sucking her thumb. I didn't even register on her radar.

"Fine." The teacher motioned for Dad to walk away. "Class will be over at twelve thirty. Sharp."

She handed me three Carmelito art camp T-shirts, and I realized everyone in the room was wearing the exact same thing. Elvis happily grabbed a shirt out of my hand and pulled it on over her dress. It came down to her knees, making it look like she was wearing nothing but the T-shirt and red tights.

Rondo shook his head. "Nope," he said, and I shoved the other two T-shirts in my bag.

We sat on the rug next to a girl with thin rows of dark braids and round glasses, and the teacher walked toward a whiteboard that had *Mrs. Doughty* written in block letters at the top. She clapped her hands together in a rhythmic pattern. *TAP. TAP. Tap-tap-TAP.*

Without a word, the class clapped it right back to her. *TAP. TAP. Tap-tap-TAP.*

"Let's tell the McDades what we've learned so far," Mrs. Doughty said in a singsong voice like she was talking to kindergartners. "How do you eat an elephant?"

She put a hand to her ear, and the whole class said in unison, "One bite at a time!"

They sounded like perfectly programmed robots. Carnivorous, elephant-eating robots.

I looked at the door. Dad was still standing in the hall, fiddling with his mustache, watching Mrs. Doughty. His nose was crinkled like it gets when he's about to throw out a bad pour of espresso. Maybe we could still get out of this.

But the moment he caught me looking at him, Dad's face changed. He brightened and shot me a thumbs-up, like this was going to be the greatest opportunity ever. Then he turned and left me, Rondo, and Elvis to fend for ourselves.

ONE BITE AT A TIME

Mrs. Doughty projected a photograph of an elephant on the whiteboard and used a ruler to draw a grid over the image.

"If we try to draw this elephant freehand, that's going to be hard, isn't it?"

Several kids nodded. Elvis murmured, "Not really."

"Now, if we break the image into dozens of smaller images," she said, pointing at one of the squares on the grid, "we can draw one bite at a time. Watch me."

The teacher began to outline the elephant, copying the image one grid square at a time. Elvis crossed and uncrossed her legs. She sat on her knees and let her arms splay out behind her. The girl in the round glasses inched away to give her room.

When Mrs. Doughty had moved on to the fourth square, Rondo elbowed me and pointed to the butt of the kid in front of us. The tip of a ten-dollar bill peeked out of the back pocket of his shorts. Rondo tapped the kid on the shoulder. "You shouldn't carry your money like that," he whispered.

The kid glanced at Mrs. Doughty, who was still drawing on the board, then back at Rondo. "What?"

"Your money," Rondo whispered louder. "Someone could steal it."

The kid twisted around to get a better look at my brother. He had a head full of thick, unruly black curls. "Like who?"

"Eugene! Listening ears please!" Mrs. Doughty snapped.

Eugene glared at Rondo before facing forward again.

After Mrs. Doughty finished outlining the elephant, we moved to tables, where each student was given one piece of white paper, a ruler, a pencil, and a small copy of the elephant photo. Eugene and the girl with the round glasses used their rulers to draw a grid over the elephant photo, then an identical grid on their white paper.

Rondo used his ruler to measure each of the fingers on his left hand.

"You gonna do this?" he asked.

"What *else* are we going to do?"

We watched Elvis, bent over her paper, drawing happily away. Art was her thing. Hopefully, now that she had a pencil in her hand, she would sit still for a minute.

I drew one grid line over the elephant, then another. As I measured out the third line, I got a brain spark. I let my pencil fly across the page, caging the elephant in an eight-by-eight grid. Sixty-four small boxes total. I numbered each one from top to bottom, then on my blank page, I drew a triangle. I broke it into fours by drawing another triangle inside it, upside-down. I did that two more times, splitting up each triangle on the page until I had one large shape made up of sixty-four small triangles.

Starting at the top, I began to sketch the elephant one grid box at a time. Transferring each "bite" of the elephant from square to triangle meant some of the images needed to be squashed or distorted to fit the new shape. It also meant that the elephant's eye, which was in box 21 of the square grid, was going to end up smack in the center of the large triangle. I grinned. It was going to look even cooler than I thought. Like seeing an elephant through a kaleidoscope.

I was working on a slice of the elephant's tail when Mrs. Doughty's voice snapped me back to reality.

"Do you need assistance, Miss McDade?"

Elvis had moved to the middle of the room with her hands and feet on the floor and her butt in the air. Her drawing was on the floor beneath her. She examined it from Down Dog position.

"I'm getting a different perspective," Elvis said. She rested her head on the carpet and lifted one foot in the air.

Mrs. Doughty reached down and plucked my sister's paper up off the floor.

"This is not an elephant," she said.

"It's an elephant bird." Elvis stood up. Her hair floated in the air from the carpet static, and her face was red from all the blood rushing to her head. "They used to live in

Madagascar. But they went extinct in the sixteen hundreds. And that"—she pointed—"is Sir Bentley. Who's staying with us."

"Cool!" Several kids left their tables and gathered to look.

"She didn't make a grid."

"It looks like an ostrich."

While Mrs. Doughty tried to hush everyone, Elvis beamed.

"Elephant birds are easy to draw," she said. "I can show you."

"Gross! What *is* that?" One of the kids had wandered over to Rondo's side of the table, and now the crowd formed behind his chair.

"An elephant," Rondo said. He was trying to look bored, but the corners of his mouth kept turning up and he had the old Rondo gleam in his eye.

On the paper in front of him was an elephant. Sort of. It had strange pockmarks and gouges all over its body and head. Half of its trunk was missing, and there were jagged lines that made it look like the legs had gotten sawn off. Next to the elephant stood a man with a knife.

"Who's that guy?" Eugene asked.

Rondo added a couple drops of blood to the knife. "The dude who's eating the elephant," he said.

"Eeeewww!"

Everyone started to talk and laugh at once. Rondo shot me a grin.

I grinned back. Maybe art camp wasn't going to be so bad.

Mrs. Doughty clapped her hands. *Tap-TAP, tap-tap-TAP.*

Every single kid stopped talking and clapped back. *Tap-TAP, tap-tap-TAP.*

"Where should you all be right now?" Mrs. Doughty asked, and everyone immediately went back to their seats. "For those of you who perhaps didn't *understand* the directions, let's have a fresh start."

She flipped Elvis's elephant bird over and tapped the blank back of the page. She picked up a ruler, drew the first two grid lines, then handed the ruler and pencil to Elvis.

She flipped Rondo's paper over quickly, but she studied my kaleidoscope elephant for a long time before turning it over to the blank back side.

"Ask a neighbor if you can't figure it out," she said.

Copying the image block by block wasn't only boring; it also didn't look good. I tried to blend the lines of the grid into the drawing, but the effect was choppy, like the elephant was made out of stacked Legos. What was the point of this?

"Hey, Eugene," Rondo said quietly. "Missing anything?"

Eugene shook his head and kept drawing, though I noticed he'd started to mix up the order of his grid squares, sort of like I had done. The trunk of his elephant was now where the tail should be. Nice.

"You sure?" Rondo waved a ten-dollar bill in Eugene's direction.

Eugene's hand went for his back pocket.

"Hey! Give it back!"

I groaned. "Rondo!"

Rondo put on an innocent face.

"I told you earlier," he said to Eugene. "Never keep money in your back pocket. It's an *invitation* to a criminal."

"Give it back!"

Rondo handed the money to Eugene just as Mrs. Doughty reappeared at our table.

Eugene pointed angrily at Rondo. "He stole my money! Right out of my pocket!"

The teacher went into high alert mode. Her eyebrows practically disengaged themselves from her forehead.

"I took it an hour ago, and he didn't even notice," Rondo said. Like Mrs. Doughty was going to be on *his* side. From the way her nostrils were flaring, she definitely wasn't.

"He didn't mean to—" I started, but Rondo interrupted.

"I *did* mean to," he said. "I'm trying to help him out!"

Eugene's voice squeaked. "By taking my money?"

Rondo's chin jutted forward. Every kid in the room had stopped drawing.

"Nobody pays attention," Rondo said. "It's like they think pickpockets and jewel thieves are only in the movies or Los Angeles. Well, they're not. They're everywhere."

"Rondo, it's not a good time . . ." I'd heard this lecture before, and it was not short.

Rondo ignored me.

"If you want to show off a whole bunch of jewels or have

money hanging out of your pocket, you have to PAY ATTEN-TION. Houdini says—"

Mrs. Doughty's hands came together in one loud *CLAP*. She was so angry, she forgot the secret code.

"Pay attention to this, young man: *Thieves* are not welcome in my classroom."

MIYON

It was ten thirty when Mom arrived at Classroom 405. She didn't seem mad, but she made us wait in the Kleenex box hall while she talked to Mrs. Doughty. I knew I'd let her down. I couldn't even get Rondo and Elvis through an hour and a half of art camp without getting kicked out.

"I wasn't going to steal it," Rondo said.

"I know you weren't."

"Of *course* you weren't," Elvis said. "Who does she think you are? A *criminal*?"

Mom came out of the classroom looking so stressed that even Elvis kept silent on the walk home. We passed the soccer field, and I tried to spot Declan in the crowd. Everyone looked the same running around in green jerseys and white socks, trying to kick the ball across the field. I finally saw him in the back, high-fiving a kid with a sweatband around his head.

It was weird. I'd never seen Dec play soccer in my life. I doubted he even knew the rules, but he was doing fine.

Good, even. He kicked the ball to a girl with a brown pony-tail, and someone yelled out, "Nice pass, Declan!" A tiny jolt of jealousy flickered through my brain, but I tried to shrug it off. Good for Dec. Day one, and he fit right in.

Back at the Perro, the backyard was a disaster. Extension cords and lighting equipment were strewn everywhere while crew members set up speakers and hammered things to the stage. The chickens were going berserk in their coop, and there was a woman setting up a ladder two inches away from Dad's organic garden.

"Please," Mom said. "Those aren't weeds, that's baby kale."

Madeleine and Asha were in the lobby, making calls and plans. The second they spotted Mom, they rushed us.

"Elly, I can't upload photos to Bentley's social media feed! We need faster internet service. Stat."

"The air in Bentley's room is sweltering. She has a photo shoot *and* a book signing tomorrow. If she gets overheated, her coat is going to be flat. I can't have flat. Also, I ordered a hundred chairs and a table for the signing. They'll arrive tomorrow after the shoot. The curtains in the lobby need to go. The photographer won't like them."

Mom crinkled her nose. "A photo shoot? And a book signing? Happening *here*?"

Elvis spotted a long, flowy tail and bolted for the lobby.

"Sir Bentley! You get to sign books!"

Mom shot me a look, and I ran after Elvis, capturing her

by the shoulders and turning her back in the direction we'd come.

"We'll go to the farmers' market," I told Mom.

She was already dialing someone on her phone—the salon or the internet provider—but she reached into her pocket and handed me her grocery list and a handful of cash. *Thank you*, she mouthed as I rushed my siblings out the door and onto Main Street.

"I can't stand this," Elvis complained. "We're missing *everything*!" We'd only gotten as far as Dogma Cafe before she started dragging her feet and begging to go back.

"I can't believe you wouldn't let me grab my book," Rondo said.

"Chill," I said. "We'll get back in time for Yappy Hour, I promise. And I have graduation money. I'll buy you a book. I'll buy you two books. You can go wild."

"Really?" Rondo asked.

"Yes."

"We can go wild?" Elvis asked.

"Well, not—" It was too late. Before I could stop him, Rondo was cheetah-sprinting down Main Street. Elvis did a little skip and galloped after him.

"Come on, guys!" I yelled. "You know what I meant!"

They barely even stopped to look for traffic on Ocean Drive. They ran across and cut through the beach parking lot. I caught up with them at the bike path. Rondo had taken his shirt off and was waving it in a circle over his head, yelling, "Woot! Woot! Woot!" and Elvis was flinging herself into Breath of Joy, her favorite yoga move. She sucked in air and threw her arms to the sky, out to the side, back up in the air, then flopped her whole body down in a forward fold.

"You guys," I started, but I couldn't help laughing. Rondo looked ridiculous dancing around shirtless with his messy long hair and his skinny ribs. And Elvis was swinging her arms faster and faster with every breath.

Somewhere in the background behind the shirt swinging and joy breathing and laughing, I heard a voice yell, "Watch out! Hey, watch out!" I turned my head in time to see a small fluffball of a dog dragging a girl on a skateboard toward us at full speed. A long blue streak of hair was tucked behind her ear—it was the surfer girl, speeding toward us like a meteor. Elvis shrieked, and in a split second, all of us were sprawled on the ground. I hit the pavement hard and felt something sharp dig into my leg. I yelled out in pain, and the pup yipped and bounced around like she'd won the game.

"Sorry," the girl said. She pulled off her headphones and untangled her foot from the dog's leash. The puppy had bright blue eyes and speckles of white, brown, and black fur all over her face, and she was licking my knee like her life depended on it. Her tongue was so rough I thought she might take off a layer of skin. The back of my leg throbbed.

"Hey! You're the surfer!" Elvis said.

"You're ri*dic*ulous," Rondo said.

I knew he meant *ridiculous* like *awesome*, like *the greatest surfer I've ever seen*, but the girl cocked her head to the side and stared him down. She was one of those girls who could be twelve or seventeen, I couldn't tell. Her dark, blue-streaked hair fell down to her biceps, which were ripped from paddling.

She made a fist and popped it in Rondo's direction.

"I know you," she said in a menacing voice. "You snaked my wave."

She leaned forward like maybe she had a lot more to say about that, and Rondo looked like he might pee his pants.

"I—I didn't mean to . . . I'm sorry . . . I—"

The girl gave Rondo a light punch in the arm and snorted while she laughed. Definitely not seventeen.

"I'm razzing you," she said. "I'm Miyon Kim. This is Layne. I got her from the shelter yesterday, and she's totally wild."

"Not as wild as us," Elvis said with pride. She held her arms out, and the pup tried to wriggle out of Miyon's grasp.

"Don't even think about it, Layne," she said. And then to Elvis, "No offense. She's trying to use you as an excuse to escape."

Something was seriously digging into my leg. I shifted my weight and Miyon grimaced. "Um, I think you're sitting on my dad's Walkman."

She was right. There was an old-school cassette player under my thigh. Scratch that. What *used* to be an old-school cassette player. The cover had been completely crushed. And there was blood all over it.

"Oh my gosh! Stand up!" Miyon commanded, and the next thing I knew, Elvis was lifting the back of my shorts and everyone was staring at me.

"Ugh," Elvis said, making gagging sounds. "Disgusting!"

"Quit it. It's fine!" I waved her away. I couldn't crane my neck far enough around to see, but the cut was high enough on my thigh that it felt like everyone was looking at my butt.

"No, she's right." Miyon held up her crushed tape player to show me there were a few missing shards of plastic. "There's shrapnel in there. You've got to get it cleaned up."

"Wash it in the ocean," Rondo said, averting his eyes. If he even caught a glimpse of the blood, he was going to puke for sure.

"What if it gets infected?" Elvis said, and turned up the theatrics. "Epic could die! And we have *nowhere* to go. We got *kicked out* of art camp, and Mom *banished* us from our own house. Maybe forever!"

"Really?" Miyon hoisted Layne onto her hip, shoved the bloody cassette player in her pocket, and picked up her skateboard. "I live close," she said. "Come with me."

HOUSEBOAT

By "close," Miyon meant about a hundred yards away at Bill's Marina. She led us down one of the docks and walked straight onto a boat painted red and orange with the words *Endless Summer* on the back. Two surfboards and wetsuits lay drying on the deck. Miyon stepped over them toward the cabin door and waved us on.

Rondo, Elvis, and I hesitated.

"It's okay," Miyon said. "My dad's not here, but he won't care."

"You live on a boat?" Elvis asked.

"That's so rad," Rondo breathed.

Miyon shrugged. "It's all right."

She led us down the stairs and into a wood-paneled cabin with a couch, a TV, and a tiny kitchen. Two guitars and a ukulele hung on one wall.

"The first aid kit's in the back," she said. We walked through a door of beads into a small bedroom with two bunks and a bathroom off to the side. The rooms had shelves and storage cabinets stacked all the way to the ceiling.

Elvis lifted the lid to the toilet. "How do you flush this thing?" she asked. "There's no handle."

"You don't," Miyon said. She took a stool out from under the sink and stood on it to reach one of the shelves. "It's a composter. There's a bin at the bottom, and you empty it every week."

"Nice." Rondo nodded with approval while Elvis made retching sounds. I really didn't care about the plumbing. I was trying to keep it together and not drip blood all over the floor.

Miyon held up a pair of tweezers and a first aid kit and hopped down from the stool. "You ready for this?"

I groaned and wished I was still at art camp.

At first, I tried to lock myself in the bathroom and fix the cut myself. But I couldn't see a thing. Then I tried to get Elvis to do it. She has terrible hand-eye coordination, and after the fifth stabbing, I'd had enough. Rondo was no help because of the whole puking-at-the-sight-of-blood thing. He wouldn't even look in my direction. It wasn't his fault, but still.

I had no choice. Rondo turned on the TV and flipped channels while I lay on my stomach on the couch and let a perfect stranger pick three pieces of Walkman shrapnel out of my thigh with the tweezers. The couch was so small that my head butted up against the wall. Built-in bookshelves reached all the way up to the ceiling, and I read the titles to distract myself. *Murder on the Orient Express. The London Eye Mystery. The Case of the Missing Moonstone.* Every single book from floor to ceiling was a mystery novel.

I flinched as Miyon put some kind of horrible stinging sauce on my leg.

"Hold still!" Elvis said, and I had to suffer for another minute while she and Miyon bandaged me up.

"I could be a nurse!" Elvis said. "That wasn't bad at all."

"For you," I mumbled.

Miyon patted my foot.

"It looked worse than it was," she said. "It's not even bleeding anymore."

"Thanks," I said to the floor. I wasn't ready to make eye contact after she'd stared at what was essentially my butt cheek for the last ten minutes.

We sat awkwardly while Miyon put her headphones on and tested the crushed cassette player.

"What is that thing?" Elvis asked.

"It's a Walkman," Miyon said. "My dad's, from elementary school. You can play music on it, but I like to record stuff."

"Like what?"

"Random things people say. I was taping some tourists this morning. There was a French couple with a bichon frise, and they were . . . Here, I'll see if it works."

She pressed a button, and the Walkman made a squeaking noise as the cassette gears slowly turned.

"Sorry," I said. "Is it ruined?"

She unplugged her headphones, rewound the tape for a second, and pressed PLAY. A tinny version of my voice said, "Sorry. Is it ruined?"

"Still works! You only crushed the cover. My dad won't care. He never uses it." She frowned at the television. "What kind of teenager walks around in bling like that, anyway? What's the point?"

Rondo had flipped to a news story about the recent Silk Bandit jewel heist at Chloe Cosmo's house in the Hollywood Hills.

"Seriously," he said.

"She's been bragging for weeks on social media about all the expensive jewelry she inherited from her famous grandma." Miyon snapped the first aid kit closed. "What a dope. It's like she was *inviting* someone to come steal it."

Rondo actually turned off the television to stare at Miyon. Even though she was at least four years older than him, I was pretty sure he'd found his ideal woman.

Elvis scooped up Layne and started smothering her with hugs and baby talk. "Sir Bentley has diamonds on her collar," she said between dog kisses. "And she wears it all the time."

"She?"

Elvis clapped her hand over her mouth and gasped dramatically.

Rondo rolled his eyes. "It's not that big of a deal. The dog's a girl. Plays a dude detective."

"Yeah, I love that show. A diamond dog collar? That's bananas."

"It has lots of other jewels on it, too," Elvis said. "I'll tell you everything. Do you have any snacks?"

"We should go," I said. "We've bothered you enough."

"I don't mind," Miyon said.

I shook my head. Rondo and Elvis glared at me.

"We've got to get the stuff on Mom's list," I said. "Thanks for . . . Well, sorry about your Walkman."

Elvis got the hiccups halfway up the stairs.

"I have the best idea!" she said, turning toward Miyon. "You should—*hic*—come to Yappy Hour. At the Perro del Mar tonight."

Miyon looked confused. "The hotel?"

"It's a bed and breakfast," I said.

My sister's Idea Hiccups were picking up speed.

"We—*hic*—live there! Yappy Hour's the best. Some of Mom and Dad's friends come over to hang out in the garden, and we listen—*hic*—to records, and the dogs eat pupsicles. I'll—*hic*—introduce you to Sir—*hic*—Bentley!"

"For real?"

Rondo nodded. "You should come."

"Okay!" Miyon turned to me. "What time?"

I cringed. I kind of thought we'd all move on and go back to barely acknowledging each other in the dark on Monday mornings. It was a lot less embarrassing.

"Five," I said.

"Great." She grinned. "And don't worry. What happens on the houseboat stays on the houseboat."

FIFI AND POO

Elvis and I were in the backyard arranging candles and flowers on the cocktail tables while Mom, Dad, and Rondo put finishing touches on the food platters in the kitchen. Dad's Buddy Holly record was on, and I could hear all three of them singing along through the open window.

"Epic! My man!" Brody Delgado held out his knuckles as he burst through the back gate. A short woman with pink hair, a man in a tight pink T-shirt, and three labradoodle puppies in pink bow ties followed behind. "Did you find that skinny dog?"

I really didn't want to fist-bump him.

"Yappy Hour doesn't start for twenty minutes," I said.

"Yeah I know, dude. I wanted to see how you guys were setting it up. This is pretty swank!"

It was, actually. Next to the stage, the crew had set up the tiki bar of Dad's dreams and strung lanterns from the house to the tree above the chicken coop. It looked like a backyard from a movie set.

Brody started placing stacks of slightly crumpled flyers under all the blown-glass candle holders Elvis and I had set out.

"Hey!" El said. "This is plagiarism."

I looked over her shoulder. She wasn't wrong.

Get your weekday wag on at the Moondoggie Inn

• **YIPS & SIPS** •

Tuesday at 5 P.M.

Featuring . . .

THE PENDLETON TRIPLETS!!!!!!

"You guys should come," Brody said. "FiFi got a DJ. It's going to be off the hook."

Seriously? It was a total rip-off of the Perro's Yappy Hour. Why would we *go*? I put one of the flyers in my messenger bag to show Mom and Dad.

"We can't," Elvis said. "It's the same time as Sir Bentley's book signing!"

"Aw, nuts. Really?" Brody seemed actually bummed. "I wanted your dad to come and give me some tips. Maybe he could get off work?"

He had to be joking.

In the back corner of the yard, the chickens started making

a ruckus. Elvis and I had locked the hens safely in their house, closed the gate to the coop, and hung my sister's goofy Yappy Hour sign on the fence: NOBODY HERE BUT US CHICKENS. PLEASE RESPECT OUR PRIVACY. SIGNED, HENHOUSE MANAGEMENT. But now the gate was wide open, and so was the door to the chicken house. The hens were skittering around outside their shed, clucking and flapping their wings like the apocalypse was coming. One had escaped from the coop and was booking it toward the garden.

"Dominique!" Elvis cried, and practically tackled her favorite chicken by its feathery feet.

The pink-haired woman and all three dogs were inside the coop posing while the man in the pink T-shirt snapped photos.

"You can't be in there," I told the photographer, then ran over to the open gate and held it while Elvis carried Dominique back inside. The dude with the camera held up a palm.

"Don't move! This lighting's perfect," he said. "There's nothing to fear, all FiFi's dogs are expertly trained."

It was true. Most dogs would be all wound up inside a coop full of berserk chickens, but the puppies sat quietly for the photos. Anytime one of them even glanced at the hens, the woman made a clicking sound with her tongue and they snapped right back to attention.

"What are they, robots?" Elvis asked, patting Dominique's feathers to calm her.

"How charmingly domestic!" The pink-haired woman plucked Dominique right out of Elvis's arms and held the terrified chicken in front of the dogs for another round of photos.

By the time the photo shoot was done and Elvis and I got all the chickens back into their house with the door locked and the gate shut, the entire backyard had filled with people and dogs. Mom and Dad had emerged from the kitchen and were passing out cocktails, snacks, and pupsicles to the biggest Yappy Hour crowd we'd ever seen.

There were the usual Monday Night Yappy Hour guests like Doug from Dogma Cafe and Miss Tabitha from Healthy Pup Natural Foods. Flo was talking with Luis, while Cookie Monster sat at their feet licking a pupsicle. Luis usually came to Yappy Hour straight from work; he was still in all his cop gear. Mr. and Mrs. Boone were at the tiki bar taking selfies with Pico. All three wore sun hats and Hawaiian shirts.

The rest of the guests were people I'd never seen. FiFi and the Pendleton Triplets were surrounded by fans asking for autographs. There was a guy with a camera on a tripod and a lady talking into an audio recorder. FiFi snapped her fingers, and one by one, the labradoodles shook hands with a reporter who had a *Los Angeles Times* badge hanging around her neck.

"Penelope. Olivia. Oleander," FiFi announced as each dog

lifted a paw. "The truth is, anyone can train *one* dog. I've trained over one hundred and fifty!"

Elvis glared at her. "Who names their dogs that? *P-O-O.* Poo!"

I hushed her and scanned the crowd for Declan. Instead, I spotted a Mohawk near the garden.

"Hey, Epic! Elvis!" Delphi waved us over. Melissa was standing next to her, holding a Yips & Sips flyer and watching the crowd intently.

"Whatever you do, don't go to *that*," Elvis said. She crouched on the ground and let Morrissey lick her hand like it was a bacon-flavored lollipop. "He's our archnemesis."

Delphi laughed. "*You* have an archnemesis? Well, then!" She took the flyer from Melissa and made a big show of ripping it into pieces. She tossed the confetti into her empty margarita cup and pretended to take a swig.

"You guys really like dragons," Elvis said, staring at Melissa's legs.

Melissa had changed into a pair of shorts, showing off a dragon tattoo with diamonds for eyes snaking around her left leg. It was identical to the jeweled dragon on Delphi's arms, which matched the large green dragon pins they each wore on their shirts.

"I love dragons," Melissa said quietly. She'd been staring intently at FiFi's labradoodles and biting her lip. "Those dogs have almost zero flight initiation distance when they're close to their trainer. Even in a huge crowd like this. I wonder if Sir Bentley has the same . . . I wish I had my notebook."

"I've got one." I handed her a notebook and pen from my messenger bag, and she shot me a grateful smile. "What's flight initiation distance?"

"It has to do with how an animal makes the decision to run away when it feels threatened. Typically, the closer a dog is to safety, the less risk it feels. If it's far from home or its owner, for instance, it might bolt at the tiniest sign of danger."

"Like Pico!" Elvis said.

Exactly. Dec and I hadn't thought to take distance from the Perro into account when we'd put together the Pico Project. Maybe next time, we should try the twenty-five-second swap closer to home. If there was a next time. Pico may have forgiven me for losing him, but Mrs. Boone definitely hadn't.

I felt a tap on my shoulder, and the minute I saw the blue-streaked hair, my own flight initiation response kicked in. My first instinct was to bolt. For some reason, I'm usually fine with adults, but kids my own age make me tongue-tied. Especially when we have an embarrassing history involving cassette-player shrapnel.

"Cool spot! My dad went inside to check it out." Miyon

looked around at the crowd. "This is a *few* of your parents' friends?"

Delphi raised her camera and shot a photo of us. I wanted to crawl into the chicken coop and hide with the hens.

"Miyon!" Elvis tore herself away from Morrissey to throw her arms around her new friend's waist. "Where's Layne?"

"Dad didn't think she was ready to behave at a party," Miyon said. She obviously didn't know what to do with Elvis's bear hug. She raised her arms awkwardly in the air. "I had to leave her in her crate. Where's Sir Bentley?"

Elvis scowled and pointed to the window above the back porch.

"Locked up in Room 3," she said. "Asha wants to be 'fashionably late.' How *boring* is that? Sir Bentley's missing all the fun."

"Super boring," Delphi agreed. She snapped a quick photo of the window, then shot us an embarrassed look. "I couldn't resist," she said. "I mean, it's *Sir Bentley's* window. That dog is even more beautiful in person than on TV."

"I know, right?" Elvis grinned.

Miyon pulled a smart phone out of her pocket and snapped a photo, too.

Melissa finished scribbling, ripped out the page, and handed my notebook back to me. Then she and Delphi led Morrissey away to refresh their cocktails. I was starting to worry that I would have to think of a conversation topic when a murmur went through the crowd. Suddenly, everyone went quiet. Dad's Buddy Holly record had been drowned out by all the voices, and now it suddenly sang out loud and clear. "Rave on, it's a crazy feeling . . ."

"Now what?" Elvis asked, standing on her tiptoes. "I can't see. Is it Bentley?"

ANIMAL UNIVERSE

It was a film crew. An actual film crew. Lights. Cameras. A giant, fuzzy boom microphone.

"Holy ravioli!" Elvis said.

The crew waltzed into our backyard like it was nothing. Like they happened to be in the neighborhood and a strawberry margarita sounded like it would hit the spot. Their hats and T-shirts all had matching Animal Universe logos.

"Clive!" I heard Mrs. Boone yelp. Animal Universe was their favorite channel. Pico could watch reruns of *Bentley Knows* and *Dogs at Work* all day long.

The crowd started to buzz again, and I spotted Declan making his way toward us with a pupsicle in his hand. Frank had been banned from Yappy Hour after he tried to take on a group of dozing golden retrievers. It didn't end well, and Dec had vowed to eat a pupsicle at every Yappy Hour in honor of his bravery.

"You know those are for dogs, right?" I asked.

"Dude, this is so gelly." He handed me his pupsicle so he could take a picture of the film crew with his phone.

"Gelly?"

Dec checked the photo he'd taken and took another. "I'm trying out some new vocabulary," he said. "Do you think I used that okay? Like, in the right context?"

I shook my head. "Don't use it. In any context."

"Right. I'll do some more resear . . ." Dec's eyes got huge, and he dropped his voice to a panicky whisper. "Okay okay okay. Don't look now, but she's standing right next to you."

"Dec—"

"No, I'm serious. Turn your head a little to the right, but be cool . . ."

Miyon leaned over and gave Dec a funny grin.

"I'm Miyon," she said.

Dec froze, then bowed, feet together, right hand twirling out with a flourish.

"Salutations," he said.

Miyon stared at us.

I shrugged. "This is Declan."

One good thing about Dec is that when he's around, you never have to worry about things like conversation topics. In sixty seconds flat, he learned more about Miyon than my siblings and I had learned all day. Her full name was Miyon Rose Kim. She was going into eighth grade and went to Carmelito Middle School (Dec elbowed me in the ribs at this piece of data), but she'd only been there since May. Her dad, Jay Kim, was a professor at UCLA, but he used to be a pro surfer. They were living on the boat as part of his sabbatical project.

"He *says* he's doing research, but I think he's mainly here to surf Mavericks."

"So will you be in school in the fall?" Dec asked.

"I don't know. Depends. Bill's Marina's pretty cheap for live-aboards, so we could stay for a while."

The sound of someone tapping on a glass shushed us all again, and we craned our necks toward the tiki bar.

"I'd like to thank you all for coming tonight, especially my dear friends from Animal Universe."

It was Madeleine Devine. She was standing on the stage in a black leather dress, flaming red lipstick, and even more bling than she'd had on when she arrived. Asha had changed into a shimmery gold dress that made her look like a sun goddess. Offstage, Thomas Scott was holding Sir Bentley's leash.

"Before we get started, I'd like to bring a very special guest to the stage."

On cue, Thomas unhooked the leash. Sir Bentley, decked out in her jeweled collar, walked up the steps to the stage alone, slowly and elegantly. Shampoo-commercial fur blowing in the breeze. Maybe Madeleine pulled a treat out of her pocket to get the dog to pause at the microphone and bark, but it was hard to tell. From the audience, Bentley appeared to be completely in charge. The crowd loved it.

"Oh my gosh!" Miyon grinned. "That's really him. *Her!*"

She and Dec held up their phones and snapped pictures.

"We're so honored to be here in America's Number One Dog-Friendly Town . . . sponsored by Dog Elegance!" Madeleine paused for the cheers and added, "Dog Elegance products are designed to boost your best friend's happiness, energy, and intelligence. How do you think Sir Bentley is able to solve all those crimes?"

The crowd laughed. Mom and Dad were stationed behind the tiki bar. Dad was laughing with everyone else, but Mom crossed and uncrossed her arms awkwardly. Being the set piece for a Dog Elegance commercial wasn't exactly on her top ten list.

Madeleine talked for a while about how Dog Elegance products helped Sir Bentley maintain a superstar lifestyle, and then she said, "Okay, Carmelito. To kick off our celebration of America's Number One Dog-Friendly Town, we have a *very* special performance for you tonight!"

She and Asha scanned the backyard while the crowd murmured.

"Elvis?" Madeleine said into the mic. "Elvis, are you out there? Come on up. I have someone I want you to meet."

"Me!" My sister leaped to her feet and elbowed her way through the crowd while some lady in a bright red pantsuit walked out of the Perro and onto the stage with a guitar. I squinted. There was a small, fluffy stuffed animal perched on top of the instrument. People gasped and hooted.

"No way!" Miyon said.

"Who is it?"

"Sharon Henderson and her dog, Newt," Dec explained. "They had a multiplatinum song this year."

"That's a real dog?"

"Pomeranian. Specially bred from an ancestor of one of Queen Victoria's dogs."

"How do you know—"

Dec held up his phone. "I'm telling you. You can learn a lot."

I can guarantee Elvis had no idea who Sharon Henderson was, but she went berserk onstage anyway, hugging Sir Bentley and jumping up and down.

When Madeleine handed over the microphone and multi-platinum Sharon plugged in her guitar and started playing "Hound Dog," Elvis looked stunned. And then she went for it. She howled into the mic. Windmilled her arms. Jiggled her hips. She practically fell off the stage diving onto her knees, and the crowd went wild.

The applause had barely died down when FiFi hopped onto the platform with the Pendleton Triplets. There wasn't any room left on the small stage, but Brody Delgado elbowed his way in behind her. Both his T-shirt and hat had giant Moondoggie Inn logos on them.

"What a wonderful performance," FiFi said, taking the microphone from Elvis.

Madeleine didn't look at all ready to turn the stage over to the Pendleton Triplets, but the platform wasn't big enough to hold all those people, dogs, speakers, and lights. Elvis leaped off the stage, but Madeleine wouldn't budge, so they all stood there smooshed together while FiFi gave a speech about Dog Elegance puppy food.

Elvis raced back to where we were standing.

"Did you see that?" she asked, bouncing from one foot to the other. "Did you see me up there?"

"No," Dec teased. "I closed my eyes."

Elvis swatted him and started doing jumping jacks.

"You were awesome, El," I said.

"You killed it!" Miyon agreed.

"Where's Rondo? Did Rondo see?"

I hadn't seen Rondo since Yappy Hour started. I scanned the crowd. A couple people leaned over to tell Elvis how great her impression was, and then something in FiFi's speech made everyone gasp.

"We signed the deal today," she was saying. "Star Wars: The Pendleton Trilogy starts shooting in September."

I'd thought the yelling and clapping for Elvis was loud, but this was out of control. People fist pumped the air. Somebody screamed. It was like she'd announced she was giving everyone a trillion dollars and free ice cream for life. Sharon Henderson started to play Darth Vader's "Imperial March" on the guitar. Somehow, the Pomeranian managed to stay balanced on top and yip on cue. FiFi smirked at Madeleine.

"That was already on all the gossip blogs," Dec shouted over the noise.

Was he serious? I couldn't even respond.

Sharon transitioned "Imperial March" into the beginning of what I assumed was the multiplatinum song. FiFi turned to slide the microphone into the singer's mic stand, but Brody grabbed it out of her hand. He put the mic up to his mouth.

"Woot! Woot! If you think this is swank . . ." he said over the music, pumping his fist. "Come on over to the Moondoggie Inn for Yips and Sips. Tomorrow at five P.M. I'll give you a private tour of America's Number One Dog-Friendly Hotel!"

He actually tried to do a mic drop. He held it straight out, *woot*ing at the audience.

"Those things aren't cheap," I said as he let go.

Madeleine and FiFi both dove for the mic, bumping into Sharon Henderson as they fumbled to catch it in midair. There was a terrible screeching sound from the speakers as the musician and the hosts collided.

The tiny Pomeranian, Newt, went flying off the top of the guitar. His miniature body hurtled high into the air, then plummeted down, mimicking the first half of a Vomit Comet's parabolic flight pattern.

Sir Bentley, who'd been lying there like a lump, instantly jumped into the air and opened her massive jaw. It was like watching the burning-building episode of *Bentley Knows*. On the brink of tragedy, just as the Pomeranian was about to crash onto the stage in a mass of fluff and bones, Sir Bentley caught the tiny dog by the scruff of his neck. She stood onstage, proudly dangling the unscathed Pomeranian in her teeth. Like she'd rehearsed the rescue a thousand times.

The audience cheered.

"Holy baloney!" Elvis screamed. "Sir Bentley is a HERO!"

Miyon and Dec compared phones to see who got the best photos, while Elvis danced around us.

"Is this thing almost over?" Rondo appeared beside me. "I'm starved."

"Me too," Dec and I said in unison.

My sister bugged her eyes out. "Who cares about food? Rondo, where have you been?"

"Reading," he said. "Why? What'd I miss?"

YAPPY HOUR

It was the longest Yappy Hour in Perro del Mar history.

Yappy Hour is supposed to be exactly as advertised: one hour. People come, they socialize, and they feed pupsicles to their dogs. Then they go home, and we clean up and have dinner and play board games. That's how it works.

But after Animal Universe showed up and FiFi said the words *Star* and *Wars*, and the whole Brody-mic-drop debacle settled down, Dad took the stage and announced that margaritas and pupsicles were on the house. I know he loves *Star Wars* and he loves dogs, but giving out a bunch of free stuff because a labradoodle is going to have a lightsaber? Seemed like an overreaction. Even Mom got into it, running upstairs and putting on the Princess Leia costume she'd worn for Halloween.

By the time seven o'clock rolled around, we'd run out of pupsicles and people were *still* hanging out. Thomas Scott pulled out a giant roll of cash and gave Mom five hundred dollars to order pizzas from Vittorio's. Luis took Rondo to pick them up in his cop car, and they whooped the sirens when they came back. People went bonkers for it. They rushed the car, cheering and carrying pizza after pizza into the backyard.

Elvis was in her element. It was past her bedtime, and she was standing on someone's picnic blanket doing her wind-mill arms and jelly legs while a crowd of people egged her on. Adding the fact that Sir Bentley was staying at our house, it was probably the greatest day of her life.

Rondo, Dec, Miyon, and I grabbed an entire pizza and a liter of soda and took it inside. All I wanted to do was sit in the quiet corner booth and stuff my face. I was starving.

It wasn't quite dark outside, but the lights were off in the dining room and some of the curtains were closed, making the guest tables and chairs look shadowy. As we entered the room, we heard a snuffling sound near the breakfast bar. Rondo immediately went into stealth mode, sneaking back to the corner and crouching to the ground.

I shook my head at him, shifted the box of pizza to one hand, and turned on the light. Delphi and Melissa were hud-dled together talking at the breakfast bar. It was Morrissey who'd been snuffling at their feet. When the light went on, Delphi jumped right off her stool.

"Yow!" she yelled. Then, embarrassed, she said, "I didn't realize it had gotten so dark in here. You guys scared the bejeebers out of me!""

"*Yow?*" Melissa raised an eyebrow at Delphi. "Who are you, Captain America?"

Delphi thought that was hilarious.

"*That* looks yummy," Melissa said.

Rondo came out of his hiding place and took the box of pizza from my hand.

"There's more outside," he said, heading to the corner booth with Dec and Miyon close behind.

"Okay, okay," Delphi said, still giggling. "No stealing. We'll get our own." She bent down to hook Morrissey's lead to his collar. "Hey, Epic," she said. "Mrs. Boone told me you're too busy to walk Pico tomorrow, so I told her I'd take him out. You don't have to worry about it."

Too busy? I wasn't too busy. I knew that Mrs. Boone was still mad, but did she honestly trust a complete stranger more than she trusted me?

"I don't think Pico will go with—"

"We did a trial run after the concert. Mel had some ideas about how to help him feel safe, and he did great. So . . . there's a load off for you."

Melissa nodded. "It's all about getting him in a *thinking* state, not a *reacting* state. You okay?"

"Sure. Thanks." I don't know why I felt let down. I *wanted* Pico to get used to walking with other people. But he hardly knew Delphi and Melissa.

"You *aren't* busy tomorrow, are you?" Melissa asked.

I shook my head.

"Aw," Delphi said. "That's not cool. We'll put in a good word, won't we, Mel?"

"Earth to Epic!" Dec snapped his fingers at me from the corner booth. "Rondo's eating all the pizza."

"Don't worry." Delphi winked as she led Morrissey toward the door. "We've got your back."

The corner booth is one of my favorite places in the Perro del Mar. It's one of those U-shaped booths big enough to fit six people. Mom built it out of headboards from beds she found at Martinez Antiques, so the walls of the booth are so tall they make you feel like you're in a fortress. There might be two hundred people wreaking chaos outside, but the four of us and our pizza were untouchable.

Almost. I'd shoved half a slice of pizza in my mouth when Mrs. Boone rushed in and peeked her head around the wall of the booth.

"Delphi told me you were here," she said. She reached over Miyon's lap and dumped Pico into mine. "Pico's freezing, and I can't find his fleece. Hold on to him while I run upstairs—I can *trust* you to do that, right?"

"Urm-hm." I started to defend myself, but my mouth was full of pizza and she was already gone.

"An Iggy!" Miyon said. "Look at his shirt!"

Whatever Delphi had said to Mrs. Boone, Pico and I were both grateful. He leaned into me, huddling for warmth. His Hawaiian shirt was paper thin. I unzipped my sweatshirt, wrapped him inside, and zipped it back up around his body so his head was below my chin.

Dec said, "If you had one more head, you could be the Hound of Hades."

"Who?"

"Cerberus. The three-headed dog-beast who guards the gates of the underworld. But you'd need another head. Obvs. That means 'obviously.' It's shorter, so it's more convenient."

While Dec jabbered on about Greek mythology and modern slang, we wolfed down the pizza. Which wasn't easy to do as a two-headed dog-beast. Every time I tried to bring a slice to my mouth, Pico opened *his* mouth and tried to get it first. I had to have Miyon distract him with small pieces of sausage and then cram the pizza in my mouth while he was looking in her direction.

By the time we'd polished off the whole box, Mrs. Boone still wasn't back. Rondo settled into the far corner of the booth with his book, and Dec scrolled on his phone looking up dog-headed gods. Miyon fed a few more pizza scraps to Pico.

"Want to play a game?" I asked. "I could get Stratego." It was our go-to. Last summer, Dec and I played a hundred-game Stratego marathon. Dad let us set up the board in the corner booth and string caution tape around the perimeter so we could leave out games in progress. Dec won the marathon 58–42, which wasn't as close as I would have liked, but he *is* an evil genius when it comes to bomb placement.

"I've got an app for that!" Dec grinned and put his phone

on the table. He tapped at it until a tiny Stratego screen popped up.

I was almost starting to hope aliens had invaded Declan's house. If he was being mind-controlled by outer space villains, it would explain how weird he'd been acting. The new vocabulary. Soccer. Playing Stratego without a board to study or actual flags to plant. At this rate, he was going to be a completely different human by the time school started. Which, apparently, was his plan.

"I have a better idea," Miyon said.

Her voice was quiet, and she leaned forward like she was about to tell us an unknown secret of the universe. Even Rondo looked up from his book.

"Let's go look at Sir Bentley's room."

ROOM 3

"This is not a good idea, guys."

I tried to lock eyes with my brother to let him know how serious I was, but Rondo pulled out his mint tin and laid two bobby pins on the table of the booth. He bent one in half and explained to Miyon how all he had to do was insert one into the lock and use the other as a handle to feel around and release the lock pins.

"Does it work?"

"I don't know," Rondo said. "It might take a while. It's probably better to use Mom's master key. She leaves a spare in the laundry room under the fabric softener."

"I'm here, I'm here!" Elvis, red-faced and out of breath, slid into the booth next to Rondo. "What's the plan?"

They'd all decided Elvis would die if we went to Sir Bentley's room without her, so Dec had gone to tear her away from the guests outside.

"This. Is. A. Terrible. Idea," I said for the thirty-seventh time.

"It's a *dog's* room," Dec said. "It's not that big of a deal."

"I'm not coming."

"You have to come!" Miyon said. "You're our alibi. If anyone sees us, we're delivering the Iggy to his owners."

She looked to Rondo for help, but he shook his head.

"My brother," he explained, "has an overdeveloped sense of responsibility."

Which, in the end, is exactly why I followed them up the guest stairs and down the hall with an Italian greyhound stuffed in my shirt. I'd promised Mom I'd look out for Elvis and Rondo. Who were the most stubborn humans on Earth. They were going to Sir Bentley's room whether I came with them or not.

I had a minor heart attack three times. Once when we got to the top of the stairs and heard Delphi and Melissa blasting music in their room.

"There are people up here," I whispered. "We've got to go back."

"They're in their room," Rondo said.

"It's fine," Dec said.

Elvis was already skipping to Room 3 at the far end of the hall.

The second heart attack happened when Rondo put Mom's master key in the door and turned. The click sounded as loud as a shotgun. I thought for sure Pico was going to leap out of my shirt and replay the great escape of the morning before.

But Pico was calm as a cucumber, and everyone else waltzed into the suite like they'd been invited.

"So this is where the magic happens," Miyon said.

"This is where she sleeps!" Elvis flopped down onto Sir Bentley's claw-footed dog bed and pulled the handcrafted dog blanket over her shoulders. "I can *feel* what it's like to be Sir Bentley."

"Okay," I said. "We saw it. Let's go."

But Dec was busy taking photos, and Miyon and Rondo were casing the joint like a couple detectives on the loose.

Rondo opened a giant box filled with copies of *Knowing Bentley Knows: The True Stories Behind the Making of a Canine Classic*.

"Jeez," he said. "How many books do they think they're going to sell?"

"Check it out." Miyon held up several packages of dog treats from the dresser. Healthy Hound Digestive Desserts. Healthy Hound Joint Pain Jerky. Healthy Hound Herbal Tea. "Didn't she say Bentley uses Dog Elegance products? What a liar!"

"Dog's got her own passport," Rondo said. "And a plane ticket to Grand Cayman Island."

"I know," Elvis sighed. "Madeleine told me Thomas is taking them on Friday. She thinks he might propose. Isn't it romantic?"

Miyon flipped through the passport. "In mystery novels,

Grand Cayman is where all the crooks go to hide their money. That's pretty romantic."

"Did you know Misty LaVa spent a million dollars on a pair of earrings?" Dec asked. "That's noodles."

"What?"

He tossed a magazine from the coffee table to me. It was open to a spread titled "Diamonds Are a Girl's Best Friend." Three photos of celebrities dripping in diamonds were splashed across the page.

"The Boones have that magazine," Elvis said. "Did you see their scrapbook? They *really* like celebrities."

Rondo grabbed the magazine from my hands. "Yeah," he scoffed. "Chloe Cosmo doesn't have *that* necklace anymore. I'd bet you a million dollars Misty LaVa doesn't get to keep those earrings either. Or this Shaunté Stevens chick? The Silk Bandit will hit her up for sure."

"Why do they call him the Silk Bandit?" Elvis asked.

"It could be a *her*," Miyon said.

"Whoever it is keeps leaving a silk handkerchief at every crime scene," Dec said. "It's weird."

"It's not weird," Rondo said. "It's a calling card. So we all know it's him. Or her. It's classy."

I took the magazine and put it back on the table. "Don't touch stuff," I said. "Put this back *exactly* how it was."

"*Chill*," Dec said, but he arranged the magazine so Chloe Cosmo's lipsticked smile pointed toward the bathroom.

The third heart attack happened when Miyon noticed the door to the adjoining room and tried to open it.

"Will the key open this one?" she asked Rondo.

"No!" Pico flinched inside my sweatshirt. He could tell I was stressed out and started to panic-breathe out of solidarity. "We are *not* breaking into Madeleine Devine's room. In fact, we're leaving. Right. *Now*."

I thought for sure my head was going to explode and someone was going to have to clean up brains and bits of skull from Sir Bentley's room, but Miyon said, "Okay. This was really cool, Epic. Thanks for showing me."

"Yeah, bro." Rondo gave me a thumbs-up.

Somehow, everything inside my head patched itself back together, Dec took one last photo of Elvis in Bentley's bed, and we snuck quietly out of Room 3. We made it past Madeleine and Thomas's room on the right. We'd almost reached the Boones' when we heard voices on the stairs.

"Act natural," Miyon whispered.

Natural? Right. Because it was perfectly normal for us to be hanging out in the guest wing at eight thirty at night. Anyone who came upstairs was going to know immediately that we'd been up to something. Specifically: breaking and entering.

Mrs. Boone was the first to reach the top of the stairs, and she raced straight toward Pico.

"Thank you for bringing him to me," she said. "You are so

responsible, Epic. I'm sorry I got mad at you. You'll come by at six tomorrow? As usual?"

My chest felt cold without Pico's body heat, but my face was burning. I couldn't figure out what to do with my hands. I couldn't even feel glad that Mrs. Boone was letting me walk Pico again. I had to stand there and lie to her face.

"Sure. Right. That's why we're up here. To bring you Pico."

Dad and Miyon's dad were right behind Mrs. Boone. Miyon ran straight over and threw her arms around her dad's waist. Which wasn't something I expected an eighth grader to do. He ruffled her hair, like Dad always does to me.

"Hey, Epic," Dad said. "Thanks for looking out for everybody. I was going to show Jay the barn door headboards Elly made—he's thinking of taking up woodworking. Maybe your friends want to see Sir Bentley's room? The celebrity *boudoir*?"

Rondo was holding the spare master key in his hand. I watched him slip it in his pocket like it was nothing. A pack of gum. Or a bookmark he'd dropped.

"Do you think that's okay?" Rondo asked. With an actual straight face. "To go into a guest's room without asking?"

"Seriously?" Dad asked. "It's a dog's room. Who's gonna care?"

Dec started to giggle. Then Elvis. And Miyon. Soon, the three of them were laughing so hard Dec was wiping away tears.

"Did I say something funny, or did you guys have a *lot* of sugar tonight?"

I looked at Rondo. I couldn't speak. My tongue felt like it was made of cotton.

"They're just really excited," he said. "They love Sir Bentley. A lot."

TUESDAY

8:00 A.M.

It's a Dog-Eat-Dog World Out There
posted by @pooperscooper1

Things are heating up in Carmelito, California. Last night's Yappy Hour at the Perro del Mar B&B was swarming with celebrities! Even Sharon Henderson took time out of her world tour to make a showing with her pocket dog, Newt. Lucky for you, Dog Dish is here with the *real* poop-scoop on the shindig.

First off, the "Sir" Bentley franchise doggedly tried to dominate the event with clickbait publicity stunts like this miniature Elvis impersonator. [CLICK HERE! CLICK HERE!] Okay, she's adorable, and we'll all spend the rest of the afternoon watching it on replay, but still . . . blatant exploitation, anyone?

From there, things got so bananas you'd have to see it to believe it. That's why we're giving you a glimpse of six exclusive photos that tell the tale:

- 📷 Check out this bling! Nope, not on the ladies. Zoom in on the dog. Show of hands if you think *Bentley Knows* is overpaying their actors . . .
- 📷 The crowd goes wild as our favorite cuddle-pups announce . . . *drumroll* . . . STAR. WARS. WITH. DOGS!!! We knew it, we knew it, we knew it!
- 📷 Owner of the Perro's rival hotel, Moondoggie Inn, throws down the gauntlet and vows to bury the Perro. Bold move from a guy in dressy board shorts.

- 📷 Madeleine Devine and FiFi Khan <u>dogfight</u> over the microphone. I swear it. You can't make this stuff up.
- 📷 <u>Sir Bentley attacks Sharon Henderson's Pomeranian!!!!!!!!</u>
- 📷 The Carmelito police show up and get <u>mobbed by the crowd</u>. Now this is a town that takes their dog-friendly revelry seriously!

And this was only day one, folks! We'll do our best to stay sane and stay safe so we can continue to scoop the poop on the furry-licious frenzy.

SO WHAT'S HAPPENING TONIGHT? You *could* choose to get a book signed by a vicious Saint Bernard, but if you want to be where the action is, all clues point toward the Moondoggie Inn. You'd better believe the Dog Dish will be there—taking notes and shaking our tails!

#dogfriendlytown #poopscoop #dogwars

Sponsored by: Healthy Hound Remedies, Canines for Caring, Dog Elegance™

BAD NEWS DAY

Madeleine scrolled through her phone and read the headlines out loud as Rondo and I shoved Dad's buckwheat blueberry pancakes into our mouths. Elvis didn't eat. She was too busy reacting to every line like it was a horror story unfolding in front of her eyes.

"CANINE ACTOR SIR BENTLEY'S NEW ROLE: ATTACK DOG."

"Attack what? No!"

"SHARON HENDERSON AND TINY NEWT REELING FROM VIOLENT ASSAULT."

"Aaaaahhhhh! *Lies!* That's not what happened at all!"

"More coffee?" Dad asked, holding up a clear glass decanter. "This pour is a direct-trade Ethiopian with notes of rose hips and stone fruit."

Madeleine looked annoyed but let him fill her cup, and he disappeared back into the kitchen to work on the next canine course.

It was bizarre to be in the dining room eating with the

guests. Usually, Rondo, Elvis, and I ate breakfast in the kitchen, but Madeleine had insisted that we sit at her table. I was stuck next to Bentley, whose massive jowls—thanks to Mom's custom dog benches—hung over the table at optimal eating height. Even at eight in the morning, the dog looked television-ready: perfectly brushed with her sparkling, jeweled collar hanging around her neck. Her movie-star eyes were locked on my pancakes, though, and there was a disgusting pool of saliva inching toward my plate.

"We could move to a different table," I said. "If your friends are coming down."

"Thomas doesn't eat breakfast, and I can't find Asha," Madeleine said. "Obviously, Bentley and I can't eat alone at a time like this."

"What are we, chopped liver?" Mr. Boone joked from the next table over. His black DOGFATHER T-shirt was on backward, and Mrs. Boone was still in her slippers and silk hair scarf. Neither of the Boones were morning people. It was the whole reason they had me walk Pico: So they could stay in their pajamas until ten.

But this morning when Pico and I got back from our walk, they'd scooped him right up and headed downstairs. He was sitting in his booster seat in an Iggy-sized ANIMAL UNIVERSE sweatshirt with the hood cinched around his head.

"The air-conditioning in our room is broken. Is yours?" Mrs. Boone asked Madeleine. "It's like a refrigerator upstairs!"

The Boones might as well have been invisible. The only person Madeleine wanted to talk to was Elvis.

"Sir Bentley is a HERO!" My sister had tears in her eyes. She hadn't even touched her pancakes.

"I know!" Madeleine agreed.

"He wasn't trying to hurt anyone. He *saved* that little guitar dog."

"Who puts a dog on their guitar?"

"Exactly!" Elvis threw her hands in the air. "Worst idea ever!"

"It never would have happened if FiFi didn't try to take over. She always has to be the star. She's been mad ever since the auditions for *Bentley Knows*. You know, she had five different dogs up for that part? *None* of them could act as well as Bentley."

"Of course they couldn't! Why does POO get all the attention? Sir Bentley's a thousand times more talented." Elvis leaned over toward Bentley and draped her arms around the dog's neck. In return, my sister got slobber all over her wrist.

Madeleine sighed. "Those Pendleton Triplets aren't even real actors. FiFi swaps them out with new dogs every three months. As soon as they lose their cuteness, they're gone."

"She's horrible!" Elvis wailed. "It's all her fault!"

"Actually, I think it's Brody's fault," I said. "He dropped the mic."

Madeleine and my sister went right on as if I hadn't said a word.

Mom and Dad came out of the kitchen carrying Tail-Wagger Smoothies and bacon cakes in fancy glass dog bowls. At the table next to us, Pico perked up in his booster seat. He sniffed toward the smoothie and his sweatshirt hood fell over his eyes. At our table, Bentley finally tore her eyes away from my plate. A thick glob of drool dripped down her chin the minute she saw the bacon cakes.

"Ugh!" Madeleine sounded like she'd been punched in the stomach.

Dad rushed to her side like he was going to have to perform the Heimlich. "Are you okay? Is there anything I can do to help?"

"No! No one can help!" she said. "Listen to this one: 'WILL SPOILING YOUR DOG TURN HIM MEAN? How a multimillion-dollar dog collar turned a beloved star VIOLENT.' I can't—I can't even."

"Why don't you ask Sharon Henderson to call the newspapers and tell them the truth?" I asked.

"She's not answering my texts," Madeleine said. "I'm being ghosted!"

"Send out a press release," Mr. Boone chimed in. "That'll do the trick."

"You think so?" Elvis brightened. She even took a hopeful mini bite of pancake.

"No," Mom said. "It's too late. You'll just fan the flames." She set a dog dish in front of Bentley and gave the guests her spiel about Barker's local grass-fed meats. The bacon cakes disappeared in one gulp. Elvis set down her fork and glared at Mom like she'd canceled Christmas.

"It's never too late," Elvis said. "We just need proof."

"Proof of what?" Asha appeared in the doorway wearing a T-shirt, jeans, and high heels so tall and spiky they could be murder weapons. Before anyone could answer, she clacked her murder-heels over to our table and started mopping up Bentley's drool. I shot her telepathic thank-you vibes for saving my breakfast from the flood.

Asha leaned toward Madeleine. "I got an email from the network," she said quietly. "Conference call at four o'clock. They want to talk about *Bentley Knows*."

Madeleine put her head in her hands.

"And *Woof Magazine* will be here in two hours for the photo shoot."

Mom looked at her watch.

"You kids need to get going, or you'll be late for art camp."

Rondo and Elvis started talking at once.

"Art camp?"

"We're going back?"

"We can't!" Elvis cried. "Not when Bentley needs us!"

Mom gave me a meaningful look. It had definite telepathic oh-good-lord-there's-a-photo-shoot-in-two-hours-please-help-me vibes.

What she *said* was "Mrs. Doughty said she'd give you a second chance. I think you should do the same for her."

MORSE CODE

"I'd say 'second chance' was an exaggeration," Rondo said.

We were standing at the soccer field trying to get Dec's attention, but he was all the way at the other end, chatting up the girl in the brown ponytail. Oblivious.

Rondo had a point. Mrs. Doughty had made the three of us sit *at her desk* all morning long. She hawkeyed us while we cut pieces of colored paper into perfect half-inch squares for a butterfly mosaic. Her design. Her color choices. We were a regular old mosaic assembly line. It didn't feel like she'd given us a second chance at all.

In a rare moment when she turned her eye on someone else, I squirreled away one of the pieces of colored paper and wrote Dec a note. Now, at the soccer field, I waved the orange note in air. Nothing. You'd almost think Dec was *trying* not to see us.

Rondo raised his voice and shouted at the soccer player closest to us. "Hey! Sweatband!"

A kid with a sweatband around his forehead turned toward us.

"Do you know Declan Harper?" Rondo asked.

Sweatband jogged over. "Yeah, I know Dec."

I handed him the note, and Rondo smirked while the kid examined the dots and dashes on the paper.

$$- \bullet \bullet \bullet \quad - \bullet - \bullet \quad \bullet \bullet \bullet \bullet$$
$$\bullet \bullet - \bullet \quad - \quad \bullet - \bullet \quad \bullet - \bullet \bullet \quad - \bullet \quad - \bullet - \bullet \quad \bullet \bullet \bullet \bullet$$

"He'll know what—" I started.

"*B-C-H*," the kid said. "*F-T-R L-N-C-H*. Hmm . . . to meet him at the . . . beach? After lunch?"

My siblings and I exchanged a look. He'd put that together really fast. Faster than Elvis, and she was a pro. To be honest, I hadn't expected anyone on the soccer field to understand International Morse Code, especially not at lightning speed.

The kid grinned. "Smart to leave out the vowels. For speed?"

Rondo nodded, impressed.

"What's this, though?" Sweatband pointed to a message that Elvis had scrawled on the bottom of the note. "Is someone in trouble?"

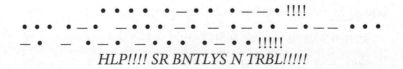

HLP!!!! SR BNTLYS N TRBL!!!!!

Elvis scowled. "It's a SECRET message!" she said, hands on her hips. "It's supposed to be *SECRET*!"

"Right. Sorry. I'll give it to Dec. He's coming to my house for lunch, so . . . maybe I'll see you at the beach?"

The whole thing left me with a spiders-down-the-neck feeling. First, it never feels good to have your secret code cracked in two seconds flat. Second, Dec never mentioned that he was going over to anyone's house. What if he didn't *want* to meet us at the beach? What if he decided he'd rather hang out with a Morse Code genius and kick a ball around?

But I forgot all about it when we got to the Perro because there was a sparkling white Tesla convertible parked outside. Elvis ran in to find Sir Bentley, but the Tesla sucked me and Rondo in like a tractor beam.

"Nice car," Rondo said.

"Go ahead. Check it out!" Thomas Scott was loading his bag and his briefcase into the trunk of a sport Roadster. It was from way back when Tesla first started using lithium ion battery cells in cars. Dec was going to flip.

At Sunny Day, we'd done one of our Innovative Thinking projects on the original Tesla Roadster. Dec was obsessed with every detail: the touch-pad door handles; the LCD panel that monitors the amount and direction of the battery's electrical charge; even safety features like the ability to cut off the electrical current in case of a crash. I'm not that into cars, but the project turned out pretty cool. Dec and I argued that the Roadster convertible should be on Sunny Day's Outlandish

Idea Board. Outlandish Ideas were either absurd or world-changing—only time could tell.

"It's a 2008," Thomas said with a grin. He had a bright pink vest on and gold-rimmed sunglasses that twinkled in the light. "Not many of those around."

Rondo whistled through his teeth. The first-generation roadsters were rare. As far as I knew, only celebrities and millionaires had them.

Madeleine Devine burst out of the Perro in a huff.

"Thomas!" she said. "We were *having* a conversation!"

I peeked into the trunk while Thomas tried to talk her off a ledge.

"I'm only going to be in the city for two nights," he said.

"At a *time like this*?"

It didn't really look like a trunk. There wasn't much room, and Thomas's bag and briefcase took up the whole space. Behind the trunk, there was a plastic panel that hid the battery. That battery was engineering genius.

"I have to, babe. It's work. Don't worry about Sir Bentley. Even if she attacked that dog—which she didn't—her fans would forgive her. She could get away with anything. She's a celebrity. A *beloved* celebrity."

Thomas put his hand on Madeleine's cheek and gave her a lovey air-kiss. Gross. I moved over to the driver's side and waved Rondo over to check out the control panel.

"You guys want me to take you for a joyride? Around the block?" Thomas grinned as he shut the trunk.

"Seriously?" I asked. I almost ran inside to call Dec to tell him to get over here. Fast. But then I remembered he was at somebody else's house for lunch.

"*Not* seriously," Madeleine said, tapping her foot. "Focus, Thomas! Did you make sure Sir Bentley has VIP status on the plane? I don't want her in some hot, sweaty compartment. And I'm worried we cut the schedule too close."

"Don't *worry*." Thomas shot us a helpless sorry-dudes look. "We'll leave right after the gala. All you and Bentley have to do is look glamorous."

While he talked, he reached into the glove box and handed me and Rondo a couple butterscotch candies as a consolation prize. I put mine in my messenger bag, but Rondo shoved his immediately in his mouth.

"Arrive in style." Thomas gave Madeleine the schmoopy lips again. "Like you always do. Put the jewels on the dog and wear that pretty red dress. The one I like. You're perfect."

Madeleine relaxed a little, and for a second, Rondo and I hung around, hoping the joyride offer might open up again. But Thomas started making a smooching motion in the air with his lips and Madeleine made air-smooches back. It was too much. Even an original Tesla Roadster wasn't worth hanging around *that* for.

Rondo tapped a Morse Code message on the hood of the Tesla.

● — ●   — ● — ●   — ● — —

RC Y. Race you.

We ran for the entrance of the Perro and hit the door within milliseconds of each other.

"I totally beat . . ." Rondo's voice faded.

It looked like an earthquake had hit the lobby of the Perro del Mar.

ASHA

The curtains from the front window lay in a heap on the floor. One of Mom's metal-pipe-and-reclaimed-walnut coffee tables had been spray-painted a shiny, bright yellow. There were white sheets, articles of clothing, combs, brushes, and bottles strewn everywhere, and Asha was curled up on one of the lounge chairs with her shoes off and Sir Bentley at her feet. She looked exhausted in a perfectly-posed-supermodel kind of way. She wasn't even trying to stop Elvis from messing up Bentley's fur.

"How'd the photo shoot go?" I asked.

"Fabulous," she said angrily. "Those curtains were hideous, so we had to take them down, but Bentley was incredible."

Elvis paused her petting frenzy to examine Asha. "Then why do you look so . . ."

Asha picked her spike heels up off the ground and shook them threateningly in the air.

"How would *you* feel?" she asked.

None of us answered. None of us moved. She shook the

heels toward the window where Madeleine and Thomas were smooching it up by the roadster.

"It's all fine for her. She's going off to a tropical island whether they cancel the show or not. But I need this job. I love this job. If *Bentley Knows* gets the axe, what am *I* supposed to do?"

Rondo snuck his book out of his pocket and quietly read while she ranted.

"They'd never do that," Elvis said. "They'd never cancel *Bentley Knows*."

Asha slipped the heels onto her feet and stood up to her full height.

"Do you know the *hours* I dedicated to that dog? The fires I've put out for Madeleine? Does she appreciate it? Does she notice? It's not even my job. I'm a *stylist*!"

"Maybe you could—" Elvis started.

"How would she like it if I *didn't* put them out? I have so much dirt on her. I could *start* some fires."

Rondo was interested now. "Real fires or metaphorical?"

Asha glared at Madeleine and Thomas through the window. "What does she see in that guy?"

"He's really nice," Elvis said. "And funny. He gave me candy yesterday, and he told Mom—"

Asha threw her hands in the air and headed for the stairs with Sir Bentley padding close behind. "Can you three clean up this mess? I have to go make a plan for my life."

After lunch, I helped Mom rehang the curtains while

Rondo and Elvis helped Dad with the laundry. Apparently, the photo shoot had a "Greek God" theme, and Asha had used every spare clean sheet in the house making Bentley appear "authentic."

"I can't believe you let them spray paint your table," I said.

Mom shrugged. "It's going to be on the cover of *Woof Magazine*."

"The cover?"

"I know!" Mom grinned. "They're going to give me credit for the furniture design."

"But you hate painted stuff." The whole point of Mom's furniture was to take things people thought were garbage and celebrate them in their raw form. *Without* chemicals like glue and paint.

"Yeah, but . . . it's *Woof Magazine*, right?"

A truck showed up with about a thousand folding chairs for Sir Bentley's book signing, and Mom gave me the Look. I rounded up Elvis, Rondo, and our surfboards, and we headed to the beach.

We searched for Dec, but found Miyon instead. She and her dad were under an umbrella with a conked-out Layne between them. Miyon's dad had a book called *Barbarian Days*, and Miyon was reading *The Screaming Staircase*.

"That looks terrifying," Elvis said.

Miyon pushed a goofy pair of kitten-shaped sunglasses on top of her head and grinned. "It is!" she said. "There's this dead girl in the wall of this creepy old house, and her ghost is pushing people down the stairs."

Elvis put her hands over her ears.

"You're going to give her nightmares," I said.

Rondo tapped his board impatiently until Miyon's dad put his book down. My brother was trying to play it cool, but I knew he was hoping to get some tips from a former pro.

"You guys want to go out?" Miyon's dad asked.

"I guess," Rondo said. All nonchalant. "I mean, if *you* do."

I wanted to wait for Declan, but I didn't see any sign of him. He was probably hanging out with the soccer dude, practicing his new vocabulary and downloading apps. I couldn't help thinking of Asha and her rant about feeling unappreciated and left behind. Even though two days ago, I would have sworn I had nothing in common with a super-model dog stylist from Los Angeles, I knew exactly how she felt. Once seventh grade started, Dec was going to be fine. No matter what. He was good at talking to people, trying new things, making new friends. But where did that leave me?

I scanned the beach one last time, then picked up my surfboard.

"Sure," I said. "Let's go out."

RESISTORS

Miyon tucked Layne into a bright blue portable puppy play-pen on the beach, and we all paddled out together. I headed for my usual spot where the soft, rolling waves were coming in.

"Hey, Epic. Come on out!" Miyon's dad waved me toward the bigger swells.

"I'm good!" I called and settled in, looking for a nice two-foot wave to ride.

Miyon's dad changed direction and paddled toward me. When he got close, he sat up on his board, keeping an eye on Miyon and my siblings as they paddled.

"I've been watching you. You're getting too comfortable over here," he said.

I checked out the swells Miyon was heading for. They weren't huge, but big enough. Some were overhead.

"I like it here."

"That's fair," he said. "But you've got this mushy stuff mastered. Your balance is right on."

"Thanks," I said, glad that he'd noticed. I worked hard

on balance. It was simple physics. Even though gravity was constantly pulling at me, as long as I kept my center of mass lined up with my base of support, I could stay strong and steady.

"You're thinking about it too much, though," he said. "At some point, you've got to let muscle memory take over."

"Muscle memory?"

"Try to balance while thinking about something else today. I don't know. Recite a poem or something. Put yourself on autopilot."

He paddled toward the lineup. His arms were so strong, he caught up with Elvis, Rondo, and Miyon in about six seconds flat.

It was an interesting challenge. I decided to try reciting the color code for electrical resistors. *Black 0, Brown 1, Red 2, Orange 3*. At Sunny Day, we learned that if you think of an electrical current like a garden hose, a resistor is a kink or a knot that holds back some of the water, keeping it from flooding out too fast and strong.

Some resistors are stronger than others, and their color bands make up a code that tells you how much electrical current they'll resist. *Yellow 4, Green 5, Blue 6*. When you're building a circuit, you want the right amount of electricity— enough to work its magic without blowing out the light bulb or the speaker or whatever it is you're trying to power on the other end. *Violet 7, Gray 8, White 9*. It's kind of like Rondo and Elvis. They have enough energy and smarts to power the planet, but without someone like me to rein them in, they would overwhelm the whole system and blow the fuse.

That was basically my job in life—at school, with Pico, with Rondo and El—I kept the current smooth and steady. I made sure there weren't any outages or power surges, and when I did my job right, everything had a nice, even flow. But recently, I felt like I had the calculations all wrong. Everything around me was changing, and I wasn't sure how much to resist and how much to let go. Maybe Miyon's dad was right. I was overthinking. I tried to shut off my brain and recite the resistor code again. *Black 0, Brown 1, Red 2 . . .*

I wiped out more times than I stayed up. But by the fourth or fifth wave, I was starting to get the hang of it. I wasn't thinking about anything but colors and numbers, and after a while, my body remembered how to balance all on its own.

"Did my dad make you do that recite-a-poem thing?" Miyon asked as we toweled off. "It's hokey, but it'll actually help when you get to faster waves."

I nodded and tried to think of something to say. I usually let Dec, Rondo, and Elvis do most of the talking when other people were around. But Dec was MIA, and Rondo was peppering Miyon's dad with questions. Elvis had paddled in early to hang out with Layne. As much as she loves surfing, she couldn't let a puppy go uncuddled. I thought of three topics and threw each of them out for different reasons. *Uninteresting. Dopey. Weird.*

Miyon squeezed water out of her hair and put her cat sunglasses back on. She made a goofy face at me and I laughed. I was overthinking it. Here was a fun, cool, interesting person. Who, for some reason, seemed to like hanging out with me and my weird family. If I couldn't talk to *her*, I wasn't going to be able to talk to *anyone* at Carmelito Middle School. I tried to put my mind on autopilot. *Black 0, Brown 1, Red 2.*

"Do you want to come to Bentley's book signing? You could stay for dinner."

"Can I bring Layne?"

"It's a dog-friendly bed and breakfast." I smiled.

As Miyon's dad packed up their stuff, I spotted Dec on the bike path with Frank in his front basket. Next to him, the kid from soccer camp rode a purple ten-speed with a brown Lab attached to a bike leash. Dec left his bike with the soccer kid while he ran toward us.

"I got your message," he said, all out of breath. "And I did some research for Elvis. On celebrities. Check this out."

He held out his phone, and Miyon grinned at me. "He never says what I think he's going to say."

Elvis and Rondo crowded Dec, trying to shade the screen from the sun.

"Why celebrities?" I asked.

"I've noticed there's a pendulum effect going on. Celebrity popularity swings up and down at a surprising velocity. Look."

Reluctantly, I watched while he scrolled through dozens of celebrity photos. Some I recognized, but most I'd never seen before.

"At first, I was correlating it with gravity. What comes up must go down, right? But then the popularity would upswing again, so I knew my model was wrong. It's more like a pendulum. Except it isn't."

Rondo was nodding, and Miyon was grinning her head off like she was watching something fantastic. On the bike path, Frank was starting to make strained, high-pitched sounds in his basket. The kid with the Lab was trying to balance his own bike and keep Frank from hopping out. Which he didn't need to do. Frank only *acts* like he's going to jump out of that basket. He never does. He's about one eighth as brave as he thinks.

"Look! It's Sweatband!" Elvis waved, but now the kid was tangled in the lab's bike leash and didn't notice.

"Sweatband? That's Carlos," Dec said. "We went to preschool with him. Anyway, it's not a pendulum because most of the time it's not a natural phenomenon that pushes the popularity back up. It's something *manufactured*."

He stood there waggling his eyebrows, like he was about to make some incredible revelation.

"Okay, I'll bite," Miyon said. "What causes the upswing?"

"A publicity stunt. Mostly fake." He scrolled through more photos. "Fake weddings, fake breakups, fake crimes, fake near-death experiences. It really doesn't matter what it is, if it's kickin' enough, people will post about it until you're back in the spotlight."

Kickin'? Who was Dec trying to be?

Frank yelped again, and Dec yelled out, "Hold on a sec!" He typed in a new URL and pulled up a website called Hollywood Dog Dish. Elvis squealed. A photo of the Pendleton Triplets in our chicken coop was on the home page.

"Why do you think these pups are on the upswing, and our big cheese is on the down?" Dec asked.

"I'd maybe drop the new vocabulary," I said.

Miyon nodded, but everyone else ignored me.

"You think last night was a setup?" Rondo asked. "For what?"

"To get publicity. For their new *Star Wars* movie!" Elvis said, outraged. "They're using Bentley's *heroism* against her!"

"Truth or dare!" Dec tried to high-five Elvis, but I shook my head at him.

"Nope," I said. "Not how that phrase is used."

"Definitely not," Miyon agreed.

"Okay," Dec said. "I'll make a note. Thanks."

"Hey! Declan!" Carlos waved his hand at us. Frank's howls were getting louder, and he was snapping his teeth at the poor kid, who was trying to pin him down inside the basket.

"You'd better go," I said. "He's making Frank madder."

"Yeah. I'll catch you kittens later."

"Not that, either," I said, but Dec was already running toward the bike path.

Elvis was spitting mad. "Those nasty labradoodles," she seethed.

"I don't think the puppies had anything to do with it," Miyon said, but backtracked when she saw my sister's scowl. "Things will turn around tonight. It's Bentley's book signing. She'll shine."

BOOK SIGNING

We spent the rest of the afternoon transforming one half of the Perro's lobby into a lecture hall. We pushed all the furniture against the walls and set up rows of folding chairs, a podium, and a long table stacked high with copies of *Knowing Bentley Knows*.

"Where's the stage crew when you need them?" Dad joked. The Dog Elegance crew had swept in, taken down the stage and the tiki bar, and disappeared without one glance at the massive stack of chairs that needed to be set up in the lobby. Apparently, Sir Bentley's book signing wasn't getting the Dog Elegance treatment.

Mom handed me a fleece she'd found under a sofa. "Pico's?" she asked.

I nodded. "I'll bring it to him."

Elvis followed me up the guest stairs, hoping to catch a glimpse of the night's honoree, but the hallway was empty.

I lifted my hand to knock on the Boones' door, but Elvis grabbed my arm. The door to Room 3 opened down the hall.

"*Bentley*," she breathed.

But it wasn't Bentley; it was Mr. Boone. He slipped quietly out of Sir Bentley's room and turned the handle so the door shut without a sound. He flinched when he saw us.

"Ah, Pico's fleece," he said, taking long strides down the hall toward us. "Thanks, Epic. Conscientious as always."

"Is Sir Bentley in there?" Elvis asked. "Is she taking visitors?"

"Oh, she's . . . sleeping." Mr. Boone tried to open the door to Room 1, but his huge hands were shaking. He fumbled the key, and it dropped to the ground.

We all looked at the floor. Two bobby pins, one bent in half, lay next to the key. I picked them up and handed them to him.

"Er, thanks, Epic. I . . ."

Mr. Boone's hands flopped to his side and he let out a heavy sigh. What was he doing? Breaking into Sir Bentley's room? Why? Elvis put her hands on her hips and waited for an explanation.

"Look," Mr. Boone said nervously. "Pico's freezing, and the thermostat for the whole floor is in Bentley's room."

"Why didn't you ask Mom or Dad?" Elvis said.

"I did. I understand they're busy, but Pico's teeth were chattering. And you know how Nicole gets."

It was strange to see a huge guy like Mr. Boone stammering and making excuses to me and my eight-year-old sister.

"Okay," I said. What else could I say? It's not like Elvis and

I hadn't broken into Room 3 ourselves. Though I wasn't about to tell that to Mr. Boone.

"Does that really work?" Elvis asked, pointing to the bobby pins. "We were going to try it, but we used Mom's master key to get into Sir Bentley's room instead."

My face flushed, and Mr. Boone's shoulders relaxed. He plucked Pico's fleece out of my hand and opened the door.

"I won't tell if you won't," he whispered as he disappeared into his suite.

Behind us, the door to Room 5 opened. Melissa and Delphi entered the hall, with Morrissey on his leash behind them. Both Delphi and Melissa were wearing all black. Delphi had on black leggings, a shiny black scarf, and a black tank top that showed off her tattoos. Melissa was wearing black cat-eye glasses, a lacy black dress, and an old-fashioned black beret. The only things to break up the color scheme were their matching dragon pins. Delphi had hers on her shoulder, and Melissa had hers on her hat.

"You look like cat burglars!" Elvis said.

Delphi laughed. "Meow!"

Melissa tipped her beret elegantly. "We decided to paint the town . . . black!"

Elvis was disappointed. "You're not coming to Bentley's book signing?"

Delphi lowered her eyes.

"Sorry," she said. "I know he's your archnemesis, but . . ."

"You're going to Yips and Sips?"

Elvis looked betrayed, and I can't say I didn't feel the same.

"For real?" I asked.

"Awww . . . kinda? He's got DJ Doggone."

"Plus, that Bentley book has been out forever. We got ours signed three years ago in Monterey."

My sister dropped dramatically to her knees and threw her arms around Morrissey. "Wittle sweetie, *you* wouldn't betray . . . What did you *do* to him?"

Delphi started giggling. Right above Morrissey's hind leg was a dragon tattoo.

"Don't worry," Melissa said, but she seemed worried. "It's completely temporary and nontoxic. I researched side effects and common reactions and—"

"It's awesome, right?" Delphi interrupted. "We got it down at Nails 'n' Tails. Now, come on. We've been at boring volunteer training all day for the Puppy Picnic, and I want to go dance!"

In the end, the only people in Sir Bentley's audience were my family, Miyon, Layne, Asha, and the Boones. Loud music from the Moondoggie Inn drifted up the street. Madeleine stood at the podium and winced every time the bass boomed.

"If you don't mind," she said, "I'll take Bentley upstairs. Everything we were going to talk about is in the book. Help yourselves."

She gestured toward the mountains of *Knowing Bentley Knows* as she walked past. The rest of us sat in our folding chairs staring at the empty podium. Rondo was reading Miyon's book *The Screaming Staircase*.

"What happened with the network?" Dad asked Asha.

She shook her head. "Animal Universe canceled the meeting. Some 'emergency' with a new series contract. They said they'd send us an email." She checked her phone. "I've been checking every two minutes. Nothing."

"You won't sleep if you check that all night," Mrs. Boone said kindly. She pulled Pico's leather "party jacket" out of her purse and snapped it around his neck. "You work so hard, Asha. Don't you deserve a night off? Why don't we all go to Yips and Sips and forget about it?"

"Great idea!" Mr. Boone said. He was holding Pico's sparkly light-up collar—the one with a remote control to change the color and duration of a hundred blinking LEDs. Had they been planning to desert us for Yips & Sips all along?

"I'm not going to that," Elvis said, crossing her arms in Sir Bentley solidarity.

"Me neither," Mom said. "I'm wiped out."

I agreed. The last thing I wanted to do was go to a loud party where Brody Delgado got to act like he was king of the world.

But Asha brightened. "That sounds nice, Mrs. Boone. Thanks."

"Well, then. How about us?" Dad asked. "What's the McDade-plus-Miyon clan up to? Family Night? You want to stay for some board games, Miyon?"

"Yes! Trivial Pursuit!" Elvis threw her arms in the air and

did a "Hound Dog" hip swivel. "Thank you," she said in her low Elvis-impersonator voice. "Thank you very much."

I cringed. Miyon had come to the Perro because she wanted to see a celebrity dog, not hang around with my goofy parents and siblings all night.

But weirdly, Miyon was smiling like she'd qualified for the World Surf Championship. "Family Night sounds great!"

BENTLEY KNOWS

When you live at a bed and breakfast, there are other people around almost all the time. But most nights, between five and nine o'clock, guests head out to town for dinner or order takeout for their rooms, and we get the Perro to ourselves. Mom puts a sign at the front desk and another on the kitchen door that says TUCKED IN FOR THE NIGHT with a picture of a sleeping pup and a number to call for emergencies.

On Family Nights, we hang out in the kitchen blasting records and making food. Mom always lights three candles and sets them on the kitchen table, and we eat dessert and play games until they burn out.

"So? Tell me about art camp," Mom said. She dished out heaps of homemade strawberry sorbet while Dad added mango slices and asked Miyon to garnish each bowl with a sprig of mint.

"It's not art," I said. "She wants it all to look the same. Like a factory."

"But how do you think it makes her feel if you don't listen to her instructions?"

"I listened," I said. "And then I built on it."

"What are you guys talking about?" Miyon asked.

"Freedom of thought," Rondo said.

"It's our moral duty to be Questioning Humans," Elvis explained. "Just because something's a rule doesn't make it right."

Dad gave Elvis a high five.

Mom gave up the conversation and lit the candles. She raised her glass for the standard Family Night toast.

"To a little peace and quiet," she said.

We'd just finished setting up Trivial Pursuit when there was a knock on the kitchen door. Sir Bentley lumbered in, and Elvis pushed back her chair and flung herself at the Saint Bernard, smothering her with kisses.

Madeleine Devine stepped around them and, without being invited, sat right down in Elvis's chair. In the dim glow of the candlelight, she looked like death warmed over. Her face was pale, and the makeup around her eyes was all smudged.

"I need a glass of wine," she said.

"Sure thing." Dad got out a bottle, opened it, and handed her a glass, but she didn't take it up to her room. She sat there and drank it while we all stared at the candlelight flickering on her horror-show face.

"The show's been canceled."

Elvis flopped, cross-legged, to the floor and pulled Sir Bentley's drooly head to her lap. The dog nuzzled in and gently put a giant paw on my sister's knee.

"There's too much bad press," Madeleine said. "And the ratings are terribly low."

"Well, I'm sure—" Mom started, but Madeleine kept talking.

"They don't understand what they're losing. The talent. The range. The emotion." Her voice cracked, and tiny candle flames reflected in her watery eyes. "All Animal Universe cares about is what's *hot* and *trending*."

"Maybe—" Mom tried again.

"Do you know what they said? They said social media is *finished* with Bentley. Social media has nothing to do with acting! That dog works harder than anyone else out there. She doesn't deserve this!"

Elvis wriggled out from under Sir Bentley's chin and moved to put her hand on Madeleine's arm.

"Sir Bentley's the best animal actor in the world," she said with tears in her eyes.

Madeleine looked at her. Then she glanced at the rest of us. And the record player. And the Trivial Pursuit.

"I'm sorry." She picked up her wine and stood up. She made a small hand gesture to Sir Bentley, who immediately stood up and padded to her side. "We didn't mean to interrupt."

But they didn't go. Madeleine stood there, looking lost. I actually felt bad for her.

"You want to play?" I asked.

Madeleine hesitated, and Miyon held out her brown playing piece.

"You can have mine," she said, scooting her chair closer to me. "Epic and I can be a team."

For a second, I forgot how to breathe.

"You have to watch out for Elvis," Rondo said. "She comes down at night and memorizes the cards."

Elvis grinned. "Maybe I do, and maybe I don't. But I always win."

By the time Elvis had collected her third piece of the pie, Madeleine had relaxed. When it wasn't her turn, Elvis peppered her with questions about Hollywood and what Sir Bentley was like as a puppy.

I pushed the dice toward Rondo, but he had his head under the table, examining Sir Bentley's dog collar.

"That thing's not real, is it?" he asked.

"Of course it is. Why wouldn't it be?"

Miyon leaned toward Madeleine. "Don't you worry? About parading around a bunch of jewels?"

Rondo sat up so quickly he hit his head on the table. "Seriously," he said, grinning at Miyon. "It's like you're inviting—"

Everyone groaned.

"Don't start that again," Dad said.

"Start what again?" Madeleine asked.

The game stayed on pause while Elvis told the whole story of the art camp disaster. I added a few choice descriptions of Mrs. Doughty's mind-control tactics, and Rondo butted in with his theories about criminal behavior. He and Miyon exchanged several high fives.

Madeleine laughed until she got a cramp in her side.

"You sound like Thomas. What's the point of having something beautiful if you don't get to enjoy it? If I locked all this up"—she pointed to the necklace and thick, jewel-encrusted bands on her wrist—"no one would ever know it exists."

"Exactly," Rondo said. "*Jewel thieves* wouldn't know it exists. Last week, a seven-hundred-and-fifty-thousand-dollar necklace disappeared right out of Chloe Cosmo's bedroom. It's not hard to do if you know what you're looking for."

"How do you know about Chloe Cosmo's bedroom?" Mom asked.

"It's everywhere," he said.

Madeleine pulled her phone out of her pocket and scrolled through her feed. "He's right," she said. "It's everywhere."

She held out her phone, still scrolling. Every other post was something about Chloe Cosmo.

"If Animal Universe wants 'trending,' they should give *her* a show," Madeleine said. Then she sighed and pushed her chair back. "I think it's time Bentley and I got some beauty rest. Thank you for cheering us up."

Elvis scrambled to her feet. She'd started to hiccup.

"Uh-oh," Dad said. "Idea Hiccups. What now, El?"

"Can I tuck Sir Bentley in?" Elvis asked. "Put her to bed? Pretty—*hic*—please?"

"We shouldn't bother the guests . . ." Mom started, but Madeleine smiled.

"I bet Bentley would love that." Madeleine held out her hand. Elvis took it and hiccuped happily out the door.

Dad checked his watch. "How about Epic and I walk you home, Miyon, while the rest of these guys clean up?"

"One of those things is more fun than the other," Mom protested. "But that's probably a good idea."

Miyon scooped up Layne, who'd fallen asleep under her chair. "Thanks so much for having me," she said. "I'm really glad I met you guys."

"Surfs like a rock star *and* she's polite," Mom said. "This girl's welcome in my house anytime."

We were halfway out the door when Mom had one more thing to say.

"Hey, Marc, do you have the spare master? I couldn't find it today."

The spare key? I turned toward Rondo, but Miyon grabbed my arm and pulled me out the kitchen door before I could say or do anything incriminating.

"Maybe," Dad said as the door swung shut. "Check the dresser upstairs. Otherwise, I'll look for it tomorrow."

YIPS & SIPS

It took forever to walk down Main Street. Miyon kept stopping every few feet to check her phone or let Layne sniff around some corner. The music from Yips & Sips was still blasting at full volume, filling the street with thumping beats. The closer we got to Ocean Drive, the louder DJ Dog-gone blared, and the slower Miyon walked. When we were almost to the end of Main Street, she stopped completely, admiring the T-shirts in the window of Furever Friends and tapping her foot to the dance music.

"That's a cute one." She pointed to a retro T-shirt with a surfing dog and checked her phone again.

"Is everything okay, Miyon?" Dad asked.

"Sure. Why?" She raised her eyebrow at me like sloth speed was perfectly normal and my dad was the one who was acting weird.

I pointed to her phone. Which she was checking. Again.

"Oh. Sorry," Miyon said, embarrassed. "My dad's out tonight. He said he'd text me when he was on his way home."

She paused and looked us over. I felt like I was being put through some kind of Trust-O-Meter before she could decide whether to tell us more.

"Okay, this is silly," she said, "but ever since I started reading that ghost series, it creeps me out to be on the boat alone at night. Even with Layne."

"That's not silly," I said. I tried to imagine being alone on a boat in the dark. Without Mom and Dad. Or Rondo and El. At the Perro, there were people and dogs around all the time. Miyon's houseboat seemed so cool, but I hadn't thought about how lonely it might be.

"You sure?" Miyon bit her lip.

"No way. It would creep *me* out. Even without ghost books."

"I agree," Dad said. He patted her on the shoulder and nodded toward the Moondoggie Inn. "Should we kill some time? See what this party's all about?"

The front patio of the Moondoggie was decked out with the exact same hanging lights, tiki bar, and stage we'd had at Yappy Hour. When the Dog Elegance crew dismantled it all, I didn't realize they were only moving it two blocks down the street. This time, the stage was filled with giant speakers, a soundboard, keyboard, and two record players. A dude in a cheesy trucker hat with floppy Dalmatian ears hanging off the sides was adjusting knobs and occasionally shouting things like "Woof! Woof!" and "*You* go fetch!" into the microphone. The music was so loud I could feel it throbbing in my chest.

I expected to see Delphi and Melissa bopping around on the dance floor, but I couldn't find them in the mob. There were people and dogs everywhere, spilling out onto Ocean Drive and even across the street to Carmelito Beach.

I scanned the crowd for Pico, and finally spotted his light-up party leash. The Boones were at a table with Asha. Their heads were bent over Mrs. Boone's notebook, and the three of them were talking intently about something. Pico caught my eye and went all wiggly, throwing his leather jacket off-kilter and letting out a bark.

Mrs. Boone slapped the notebook closed and waved us over. "Isn't this the limit? You know George Lucas's *assistant* is here? Asha spotted him. She's amazing. She knows *everybody*."

Mrs. Boone was interrupted by Brody Delgado locking Dad in a bear hug.

"Aw, man, thanks for coming!" Brody said, patting Dad's back. "Seriously. It means a lot to me. Can you believe this crowd? It's even bigger than yours was. I just talked to a couple from Sweden. Sweden! And George Lucas's assistant is here!"

"Yeah, we heard." Dad winked at Mrs. Boone.

"Will you come test my margaritas?" Brody asked. "I tried that infusion thing you told me about, but it's not working out exactly the same as yours."

Dad's smile froze while Brody went on to explain his infusion method in detail. I could practically see Dad thinking up an exit strategy, which was fine by me. DJ Doggone was giving me a headache. Pico looked miserable, too. Masses of people, loud music, and some guy randomly barking into a mic—Yips & Sips was pretty much his worst nightmare.

We all relaxed when Miyon's phone dinged.

"He's home!" she said.

Dad grinned. "That's our cue. Great event, Brody. See you all back at the ranch?"

Pico gave a desperate yelp as we backed away. His eyes locked onto mine, and he shivered. I couldn't ditch him. I went back to the Boones' table.

"Want me to bring Pico home?" I yelled over the music. "He looks cold."

Mrs. Boone blinked at me like I'd solved a problem she didn't know she had. She glanced at Mr. Boone, who was already handing over his key to Room 3.

"To Epic!" Mrs. Boone lifted her glass and winked at Asha. "And to new partnerships!"

The Boones might be celebrating, but I swear I saw Asha frown as the three glasses clinked.

That night, I had a hard time falling asleep. Elvis was snoring like a jackhammer, and Rondo kept tossing and turning on his top bunk.

"Hey, Rondo," I said into the darkness. "Chill out."

"Sorry, bro." But he tossed again, and the bed springs squeaked. "Thanks for not ratting me out about the key."

"I'm not a snitch."

"I know."

"Why didn't you put it back?"

There was a pause.

"I *may* have used it to watch TV in the Boones' room when we were supposed to be doing the laundry."

"*Rondo.*"

"I know. I'll put it back tomorrow. I swear."

The squeaking continued, so I focused on counting Elvis's snores and deepening my breath. It was the old electrical resistor calculation again, and I'd let too much energy flow through. I hadn't checked to make sure Rondo put the key back, so of course he didn't. How was he going to manage without me at Sunny Day? I spent about fifty-seven of my sister's snores wondering if there was anything else I'd let slip through the cracks. One hundred eighty-four is the last number I remember before I finally drifted off to sleep.

The next thing I knew, Madeleine Devine was screaming her lungs out, and Sir Bentley's half-a-million-dollar dog collar was gone.

WEDNESDAY

1:45 A.M.

THE LOBBY

Turns out, when someone starts screaming her head off in a bed and breakfast, people want to know what's going on. At least at the Perro del Mar they did. Instead of turning over and going back to sleep, the guests had all gathered in the hall and then filed down to the lobby to see what Mom and Dad were going to do about it.

They didn't do much. After Mom called Luis, she brought out a plate of muffins, and Dad served everyone fair-trade coffee from Guatemala. Which seemed to calm Madeleine down, but got Mrs. Boone all wound up. She worked her way around the room, talking a mile a minute at anyone who would listen while we all waited for the police to arrive.

All except Rondo. Where was he? I checked my watch. It had been at least ten minutes since he'd bolted out of our room. I'd told Mom he was in the bathroom, and she was so busy trying to calm everyone down that she believed me. It was only a matter of time before she asked me again. Ten minutes is a long time on the toilet.

"Can you believe it, Epic?" Mrs. Boone fretted. "After we'd all had such a lovely evening! I can't imagine who—OH!"

As Luis walked into the Perro, Mrs. Boone adjusted her head scarf and smoothed out her polka dot pajamas.

"Too much coffee," she mumbled. "I'd better sit down."

Luis's entrance spooked everyone. It was the police uniform—it made the whole thing feel real. A criminal had broken into the Perro del Mar. Into my *house*. We were literally living in a crime scene.

Elvis tugged at my hand. Her palm was sweaty and shaky. As much as it creeped *me* out, my sister probably felt like she was living in one of her own nightmares. She'd been quieter than usual, staring at Sir Bentley like she was sending telepathic condolences to the victim of the crime.

"It's going to be okay, El," I whispered.

She tugged my palm again and nodded toward the guest stairs.

While everyone's attention was on Luis and Madeleine, my brother waltzed down the stairs. Walked right down and gave me a nod like it wasn't at all strange that everyone but him was gathered in the lobby in the middle of the night and a police officer was walking around taking names and phone numbers from all our guests.

"Where were you?" I hissed.

Rondo scanned the room.

"Investigating," he said. "What's he doing here?"

I followed his gaze to Brody Delgado. He was talking to

Luis while the Pendleton Triplets sniffed at the police officer's shoes.

"He told Mom he was out walking FiFi's dogs and heard the screaming," I said. "He came in to see if everyone was okay."

"Dog walking at one thirty in the morning?"

"That's what he says." It sounded fishy to me, too. "What do you mean you were investigating?"

"Did you find anything?" El's eyes were wide.

"Too early to tell," Rondo said. "But it was definitely an inside job. Someone in this room is the culprit."

Elvis looked like she might cry. "How do you know?"

"Shhh," Rondo said. "I need a minute."

He scanned the room, examining each guest like they could be a criminal. An inside job? Who here would even *think* about stealing a dog collar?

Delphi and Melissa were cross-legged on a couch that had been pushed up against the wall for the book signing. Morrissey was sacked out between them, tongue lolling, like coming down the stairs in the middle of the night had taken all the life out of him. The girls were glued to their phones, still in their black dancing clothes. Which reminded me: I hadn't seen them on the dance floor.

Mrs. Boone had settled onto a lounge chair next to Mr. Boone and Pico. All three of them wore polka dot pajamas that matched Mrs. Boone's silk sleeping scarf. She'd stopped talking, but her hands were fluttering on her lap. I'd seen

Mrs. Boone in a nervous tizzy lots of times, but she was acting odd even for her. She tapped Mr. Boone several times, but he was in a daze, scratching Pico's head and watching Madeleine pace while Mom followed her around with a box of tissues.

Asha was near the front desk with Sir Bentley, glaring in Delphi and Melissa's direction. She hadn't been to bed yet either. Her spiky heels and makeup were still intact, and her Afro puffed out in a perfect cloud around her head.

Brody was still talking to Luis, who was writing everything down in a notebook but pausing every few seconds to crouch down and rub the ears of one of the Pendleton Triplets. Like, even in the middle of a police investigation, he couldn't resist the labradoodle charm.

What was *Brody doing here?*

"Come on," Rondo said to me and Elvis. "We need to talk."

He headed for the dining room, grabbing three muffins on the way. Dad was refilling Mrs. Boone's coffee cup, and he waved me over as Rondo and Elvis passed by.

"Those guys okay?" he asked.

"Yeah," I said. Though I wasn't 100 percent sure it was the truth. Elvis was all jittery, and Rondo had been who-knew-where tampering with evidence.

"Keep them out of trouble, okay? Go ahead and have a snack, but then make them go back to bed. Cool?"

He was trying to act all calm, but I could tell he was rattled, too. He couldn't be in his right mind if he thought anyone could make my siblings do anything. I gave him a thumbs-up anyway and went to find Rondo and Elvis in the corner booth.

"Okay," Rondo said. He pulled a tiny notebook and a golf pencil out of his mint tin.

"How many things can you fit in there?" Elvis asked.

Rondo ignored her. "I checked out the crime scene. There were no signs of forced entry."

Crime scene. It was still sinking in.

"How'd you get inside?" Elvis asked.

"Inside what?"

"The crime scene."

"He's still got the key," I said.

"Shhh!" Rondo waved his hands at us and quickly slipped off the booth seat and crouched under the table. We didn't even pause to think about it. Elvis and I slid down, too. As we squatted on the floor, we heard stools scrape and someone sat down at the breakfast bar.

SPIES

"We'll hit the standard questions first. You cool with that?" said Luis from the breakfast bar. Even in police officer mode, he talked like a surfer. "When did you catch on that the collar was missing?"

Rondo, Elvis, and I crouched under the corner booth table, which was ridiculous because we were actually *more* exposed on the ground than we would have been sitting in the booth like normal humans. The tall headboards that made up the back of the booth didn't go all the way to the floor. I could see Luis's shiny black cop shoes tapping against the breakfast bar next to a pair of bare feet with bright red toenails.

I glared at my brother. There had to be a law against spying on a police investigation. I thought about coughing or sitting back up on the seat and making a noise. Why had I followed Rondo's lead? Now that we were crouched on the floor, everything we did looked suspicious. Especially with my brother writing down everything we heard.

"I couldn't sleep," Madeleine said. "So I went to Bentley's room for some company."

"Was she sleeping in the collar?"

"*Yes.*" Madeleine sounded defensive. "It's perfectly comfortable."

"Was there something that woke you up? Any noise? Any sounds that could be forced entry?"

Rondo shook his head and tapped his notebook on the spot where he'd written *No forced entry.*

"I was up anyway," she said. "Thanks to that nonstop music down the street. Plus, Asha came to see me when she got in."

"What time was that?"

"I don't know. Midnight? It was before those giggling girls."

"Delphi and Melissa? When did they get in?"

"Not long ago. Maybe one o'clock."

Rondo was writing as fast as he could. My foot was starting to fall asleep.

"Does Asha usually visit you so late at night?"

Madeleine sighed and started swinging her left foot. "She wanted to know if I was going to fire her. Because of the show getting canceled. She said she needed to know if she should 'explore other opportunities.'"

"What'd you tell her?"

Madeleine stopped swinging her foot. "I don't see how

this is relevant," she snapped. "But of course I'll have to let her go. What else am I supposed to do? We're *finished*! Bentley's washed up!"

"*She is not!*" Elvis whispered.

Rondo put his finger to his lips, and I sent him more dagger-eyes. I didn't want to spy on Luis. I wished all of this was over. I wished it had never begun.

"Oh . . . okay, sorry," Luis said. "Has anything else strange happened recently?"

"Strange?" Madeleine blurted. "Officer Sánchez, *everything* is strange. Those terrible little petri dish puppies are everyone's darlings while my Bentley is wrongly accused, stripped of her show, and now *robbed* in the middle of the night . . ."

There was a pause while Madeleine ripped out a few sobs.

"Sure. But . . . weird behavior? From other guests, or maybe, like, out in town?"

Luis sounded tired. I was, too. Elvis had her thumb in her mouth, and her eyelids were drooping.

"Jewel thieves are good at what they do," Luis explained. "They'll spend *days* waiting for you to let your guard down. Even for a second, like when you stop to pick up a latte or something."

"You think someone's been *following* me?"

"Maybe. Think of how many people on social media saw that bling."

"Not *that* many," Madeleine said bitterly.

There was another pause and more foot swinging before

she added, "Well . . . Clive Boone was in the laundry room three times yesterday. Without laundry."

"The one upstairs?"

"Yes. Across the hall from Bentley's room. You don't think he was *spying* on me?"

"Hm. Anyone else?"

"Melissa gave me a pill. But I can't imagine . . ."

"What kind of pill? When did she give it to you?"

"Before the book signing. She said I looked worried, which is a whole other disaster. All this stress is giving me premature wrinkles. I'm going to have to—"

"Melissa's a vet, right? You're sure the pill wasn't for the dog?"

"She said to take it before bed so I could sleep."

Rondo was writing furiously now, underlining and drawing stars and arrows all over the place. If this went on a minute more, I was going to burst. My foot was seriously asleep, and I had to move.

"Did you take the pill?" Luis asked.

"No. It's still up in my room."

"Okay. Let's go secure the scene and give it a look."

The stools scraped the floor, and we listened to their footsteps fade as they walked out of the room. Rondo held up his hand and made me wait a full sixty seconds before saying anything. There were a bunch of things I *could* say. Mr. Boone was obviously innocent. He'd told us straight out that he was stalking Sir Bentley's room so he could turn down the air-conditioning. And I was certain Melissa was only trying to help. Sure, it was weird to knock on someone's door and give them a sleeping pill, but Madeleine *had* been pretty worked up. Maybe Asha could have waited to talk to Madeleine in the morning, but I didn't blame her. How could she sleep, not knowing if she was getting fired or not? I wondered what *other opportunities* dog stylists could explore. That pretty much left Brody. Who had absolutely no business being in the Perro with three dogs at one thirty in the morning.

My mind was spinning, but the last thing I needed was to get Rondo more worked up. I did the responsible thing. I said, "We should get to bed."

Rondo laughed. "You're hilarious, bro."

"I'm serious."

"No you're not. That's the overdeveloped sense of responsibility talking."

He was right. I didn't want to go to bed. "But Dad said—"

Rondo pulled on his hair like I was killing him. "Epic! There's an investigation going on. Of an actual, real-life crime. And someone in this house pulled it off. Aren't you at all curious?"

I was, actually. I was very curious.

"Do you think it was Brody?" I asked.

Rondo rolled his eyes. "You give that guy way too much credit. Besides, it's always the person you least expect."

"Like?"

"The Boones?"

"No way," I said. "They're already rich."

"We don't know how they get their money."

"He broke into Room 3 with your bobby pin trick," I said.

"What?" Rondo looked shocked. And impressed.

"It was for the air conditioner, though."

"Are you sure?"

"Pretty sure."

"What about Melissa?"

"She's too . . . quiet."

"I know. But the sleeping pill?" Rondo flipped back a page in his notebook. "I started to check out Room 5 while I was up there."

"Rondo!"

"It was only for a second. Luis got here, so I had to bail. But you know that bag Melissa has? The one they said is full of emergency vet stuff? Guess what's in there."

"What?"

"Mini chocolate bars."

That got me. "Chocolate? How many?"

"A lot."

"Why would she lie? *Did* she lie?" I tried to remember exactly what Delphi and Melissa had said about the bag. I took a deep breath. "It doesn't matter. Dad said we've got to go to bed. Luis will figure it out."

"Luis," Rondo said, "doesn't know the Perro like we do. Luis needs our help."

We did know things that might help. The air-conditioning. The doctor bag.

"Fine," I said. "But we've got a problem."

Elvis was asleep.

INVESTIGATION

We shook Elvis until she snorted herself awake. Sort of awake. When Elvis is overtired, she goes into this strange half-sleepwalking zone. Her body can walk and talk like a normal person, but her brain is in a bizarro-land dream-world.

"Come on, El," I said. "We'll put you to bed." I led her toward the back staircase, but she kept pulling away from me, trying to stumble toward the lobby.

"Sir Bentley," she mumbled. "She has to come with us. She'll solve it. She'll solve the crime."

Rondo looked at me for help. "We don't have time for this," he said.

I grabbed Elvis by the shoulders and steered her toward the family stairs.

"Bentley's probably upstairs already," I said, even though we could all see Asha and the Saint Bernard with the Boones. Elvis wouldn't know the difference. When she's in the dream zone, you could tell her she's got six thumbs, and she'd believe you.

"Right!" Rondo chimed in. "Bentley's up there solving the crime right now. She's got her magnifying glass and everything. We've got to be her assistants."

"Okay. Good," Elvis said, but she insisted on crawling up each step on all fours like a toddler. Halfway up, she paused, resting her head on the Ghost Stair. Which was proof she was 99 percent asleep. Even her fear of creaky ghosts couldn't revive her.

"I'll wait for Bentley here," she murmured. "On the Screaming Staircase." Then she closed her eyes. She was out.

Rondo groaned.

"Come on, El," I said. "We're almost there."

We pulled on her arms, trying to lift her up, but when my sister goes into rag doll mode, she's heavier than a sleeping elephant.

"We have to leave her here," Rondo said. "She won't move."

"But Mom and Dad . . ."

"We'll be back before they come upstairs. Luis needs us *now*. Do you want to miss everything?"

I didn't. I *wanted* to help Luis figure out who had broken into our house and why. But I knew leaving Elvis asleep on the stairs—especially on the Ghost Stair that haunted her twenty-four-seven—was not the right thing to do. It felt like there was a pendulum in my brain, swinging wildly from one side to the other.

"'Follow your curiosity,'" Rondo said. "Or do you not believe in the school motto anymore? Now that you and Dec are *mainstreaming*?"

It was a low blow, but it worked. We left my sister snoozing on the stairs and used Rondo's mirror trick to check out the lobby.

"Stick to the wall by the dining room," Rondo said. "Nobody's over there right now."

"If Dad sees us—"

"We'll say you left your messenger bag in Pico's room."

"But I didn't."

Rondo's eyes rolled so far back into his head, I thought he might not get them back.

"Fine."

I followed him past the dining room doors and hugged the wall to the right. No one paid any attention to us sneaking past the folding chairs, or even walking blatantly up the guest stairs. By the time we got to the top step, my stomach organs had squeezed themselves into a knot so tight I was pretty sure I'd never be able to eat another piece of pizza again.

Rondo paused and held up his hand. Luis was examining the doorway of Sir Bentley's room.

"No sign of forced entry from the hallway," we heard him say. "Let's go check the windows."

"I told you. Those windows are fine," Rondo whispered to me.

Luis and Madeleine disappeared into Sir Bentley's room, leaving the door wide open.

"Now what?" I asked.

"We help." Rondo walked right into Room 3. My brain pendulum took a swing. We should definitely have gone to bed. *How did I let Rondo talk me into this?*

". . . standard sleeping pill," Luis was saying. "Nothing dangerous. Though if you'd taken it, you wouldn't be on your feet right now, that's for sure. Uh . . . hey, guys. We're busy right now."

"That's okay," Rondo said. He walked across the room toward the window overlooking the backyard. "All these windows are secure. I checked them already."

"We wanted to . . ." I started, but Luis frowned like we were a couple of naughty kids, not Questioning Humans who might have information relative to the case.

"You *checked* them already?" Luis did not look pleased.

I wished I could rewind my life. Walk backward up the family stairs and straight into our room. If Elvis woke up on the Ghost Stair before we got back, she was going to freak.

"Yeah," Rondo said. "I thought you might want to—"

"Dude." Luis lowered his voice. "You can't be here right now."

"We won't mess around. We're here to help," Rondo said.

Luis ignored him and stared me down. "Epic. Seriously? You're old enough to know better."

Maybe we could still salvage it. Get back to the stairs before Elvis moved and Mom and Dad found out we were bugging Luis. I pulled on Rondo's arm, but he shook my hand away and let his hair fall in front of his face.

Luis softened his voice. "I know you're really into this stuff, but it isn't a game. I need you to leave."

Rondo stayed put for a second longer, looking like he had a lot more to say. Then he shrugged like he couldn't care less.

"Your loss," he said, and marched out to the hall.

We only made it halfway down the stairs before all my bad decisions came crashing down on us.

From the guest staircase, we had a view of the whole lobby. Asha had propped the front door open and was fanning Sir Bentley with a magazine while the Boones covered Pico with a throw blanket. Brody was waving his hands in the air, talking to Mom like they were BFFs. The Pendleton Triplets were asleep in a heap in the middle of the room. Melissa and Delphi were still on the couch with Morrissey. My mouth went dry as I watched Dad empty the last of his Guatemalan coffee into Mr. Boone's cup and head toward the kitchen with the empty carafe.

I don't know what went through Dad's head. All I know is that one step from the kitchen door, something made him turn. Not a huge pivot. A small swivel in the direction of the family stairs. Where my sister was sacked out like a pile of laundry. The way Elvis sleeps, he probably thought she was dead.

The glass coffee carafe slipped out of his hand, and gravity did its thing.

The carafe shattered, and Dad let out a curse so loud that it woke up Elvis.

Who let out a bloodcurdling scream.

Which sent the sleeping heap of Pendleton Triplets into terrified spasms.

Without FiFi there to make clicking sounds and feed them treats, the dogs went berserk, barking and flailing around. They tried to stand up but knocked one another over, paws sliding on the wood floor. Morrissey got up the energy to jump off the couch and growl at a labradoodle who took one look at the bulldog lumbering toward her and started booking it in the direction of Pico's corner.

Pico, already stressed to the max, pointed his nose to the ceiling and started to howl. It was the sound of agony, and it sent Sir Bentley into motion.

The Saint Bernard lifted her one-hundred-fifty-pound bulk from the doorway and sprang into hero-dog action, lunging for the rogue labradoodle and knocking over a coffee table and two entire rows of folding chairs in the process. One of the folding chairs caught on the curtains Mom and I had rehung, and the curtain rod came crashing down. The sense of dread, which had been piling up ever since Madeleine's first scream, broke over me like a heavy sixteen-foot wave.

As Bentley tried to "rescue" the labradoodle, her tail

swiped a potted cactus from a display table and dumped the spiny plant and two gallons of dirt crashing onto the floor. The labradoodle yelped, put on an extra burst of speed, and ran out the open door, Sir Bentley close behind.

Brody froze, but Asha shrieked and ran after them into the night.

Everyone looked at Dad. He swore again.

"I'm sorry," he said, miserably. "It's been a long night."

I hadn't noticed that Luis and Madeleine had appeared behind us on the stairs. Madeleine was frozen in place, tears welling up in her eyes.

"They won't get far," Luis said. He sprinted into action. "I'll go pick them up in my car."

While everyone else rounded up their dogs, Rondo and I walked silently down the stairs. Rondo folded a few chairs and I tried to stuff the cactus back into its wooden pot. I was shoveling in a handful of dirt when I felt Dad's hand on my head. He didn't say a word. He took the pot out of my hands and lifted his eyebrows.

"Bro," Rondo said. "We should go to bed."

Upstairs, Mom was sitting on the bottom bunk, rubbing El's back.

"Elvis said you abandoned her on the stairs?"

Even though I knew it was ultimately my fault, that stung. "She wouldn't come with us," I said. "We tried. She wouldn't move."

"So you left your sister on the stairs? Alone. On a night like this?"

Even Rondo knew better than to say anything. Elvis was shuddering her nightmare shudder as Mom's hand moved in a circular pattern, soothing her.

"How do you think she felt?" Mom asked.

"Not good," I said. Terrified was more like it. The dim lighting and the creaky Ghost Stair. She was probably going to have nightmares for a week.

Mom shook her head at me. "Your dad and I had a lot to deal with tonight," she said. "We needed you to step up and help out." She sighed. "You're in middle school now, Epic. You should know better."

"I'm sorry, El," I said. I really was. But I was also tired. In an electrical circuit, if there's too much voltage, even a resistor can melt or catch fire. I was *trying* to step up and help, but to be honest, I was starting to feel a little melty on the edges.

Even in the barely there glow of the night-light, I could see my sister's swollen red eyes blinking up at me.

"Sir Bentley didn't do it," she said with a frown. "She didn't solve the crime."

BREAKING NEWS: MAJOR JEWEL HEIST IN NOT-SO-DOG-FRIENDLY TOWN

posted by @pooperscooper1

Remember when we first heard about Carmelito? That yawns-ville halfway point between LA and San Francisco? Turns out Carmelito's not so sleepy after all. Late last night, most of the town was awake . . . investigating the disappearance of a $500,000 dog collar!

That's right, folks. That sparkly bangle Sir Bentley was sporting at the Perro del Mar's Yappy Hour? Half a mil of dog bling. Gone in the shake of a tail.

Here's the poop-scoop on the drama rolling out:

First off, we *thought* today's big news item would be the rollicking party at the Moondoggie Inn. Yips & Sips had it all: DJ Doggone, tattooed pooches, and (wait for it) George Lucas's *personal assistant*. With up-to-the-minute dish about The Pendleton Trilogy! Don't you worry. The HDD got the exclusive scoop!

But *Star Wars* will have to wait because there's a criminal on the loose! Just two blocks up the street from the Moondoggie shindig, police held several sketchy suspects for questioning, and trust this newshound, it didn't take long for tempers to flare.

By 2:00 A.M., the crime scene was a war zone. Seriously, put your imagination to work, then turn it up to *eleven*.

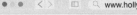

Need a visual aid? <u>Check out this bomb-tastic video</u> of Perro del Mar owner Marc McDade going bonkers with rage [warning: explicit language]. Flying furniture? Yep. Curtains ripped off the windows? You betcha.

High-speed car chase? Yes, please! At approximately 2:45 A.M., the police left the premises to chase down a lead suspect! We almost believed we were on the set of *Bentley Knows*, except if this were a BK episode, we'd be drooling like a Saint Bernard out of sheer boredom.

What's next? Maybe this is Sir Bentley's real-life chance to prove he's a detective worth his kibble. *Maybe* he can use those droopy eyes to solve one last crime. Don't count on it, folks. Some days you're the dog, some days you're the hydrant.

#dogfriendlytown #poopscoop #byebyebling

Sponsored by: PetzPlay Sporting Goods, Dog Elegance™, KhanArts Training Treats

DELPHI & ASHA

Even though I'd barely slept, I was up knocking on the Boones' door at 6:00 A.M. sharp. No one answered. I knocked again. There was a scuffling sound, and I heard Pico's dog tags jingle on the other side of the door.

I knocked a third time.

Pico pawed at the door. His claw made a *scritch-scratch* sound on the wood.

"Hey, buddy." I fished a treat out of my messenger bag and slipped it under the door. "Where is everybody?"

Long after Elvis and Rondo were snoozing in their bunks, I'd lain awake listening to the sounds of people talking and cleaning up downstairs. It was unbelievable how tired I could be and *still* my body wouldn't fall asleep. Eventually, everything quieted down, and I'd assumed all the guests went back to bed. But now it was six in the morning. Where were the Boones? I tapped my feet as I considered the possibilities. Had they taken off? With the jewels?

Mr. Boone had *seemed* like he was telling the truth about

the air conditioner, but last night at Yips & Sips, they were planning something with Asha. Something that made Asha uncomfortable. I shook it off. They wouldn't have left without Pico. Even criminals wouldn't be that cruel.

I leaned my ear against the hollow wooden door and listened. I could hear Pico panting and pacing. I could also hear a faint series of short snorts and a drawn-out sound like a chainsaw revving. It was the Boones. Snoring.

Pico's dog tags jingled faster. He wasn't going to be able to hold out much longer. For one, I knew he had to pee. And based on the look in his eyes as he'd howled to the ceiling last night, I also knew he was losing it. Pico needed his routine, and the past few days had not gone as planned, to say the least. He was starting to remind me of a shaken-up soda can. When that tab finally got pulled, it was not going to be pretty.

I pounded on the door.

Behind me, the door to Room 5 opened instead. Delphi leaned against it with her eyes half closed.

"Epic, come on," she said in a gravelly voice. "Give it a rest. We all had a really long night."

"Some of us longer than others!" Asha said.

I jumped and swiveled toward Room 4. I hadn't heard her door open at all. Asha didn't look like herself. She stood in the hallway in her bare feet and a baggy sweatsuit. Her usually explosive hair was tucked away under a satin cap. Without her makeup, her eyes appeared tiny, and she seemed about a foot shorter. Which of course was physically impossible. At six in the morning, there was nothing supermodel about Asha. And she definitely wanted to throttle somebody.

"Sorry," I whispered, but she wasn't glaring at me. She was glaring at Delphi. I shifted my messenger bag on my shoulder as the two of them shot dagger-eyes at each other across the hall.

"I was trying to wake up the Boones," I explained. "I'm supposed to walk Pico."

Delphi shook her head. "Not gonna happen," she said. "Melissa was handing out sleeping pills like candy last night. They won't wake up until noon."

"I. Saw. Everything. *Delphi*," Asha hissed.

"Saw what?" I asked. *The jewel thief?* Whatever it was, Asha was not messing around.

"Don't worry about it, Epic," Delphi said. "She didn't get enough beauty sleep, and now she's short-circuiting."

"I told Officer Sánchez," Asha said.

Delphi rolled her eyes. "Trying to take the heat off yourself? You're not as loyal to Madeleine as the little act you put on. I've been watching you, too."

"I don't know why you're not already in jail." Asha stepped back into her room and slammed the door.

Jail. Pico's claws *scritch-scratch*ed at the door more frantically now. I couldn't believe the Boones were sleeping through all of this. My feet froze in place, but my eyes started counting all the jewels hidden in Delphi's arm tattoos. Once you started looking, they were everywhere. Rubies, diamonds, sapphires. The dragon was practically wearing a coat of armor made out of bling.

Delphi was biting her lip and staring at Asha's door like she'd forgotten I was there. *Was Delphi the jewel thief?* I tried to think like Rondo. What would he do? I wasn't sure how to investigate a crime, but I could at least gather intel.

I dug around in my messenger bag and found a pencil.

"Do you have a piece of paper?" I asked. "I should leave a note."

"I guess. Hold on."

Delphi shut the door. Weirdly, with all that had happened in the last minute, my brain was still stuck on how bizarre it was to see Asha looking like a normal human being. Rondo and Declan were never going to believe me. Even Delphi had been more pulled together. Which was odd, too. Her eyes had been half-closed like she was sleepy, but her Mohawk was still perfect. Not squashed down or tied up in knots like Asha's Afro. What did she use to keep it so pointy? Superglue?

"Here you go," Delphi produced a journal and ripped out a page. She grinned as she handed it to me. She was back to her relaxed, chill self. "*Now* can you let everybody get some sleep?"

Only, by now I was convinced she hadn't been sleeping.

When she'd opened the door, I'd gotten a quick glimpse of the room. Enough to see that all the lights were on. And Melissa was sitting on the bed with a phone to her ear, surrounded by clothes and a . . . suitcase? I tried to angle myself to get a better view.

"Who's Melissa talking to?" I asked.

Delphi rolled her eyes. "Her PhD advisor," she said.

"At six in the morning?"

"Tell me about it. She's all revved up about the way the doggos bolted last night," Delphi said. "Something about the number of triggers it took to put each of them 'over threshold.'" She faked a yawn and waved me away. "It's boring. Go on. Leave your note."

I scribbled a note to the Boones. *6am: Came by for Pico. Tried to wake you. I can take him to Dog Run after camp if you want.—Ep . . .*

Delphi's door shut behind me. I paused writing, took a deep breath, and quietly inched my way closer to Room 5. As quietly as I could, I held my ear to the door.

I couldn't swear to it in a court of law, but what it sounded like to me was, "Asha. Knows. Everything."

I tried to keep my breathing slow and steady as I folded my note and slid it under the Boones' door. Immediately, I heard a frustrated growl and the sound of paper being pounced on, crumpled, and torn to shreds.

None of this was going to end well if I didn't do *something*.

First I had to bust Pico out, which meant I had to wake Rondo or find the master key. Then I had to find Luis. My brother was right. Luis might not want us meddling, but he didn't know the Perro—or the guests—like we did.

Luis needed us.

TRENDING

I ran into Dad on the family stairs.

"Can I have the master key?" I asked. "I've got to get Pico outside."

He put his finger to his lips. "Don't wake your mom. She barely slept last night. Come to the kitchen."

I didn't have time for that.

"He's dying up there," I said.

If I couldn't wake Mom, I was going to have to get the spare key from Rondo. I ran up a few more steps, but Dad stood in my way. He pulled at his mustache. He looked awful. Bloodshot eyes. Droopy lids.

"Come on down," he said. "Just for a sec. Pico can wait."

What else could I do? I followed him to the kitchen. Madeleine was sitting on a bar stool, scrolling on her phone, with Sir Bentley sprawled on the floor at her feet. Bentley looked surprisingly different without the collar. Less like a celebrity posing for cameras. More like somebody's lazy pet eyeing you for treats. She turned her nose in my direction and sniffed. I wondered if she *felt* any different.

"Good morning!" Madeleine said, awfully cheery for someone who'd been screaming her lungs out a handful of hours ago. "I came down for coffee, but I don't know how to use all . . . that."

She waved her hand toward Dad's coffee bar, which was more like a science lab than a kitchen counter. It was covered with grinders, scales, vacuum brewers, and several glass funnels and beakers—minus the one that shattered last night.

"I got you," Dad said. "The Chemex is obviously out of commission, but I can make you a pour-over, or would you rather have espresso?"

"Anything caffeinated will do."

This was going to take forever. I bounced from foot to foot while Dad put on "Stormy Monday" by Etta James—his go-to album for depressing times—and started measuring out coffee beans on the scale. Madeleine's toes tapped to the rhythm.

She handed me her phone. "Did you know your dad is trending online?"

I watched a video of Dad's Chemex shattering as he shouted obscenities. "Who recorded that?"

Dad groaned. "Big Brother is everywhere."

I played the video again.

"Mom's going to flip."

Madeleine's phone beeped, and a text message with about

four lines of kiss and heart emojis popped up: *Hang in there. Love.*

I handed the phone back. "You got a text," I said.

Madeleine got the schmoopy look on her face she usually reserved for Thomas Scott. "Everyone's being so supportive," she said. "And see?" She scrolled through her feed. "Not a single Pendleton Triplet!"

She was right. Instead of POO, Bentley was in half the trending topics.

#dogbling

#saveBentleyKnows

#PerroPurloin

"I mean, I'm not *glad* the collar was stolen, but don't you think sometimes things happen for a reason . . ." Her voice drifted off as she scrolled some more. "Someone's posting Bentley's highlights! 'Top Five Bentley Tearjerkers (Tissues Required).' Oh my . . . EEEEEK!!!"

She shoved her phone in my face again.

@SharonHenderson posted 6:45 A.M.: Fresh out of a 24- hr recording sesh (you will 💜💜💜 these tunes). Saw the news. DON'T BELIEVE EVERYTHING YOU READ.

@SharonHenderson posted 6:46 A.M.: @SirBentley SAVED Newt from falling. DON'T LISTEN TO EVERYTHING YOU HEAR.

@SharonHenderson posted 6:47 A.M.: @SirBentley is a ROCK STAR. #grateful #blessed #savebentleyknows

"Bentley! You're redeemed!!" Madeleine was almost

crying now. She dropped down from her stool and covered the dog in hugs and kisses.

I backed away from them and tried to get Dad's attention at the coffee bar.

"Dad. Pico? The key?" I reminded him.

He glanced at Madeleine and waved me closer. I stood next to him while he dumped the beans into the grinder.

"I'm sorry I put all that on you last night," he said quietly. "It was too much. I should have been looking out for Rondo and El myself. I'm the adult."

We waited thirty seconds while the grinder loudly crushed the coffee beans into a fine powder. It was nice of him to say, but really, I didn't care. We had a known criminal in our house, and Pico was getting ready to spray. Or worse.

"Can I go now?" I asked the second the grinder stopped.

Dad lowered his voice even more. "Luis told me you guys were poking around upstairs and messing with his investigation."

I felt the blood drain from my face.

"We were trying to help."

"You can't. This is a big deal. I need you to take the kids to camp this morning and keep them out of Luis's hair."

"But I think I know who did it."

"Epic. For real." Dad stopped making coffee. His red hair was sticking up Elvis-style, and he had a desperate, tired look in his eyes.

"We probably can't go to camp during an investigation," I said. "Shouldn't we all be on lockdown?"

"That's not a thing," Dad said. "Take them to camp. Keep them out of this. You're in charge today."

"But you said *you* should be the adult."

Dad ran his hand through his bedhead and set a mad-scientist vacuum pot on the stove.

"I don't know, Epic." He sighed. "Just. Please?"

The swinging door to the kitchen started to sway, and I heard someone fumbling at it. Bentley shook herself out of Madeleine's arms and pricked up her ears.

The scratching got louder.

"Stay there," Dad said quietly, nodding to me and Madeleine. He picked up his cast-iron frying pan, and my heart started to race. If there was something dangerous behind the door, what was he going to do? This wasn't a cartoon. You couldn't just *pan* someone.

The door creaked open a centimeter, and then another. Bentley stiffened and let out a low, rumbling growl. As the opening widened, we saw a giant hand, then a face, and finally, Mr. Boone's body slow-motion stumbled into the room. Madeleine yelped. Dad dropped his pan onto the butcher block. Bentley rushed to Mr. Boone's side, and Pico came hurtling toward me like a terrified bullet.

"Clive! Are you all right? What happened?"

Dad and Madeleine rushed to Mr. Boone, who'd slumped

onto his knees and was draped over Sir Bentley for support. The first thought that crossed my mind was that he'd been attacked. But he didn't look hurt. Maybe he was sick.

"Pico needs a waaaalk," Mr. Boone said in a slurry, sing-song voice. "I need coooffeeee." He drooped further onto Sir Bentley's back, and his eyes started to close. Before he could totally collapse, Dad put his shoulder under Mr. Boone's arm and hoisted him to his feet.

"Come on, Clive," Dad said. "Let's get you to a chair. We'll find out what's wrong."

Madeleine supported Mr. Boone's other side, and they all stumbled toward the kitchen table. Pico stuck his nose right in my ear and let out a loud howl. I ran for the back door.

"Epic! Where are you going?"

"Pee!" I said over my shoulder.

While Pico did his business in the bushes, I watched through the kitchen window. As soon as Dad and Madeleine lowered him safely into a chair, Mr. Boone put his arms on the table and his head slumped forward. I could hear his loud chainsaw snores even from the backyard.

I led Pico back into the kitchen. Dad was dialing someone on his phone.

"Melissa drugged him," I said.

"What?" Dad held the phone in midair.

"She gave him a sleeping pill," I said. "I think."

"Oh!" Madeleine said. "That makes sense."

"It does?" Dad wrinkled his forehead.

A person on the other end of his phone answered. "Hello . . . Hello?"

Dad stared at it for a minute like he'd forgotten who he'd called, and the kitchen door swung open again. Frank scrambled into the kitchen with Dec close behind.

"We've been waiting out front forever," Dec said. "Are we walking or what?"

Frank took one look at Sir Bentley and started to yip his you-might-be-bigger-than-me-but-I-can-totally-take-you yip. If anyone in the house was still sleeping, they were awake now. Except, obviously, Mr. Boone. He snored away on the kitchen table with his mouth half open. Dad gave me and Declan a frustrated shake of the head and pointed to the back door.

"Walk Pico. Bring him straight to the Boones' room when you're done. Then get the kids ready for camp," he said. "I'll take care of Clive."

DECLAN'S ADVICE

Flo put Pico on the massage table and shooed us away.

"I need extra time," she said. "I've never seen his aura so frizzy."

Dec and I moved over to check out the junk at the Martinez Antiques booth and gave Frank a bacon-scented rope to keep him busy. Frank attacked it like the rope had insulted his family.

"The good news is the Pico Project's back on track," Dec said. He typed the results of our leash swap into his phone. "That was smart thinking to front-load the swaps closer to home."

Maybe it was because Pico was so frazzled he couldn't be bothered to care, but he'd let us swap leashes for a full minute outside the Perro without making any kind of fuss.

"Flight initiation distance," I said. "One of our guests told me about it." I winced. A guest who was possibly an accomplice to theft.

"At this rate, he'll be totally fine by September," Dec said. "He won't even need you."

That should have made me happy. The whole goal was to help Pico get comfortable with other people. But hearing it come out of Dec's mouth, it felt like an insult.

"Whoa!" Dec shook his phone at me. "Check it out! Your brother was right. Shaunté Stevens got hit by the Silk Bandit last night."

"Who?"

"The actress from the magazine. Remember? In Sir Bentley's room?"

"I guess."

"Rondo said she and Misty LaVa were going to be the next Hollywood Heists. He was right. At least about one of them. Luis should hire *him* to solve the dog collar crime."

"Seriously." I wondered what Rondo would say about Delphi and Melissa. I'd been running through every interaction we'd had with them, trying to pick up clues I'd missed. "Remember when we walked in on Delphi and Melissa in the dining room after Yappy Hour?"

"Yeah." Dec picked up an old radio and fiddled with the knobs.

"Do you think they were plotting?"

"Doubtful. They don't seem like the type."

"What type?"

"Diabolical? Evil to the core?"

"Do they have to be evil? Maybe they need the money to save a dying grandmother."

I spotted a vintage cassette player almost identical to Miyon's in the Martinez Antiques trash pile.

"How much is that Walkman?" I asked Mr. Martinez.

"It's dead," he said, handing it over. "So . . . free?"

"I only need the cover anyway." At least there was *one* thing I could fix. I put the Walkman in my bag for later and went back to worrying about the missing jewels.

When Flo finished with Pico, he was so zoned out he could hardly walk in a straight line. He was in no shape to chase a ball, so we skipped Dog Run and headed back toward the beach. All the way down Ocean Drive, Dec went on a tangent about soccer rules. He'd suddenly memorized a thousand statistics about players and tournaments, and every time I tried to bring up Delphi or the stolen collar, Dec changed the subject back to soccer. The more he talked, the more annoyed I felt.

"You don't even seem to care," I said.

"What?" Dec looked all innocent.

"A criminal was *at my house*," I said. "Don't you want to help figure this out?"

Frank stuck his nose into a patch of flowers and ice plants on the edge of the sidewalk, and Dec paused to let him root around. Pico gave me the side-eye and stepped behind me in case something threatening like a bunny or chipmunk scooted out.

"I just think things are more complicated than they seem," Dec said.

"Meaning?"

"People are unpredictable," he said. "You don't have any evidence to go on. And you guys . . . tend to get worked up about stuff, you know? Make things a bigger deal than they are?"

"This *is* a big deal!"

"I'm just saying, if it were me . . . Luis is the expert, right?"

"Yeah, but—"

"He'll figure it out. Don't distract him. Stay out of it."

Seriously? That was his advice? Stay out of it? How many times had Dec and Rondo made fun of *me* for having an over-developed sense of responsibility?

"What happened to Follow Your Curiosity and Be a Questioning Human? All of that's over now? Because you're main-streaming?" It wasn't until after I'd said it that I realized I was using Rondo's words. I'd hated it when my brother said them to me, but they didn't seem to bother Dec at all.

"You asked what I thought." He pulled Frank out of the bush and kept walking. "Don't jump down my throat."

But I was already jumping. Pico and I walked a little faster to catch up, and maybe it was exhaustion or maybe it was stress, but something I'd been thinking about for days popped out of my mouth.

"I feel like you're trying to be a different person," I said. "Like you want to leave Sunny Day as far behind as you can.

The cell phone, soccer, the new vocabulary. What's going on? It's weird."

"I'm not doing the vocabulary anymore," Dec said.

"You aren't?" It was true he hadn't used it once all morning.

"Carlos advised me to drop it."

I'd hated Dec's new vocabulary, but the fact that he quit it because of some kid we didn't even know was annoying to say the least.

"*I* told you to drop it," I said. "And what's up with Carlos? You've known this kid for one minute, and suddenly he's your new best friend?"

"We've *both* known him since preschool. That's seven years."

"No one remembers preschool," I said.

"Listen. Epic . . ." Dec stopped, picked up Frank, and rubbed some dirt off his nose. "I don't think you should be so down on Carmelito Middle School. There are a lot of opportunities we didn't have at Sunny Day."

I frowned. "Like what? Soccer?"

"Exactly!" Dec grinned like we'd had a mind-meld, which we definitely did not.

"That's what I mean," I said. "Since when do you care about running around and kicking some worthless ball?" It came out harsher than I wanted it to, and Dec's grin disappeared.

Pico nudged my ankle with his nose. He wanted to be

picked up, too. But right now, I was focused on Dec's eyebrows. They weren't wagging up and down all goofy or raised in amazement at whatever new thing he was obsessed with. They were scrunched into a low, angry V. Dec was losing his cool.

"You know you're being super closed-minded, right?" he said. "It's like you didn't even listen at graduation. This is our opportunity to evolve. I've got *new* curiosities. And I'm following them. Why wouldn't you want me to do that?"

Carmelito Beach stretched out in front of us, and I stared out at the ocean through the gloom. There were barely any waves. Just soup. Not a single surfer in sight. It was a good question. Why *should* I care what Dec wanted to do?

"I feel like you're leaving me behind," I said. Once the words were out of my mouth, I knew they were true.

"You *what*?" Dec practically dropped Frank. "I'm right *here*! You're the one who's been ditching *me*."

"*Me?*"

Dec rolled his eyes. "That urgent note to meet you at the beach? I did all that research and raced over there and then Carlos and I had to ride around the bike path for an *hour* to kill time while you guys surfed with Miyon."

"I didn't—"

"And she's part of Family Night now?"

"She's not . . . She's . . . nice."

"Yeah, she is," Dec said. "Which is the main reason I didn't want to get dragged into your whole jewel thief investigation."

He mumbled it, but I heard every word.

"What does *that* have to do with anything?"

Dec shook his head. "You're not including all the data."

"Like?"

"I don't know. Some cool girl who moved to town on a boat suddenly wants to hang out with us all the time and do recon in Sir Bentley's room?"

I couldn't believe him. "She's an eighth grader, not a jewel thief."

"I'm not saying she *did* it," he said. "I'm saying you're not being objective. About any of it. You talk about *me* acting strange, but leaving someone off a suspect list because of bias isn't your style. Neither is writing people off for making different choices than you." He glanced at his phone. "I've got to go. You know, kick a worthless ball around."

I stood, frozen, watching Dec and Frank disappear into the fog until Pico pawed at my leg. His brown, watery eyes gazed up at me, and he tilted his chin to the side until one of his ears flopped inside out.

"I know, Pico," I said. I picked him up and rested my chin on his head. "I wish I never said any of it, either."

BRODY

Pico and I were almost to the Perro when the door to Dogma Cafe opened and three small labradoodles dragged Brody Delgado out of the shop. Brody was holding a cardboard tray full of coffees. He had dark circles under his eyes. Board shorts that were even more rumpled than usual. He looked almost as bad as I felt.

"Aw, I'm glad to see a Mighty McDade." Brody tried to hold out his hand for a fist bump, but the labradoodles dragged the leash in the opposite direction, tangling themselves around a lamppost, and he almost spilled the coffee tray.

I didn't have the time or the energy for Brody's nonsense. I'd just had a fight with my best friend, and to add insult to injury, I had to go get Rondo and El out of bed and ready for art camp. I tugged Pico's leash and moved toward the curb.

"Help me out, dude?" Brody asked before we could cross the street. "I'm supposed to stop by the Perro and give a message to the guest in Room 5."

That was weird. "Delphi? Or Melissa?"

"I guess." His eyes drifted to the sky like he was trying to remember the message. "*Emergency vet meeting. Nine a.m. The usual place.* Can you do that for me?"

Emergency vet meeting? "Who's the message from?" I asked.

"Yeah . . . I'm not supposed to say. It's on the down-low. But you got this, right? You're a lifesaver, brah. I'm barely keeping it together."

He wasn't the only one.

Brody jutted his chin toward POO. "FiFi's got me walking these guys all hours of the night. And last night was totally wild, right? After I heard those screams. I mean, that was the worst. I thought something *happened* to you guys. You're family to me. You know, not literally. But seriously, I'm glad you're okay."

"Um. Thanks," I said. Brody didn't look like he was being sarcastic. He looked like he'd been up all night. Worrying about my family.

Dec had been right about one thing. People are unpredictable. But he was wrong about everything else. You didn't have to be biased to know that putting Miyon and her dad on the suspect list was absurd. Especially when all the evidence pointed to Delphi and Melissa. Clearly they hadn't gone to bed, and they were packing. They'd lied about the doctor's bag full of chocolate. Asha saw them do *something* incriminating. And a top secret "emergency vet" meeting at an undisclosed location? Tell me that wasn't sketchy.

Except, objectively, I had to admit none of that was actual evidence. So Dec had been right about *two* things. Maybe I wasn't exactly going about this scientifically.

As Pico and I crossed the street toward the Perro, I made up my mind. Declan Harper was the smartest person I knew. If I couldn't convince *him* that Delphi was a jewel thief, Luis wasn't going to take me seriously either. He didn't want to be distracted with theories and hunches. Luis needed concrete information. Something he could use to build a case.

And I knew when and where to find it.

HOOKY

I stood on the ladder to Rondo's bunk and dropped Pico on the bed. My brother was dead asleep. As usual, his sheets were all tangled and knotted up. I don't know what he does in his sleep to get them so twisted. He didn't move as Pico tiptoed around, sniffing Rondo's head and neck.

"Hey, Pico," I whispered, pointing at Rondo's face. "Over here."

Pico's a smart dog. He hopped right onto Rondo's shoulder and started licking my brother's face.

"Ugh!" Rondo rolled onto his stomach. "What do you want?"

"Art camp starts in fifteen minutes," I said, pointing Pico toward Rondo's face again.

"That's disgusting!" My brother pulled the sheet over his head.

"We're not going," I said quietly. "But we have to *look* like we're going."

Rondo sat up so fast, Pico jumped to the far end of the bed.

"You're going to let us ditch camp?"

I felt a tug on my pant leg. Elvis stuck her head out from the bottom bunk.

"Can we go to the beach?" she asked with her thumb in her mouth.

Rondo was already putting on his swim trunks. If I'd known playing hooky would get my siblings out of bed so fast, I would have tried it a long time ago. Maybe. I'd thought it through from all angles, and it had to be done, but I still felt guilty. My palms were sweating, and butterflies fluttered around in my stomach.

"Don't make a big deal out of it," I said. "Act normal."

Elvis was doing Flamingo-Dances-the-Disco in the middle of the room. It was her own yoga move she saved for special occasions. Rondo was stuffing his backpack with ancient criminal behavior books, his mint-tin spy kit, a pair of binoculars, and his hollowed-out *Sherlock Holmes* book, jangling with coins.

"Or . . ." I picked up my own messenger bag filled with electronics, a stuffed octopus, and tiny dog clothes before clipping on Pico's leash. "Normal-ish."

My sister's mood changed the minute we got out into the hall.

"We can't go anywhere," she said. She stood at the top of the stairs and held her arms straight out, blocking our way down. "We have to help Sir Bentley find the collar."

Rondo tried to duck under her arm, but she scissored

it up and down as fast as she could. He broke through and raced down the stairs. Elvis shrieked when his foot hit the Ghost Stair, and it let out an eerie snap and creak.

"Rondo!" she scolded, and Pico yipped.

"Come on, Elvis." I leaned close and whispered in her ear. "We're going to help find the collar. I promise. And we'll get donuts."

We had time to kill, so Rondo used the five dollars he owed me to buy us donuts at Dogma Cafe. It took about five minutes for him to count out the change and about five seconds for most of the dollar fifty we'd spent on Elvis's gourmet raspberry filling to dribble straight down her shirt.

I handed her three napkins.

"Melissa and Delphi would never steal," Elvis said through a mouthful of donut. "If Asha says so, she's a liar."

"That's why we've got to follow them," I said. "To find out where they're going and who they're meeting with. Then we'll know the truth."

It was an objective, unbiased plan to gather evidence. Which we could use to prove to Luis *and* Dec that I wasn't making a big deal out of nothing. Or leaving data points out of the equation.

I hugged Pico close and kept my eye on the Perro's front entrance across the street. Rondo said it was risky to choose the window seat, especially since we were fugitives with a stolen dog in our possession.

"We're not fugitives," I said.

Rondo grinned. "Sure we are."

Pico adjusted his position on my lap and rested his head on my chest. I wondered if he could feel my adrenaline levels rising and speeding up my heart rate. I was so focused on the plan that I'd completely forgotten to drop him off at the Boones, and even though I felt bad about it, we didn't have time to go back. It was almost nine. Besides, Mr. Boone probably went back to bed, and if Delphi was right about the sleeping pill, they'd both sleep until noon. By then, we'd be home and the jewels would be back in Sir Bentley's possession. Everything would be fine.

"We have to go back," Elvis said. "Bentley needs us."

"What did Delphi say when you told them about the meeting?" Rondo asked.

I shook my head. "Nothing. They acted like it was normal."

"It *is* normal," Elvis said. "Melissa's a vet. She goes to vet meetings."

"Then why are they both going?" I asked.

We watched as the door to the Perro del Mar swung open and Melissa, Delphi, and Morrissey walked outside. I checked my watch. It was 8:56. Either they were running late or their meeting spot was close by.

Delphi bent down to adjust Morrissey's collar. She was wearing her dragon pin on a bright pink tank top.

"Well, that shirt'll be easy to follow," Rondo said. He opened his notebook to an on-the-ready page and tucked his pencil behind his ear. "Exit the building to the right. Pause at Dog Days. Watch for my signal. We'll stay a block behind them at all times. Got it?"

He shoved the rest of his donut in his mouth while we nodded.

"Let's roll."

Outside Dogma Cafe, we paused at the window of Dunham's Dog Days Photography, waiting for Rondo to give us the signal. I fiddled with Pico's leash and tried to distract myself from my growing panic by studying the display photos of poodles in poodle skirts, German shepherds in lederhosen, and Scottish terriers in kilts. Mr. Dunham might be a good dog photographer, but he has a terrible imagination.

"Okay," Rondo said. "They're walking up Main Street toward Healthy Pup."

Staying a block behind was easier said than done. Melissa stopped dead in her tracks to check her phone twice, and we had to turn around and walk backward for half a block. When Morrissey stopped to sniff down the alley next to Barker Bisson's Butcher Shop, we had to pretend to stop in the ATM booth at Carmelito First Bank. All the starting and stopping was driving Pico nuts. He pulled at his leash as Elvis pretended to push buttons on the machine. Rondo peered around the ATM and gave us a running commentary.

"Still sniffing. Now Barker is outside. He's petting the dog. Still talking. Still talking. We should start a detective agency, by the way. People would totally pay us to do this kind of surveillance."

I didn't blame Pico for being nervous. My hands had gone sweaty again. I couldn't help imagining Mrs. Doughty running through the roll call and scrunching up her nose when no one answered to the name McDade. What would she do? Call Dad? Hopefully Dad and not Mom. Dad might be glad we were acting on our instincts and doing the right thing for our family even though it meant breaking the rules. Or he might freak and call out a search party. One of the two.

"Earth to Epic," Rondo said. "They're on the move."

We were only back on the trail for about five seconds before Delphi and Melissa led Morrissey into the doorway of Nails 'n' Tails. We stepped into the alley next to Healthy Pup Natural Foods and waited.

"See?" Elvis said. "I told you it was nothing."

"A veterinarian meeting at a dog salon?"

"Look," I said. A large sign in the Nails 'n' Tails window read NONTOXIC, TEMPORARY DOGGO TATTOOS—2 FOR 1 SALE. "I bet they met here yesterday, too."

"So?" Elvis said. "That's a good deal. They came back for another one."

Maybe she was right. Maybe the Dog Elegance team of emergency vets was doubling down on the doggy tattoos, but I doubted it.

Rondo made a note in his notebook.

"I think we should go in," I said.

"Hold on!" Rondo glowered at us behind his hair. "You'll blow our cover. Wait a few minutes. See what happens."

"A few *minutes*?" Elvis said it like it was a life sentence. "What are we supposed to do? *Stand* here?"

Pico whimpered in solidarity. Knowing him, he probably didn't care what we did as long as we made up our minds and did *something*.

"We've got to find out why they're meeting," I said.

"*You* want to go confront potentially dangerous criminals, and Elvis and I want to play it safe? Are we living in an alternate universe right now?"

I didn't have a good answer. It was a gut feeling. We had to go in, and we had to go in now. Before whatever it was they were doing was over.

"Follow Your Curiosity, right?" I said. "I'm not going to confront them. They won't even know we're spying. We'll tell them we're there for Pico."

Elvis brightened. "We get to give Pico a tattoo?"

"No!"

"Well then, what's your excuse? What are we there for? Nails?"

She had a point. Reluctantly, I checked my wallet. Pico looked up at me like he knew I was getting ready to sell him out.

Elvis bounced on her toes and grinned. "Can I choose it?"

"Fine."

"I wouldn't advise it," Rondo said. "But . . . why not? It's not every day Epic goes rogue."

I led them across the street with a sudden burst of confidence. I was doing it. I was following through. Like a real Questioning Human about to turn an Outlandish Idea into reality.

Until we opened the door and filed into Nails 'n' Tails. That's when the smell of hair spray, nail polish, and reality slapped me in the face. My eyes started to water, and my voice wouldn't work. Delphi was sitting next to pink-haired FiFi Khan in the waiting area. FiFi was counting out a thick wad of cash. The dragon tattoo on Delphi's arm stared straight at me with its diamond eyes.

"Epic? What are you guys doing here?" Delphi put on a huge smile, quickly took the cash from FiFi, and shoved it in her purse. "Your mom told us you went to art camp."

Even Rondo couldn't say a word. It was Elvis who matched Delphi's smile and chirped, "We're getting a tattoo!"

OUR RIVAL, THE RASCAL

You would expect a jewel thief who'd been caught red-handed to make excuses or threats, or bolt out of the room. I was half expecting FiFi to kidnap us and hold us for ransom or for Melissa to jump out from behind the salon curtain with a loaded revolver. What had I been thinking? *Following* criminals. Waltzing into a doggy salon with a half-baked plan to catch them in the act.

Well, now I had. And what happened?

The Pendleton Triplets got a fur-conditioning treatment.

Morrissey got his nails painted black.

And poor Pico shook like a leaf while a stylist in a white apron attached rhinestones in the shape of a skull and cross-bones to his butt.

Elvis hovered over Pico and peppered the stylist with questions about stenciling and painting techniques. Rondo sat next to Melissa and pulled *Our Rival, the Rascal* out of his backpack. He pretended to read, but every few minutes, he snuck his tiny notebook out and wrote something down. Real discreet.

I tried to sit still, but my legs didn't want to stay put. I crossed and uncrossed my feet, trying not to choke every time one of the adults asked me a question. On the surface, it seemed like they were making small talk, but I was afraid if I opened my mouth, I'd say something incriminating. Blow our cover, like Rondo said. Right now, as far as they knew, we were just kids getting a doggo tattoo for Pico. I decided to answer nothing.

"How do you like art camp? Are you headed there after this?"

"Your dad said you go to some kind of expeditionary school. What's that like?"

"They teach you to be good problem solvers and all that?"

"Boy, somebody's not talkative today."

After a while, they gave up. Delphi scrolled on her phone, Melissa wrote something in a notebook, and FiFi read *Glitz Magazine*. I hadn't even considered that the owner of the Pendleton Triplets might be involved in stealing Sir Bentley's jewels. Obviously, our list of suspects was less complete than I'd thought. Why would she do it? Jealousy? Revenge? And did that mean Brody *was* involved, after all that talk about us being like his family? Maybe she'd sent him over in the middle of the night to be a lookout or a decoy.

Dec was right. I was in way over my head. None of it made

any sense. But at least we knew something. We'd seen money exchanged. A lot of money. That *had* to be useful to Luis.

Finally, Pico's stylist applied a finishing spray and declared that his new look was "dogalicious."

"You're a tough guy now, aren't you, Pico?" she said.

The rhinestone skull and crossbones didn't exactly scream "tough guy," but Pico didn't seem to mind it. He held his head high while I fastened his leash, and he almost strutted toward the door.

"See you back at the Perro," Delphi said.

I stared at her. She had no idea that the minute we left Nails 'n' Tails, we were going straight to the police.

Rondo held the door open with a don't-blow-our-cover glare. Elvis was blabbering on about how Pico should get the unicorn tattoo next, or maybe the kissing lips. I had to pull her by the sleeve to get her outside. She could have stayed in Nails 'n' Tails chatting with jewel thieves all day.

"I don't know how nontoxic that was," Rondo said after the door shut behind him.

I picked up Pico, and we gulped in fresh air before sprinting all the way to the Carmelito Police Department.

LUIS

"Dudes, I told you to leave this alone."

It was weird to see Luis at work. It was weird to be in the police station, period. I'd lived in Carmelito my whole life, walked past the station every morning with Pico, and I'd never been inside. I don't know what I was expecting. Handcuffed criminals? Bulletproof glass? A head cop barking orders from a control room with maps and blinking lights? It looked like any kind of office. A waiting room. Receptionist. Luis had a tiny desk with a dog bed on the floor for Cookie. Instead of cowering in my arms, Pico strode straight toward the terrier and sniffed her.

"See?" Elvis said. "I knew I picked the best one. That tattoo gives him confidence."

Luis ran his hand over his bald head, clearly annoyed.

"FiFi was giving her a *lot* of money," I said. I felt like I was on a sugar high from all the running and spying and donuts. "And you heard Rondo. That's solid evidence, isn't it?"

It turned out Rondo had been doing legit detective work

inside Nails 'n' Tails. He'd been spying on Delphi—her phone, in particular. She was staring at it like she was checking email or reading an article, but she was actually watching a real-time video of Pico getting his tattoo.

"I think the dragon pins are hidden cameras," he said to Luis. "She was controlling it with her phone. She could zoom in and out and turn it almost a full one hundred and eighty degrees."

This was news to Luis, I could tell. But he played it off like it was nothing.

"Asha already reported Delphi," Luis said. "We've got bigger problems."

That made me pause. What bigger problems? If he already knew about Delphi, why wasn't he doing something about it?

"FiFi Khan!" Rondo said, and I nodded. Luis probably didn't want to waste time on Delphi and Melissa if they were only hired help.

"What kind of evidence do you need?" I asked. "Like, if we recorded a confession—"

"Epic! I'm going to lose it any second now. Do I have to call your parents and have them come get you? I love you guys, but I'll put you in a cell if I have to."

He was joking. Maybe.

I pried Cookie out of my sister's arms. "We're going," I said.

Outside the police station, we stood on the sidewalk

planning our next move. Rondo tucked his pencil behind his ear. Elvis did a few jumping jacks. Pico used the slack on his leash to explore the underside of a juniper bush. Maybe the tattoo did make him more confident. I felt different, too. Across the street, the Carmelito Kleenex Box Middle School stared us in the face. I stared back, without a single heart palpitation. For all I knew, Mrs. Doughty could be watching us from the window, but my palms were dry. My throat wasn't choked up or filled with cotton. I felt calm. Confident. We'd taken a risk, and we'd lived to tell about it. More than that, we'd found out important information. We were on to something with FiFi being the ring leader. All we needed was more proof.

I was starting to get why Rondo liked this stuff. It was like solving a puzzle. For justice.

"I like your recording idea," Rondo said. "I bet we could get Delphi to talk. We need to hide a bug or carry one on us. Those camera pins are genius. That's some serious equipment."

I rummaged through the electronics in my messenger bag to see if there was anything we could use. I pulled out the broken Walkman I'd picked up at Martinez Antiques, and had a brain spark. "Could we fit this in your book safe?"

"Nice!" Rondo unzipped his backpack and removed the box of change from inside *Sherlock Holmes*. The Walkman didn't fit perfectly, but if you held the book shut, it looked completely innocent. No one would be able to tell you were recording.

The problem was, the RECORD button didn't work.

"Maybe I could fix it," I said. "We'd have to find a cassette."

"Let's go borrow Miyon's," Rondo said. "Hers works fine."

It was a good call.

"How much jail time does a jewel thief get?" I asked as Rondo stuffed the book safe back in his bag and I pulled Pico out of the juniper bush. He shook his tail happily at me, satisfied with his new adventure.

"Depends. It's grand larceny, so at least a few years."

"We *should* start a detective agency," I said. "We're awesome at this."

Rondo grinned, but Elvis stopped jumping.

"I don't want to do this anymore," she said.

"What? Why?"

"It got boring. I want to go home."

"It's not boring! We're about to catch a criminal."

"I like Delphi and Melissa."

"Me too, but that doesn't mean they should get away with grand larceny. Besides, it's FiFi we're after. Come on."

Rondo, Pico, and I started walking toward the marina. Elvis stuck her thumb in her mouth and stayed put.

"You can stay with Luis if you want," I said over my shoulder.

We heard her feet scuffle on the pavement as she hurried to catch up with us.

"The thing about a detective agency," Rondo said, "is you'd

have to decide whether you'd take multiple cases at once or if one at a time is the way to go."

"The more the better, right?"

"You'd think, but not every case would be this easy. Sometimes it's right in front of your eyes, but the clues are misleading. One extra detail, one new piece of information, and you've got to scrap everything and start all over. I think I'm a one-case-at-a-time detective."

Elvis had been hanging back, but now she caught up with us, tugged at my hand, and gave me her droopiest puppy-dog eyes.

"Please don't solve it," she said. She looked tired. And scared. "*Please.*"

"El. Don't worry. We'll be okay."

"It's better if Sir Bentley figures it out." She mumbled it quietly, but we all heard it.

Rondo gaped at her. "The dog?"

"She's a professional. It's what she does for a job. She'll solve the crime and get her jewels back, and everyone will see she's a hero."

"You know that's just a TV show," I said. "Right?" It was a silly question, but I had to check.

Elvis rolled her eyes. "I know that. But she's lead detective on the show. She knows how to do it."

I can't stand it when people treat Elvis like a baby because she sucks her thumb, but sometimes I forget she's only eight and still believes in unicorns and stuff.

"She's a dog, El," I said. "They train her to do tasks, and she does them so it *looks* like she's acting."

My sister glared at me. "Sir Bentley's smarter than that," she said.

"No way," Rondo said. "Dog acting is all tricks. The trainers use rewards to get them to look in the right direction or run a certain way. The dogs don't know what they're doing."

"Sir Bentley does," Elvis said, but she furrowed her forehead.

We were almost to Bill's Marina. The fog had burned off a little, but it still hovered around the boats, covering them with a soft gray mist. Even our footsteps on the dock sounded muffled. Pico's claws *clip-clipped* on the wood with a spooky echo.

At first I thought we'd missed it. Gone down the wrong pier. But it was definitely Miyon's spot. Except there was nothing but water lapping up against the dock where *Endless Summer* used to be.

"Well, *that's* a new piece of information," Rondo said.

ELVIS

Elvis looked like her heart was going to break.

"Miyon's gone? Why?"

Rondo and I locked eyes, and I felt like all the air had been vacuumed out of my lungs. I couldn't get a decent breath.

"Did she say anything when you and Dad dropped her off last night?" Rondo asked.

"No. 'See you later.' Although . . ." I bent down to pick up Pico. I suddenly needed to hold on to him. "She was acting sort of strange."

"Strange how?"

Pico nuzzled his nose against my neck. He could tell something was wrong. Very wrong.

"She kept checking her cell phone. And she didn't want go back to the boat because her dad was out. You don't think . . ."

Dec's words were on repeat in my brain: *Some cool girl who moved to town on a boat suddenly wants to hang out with us and do recon in Sir Bentley's room?* I hadn't wanted to admit it, but it *was* odd that she'd wanted to stay for Family Night. Who volunteers to play trivia games with a rowdy bunch of strangers? I'd convinced myself that it was because she liked us. But really, when I thought about it, that seemed delusional. She barely knew us. And we didn't know anything about Miyon. She'd said they were in town on sabbatical, but she didn't say what her dad was "researching" or why they couldn't do it in Los Angeles. Her dad was "out" last night—and Miyon was all stressed about it. What if he was "out" committing grand larceny? What if she'd only come over to distract us? What if the clues we'd been following were the wrong ones all along?

I rested my chin on Pico's head, and Rondo and I locked eyes again. Elvis put her hands on her hips.

"What?" she asked. *"You don't think . . .* what?

"Miyon and her dad might be jewel thieves," I whispered. It was too depressing to say any louder.

Elvis lost it. Her eyes went wild, and she stomped her foot.

"Epic! Stop it! No!" she shouted.

Then my sister sat down on the dock and started to cry.

"Okay, this is getting weird," Rondo said.

Elvis buried her face in her knees and sobbed big, heaving sobs. Rondo looked to me, but I didn't know what to do. We sat down on either side of her. Pico sniffed in her direction. Rondo put his hand on her foot. I tried to rub her back like Mom had done the other night after we'd left her on the stairs. None of it worked. Elvis wiggled and shook both our hands away, curling herself into an even tighter ball.

"I wanted to help." Her voice was muffled.

"You can help," I said.

"No!" she wailed.

I raised my eyebrows at Rondo. He shrugged.

"I don't want anybody to go to jail," Elvis said.

"*Somebody* has to," Rondo said, and Elvis wailed louder. I shook my head at him.

"Don't worry, El. The faster we catch the thief, the faster it'll be over. Everything will go back to normal. You'll see."

Elvis lowered her voice so we could barely hear it. "I want to help Sir Bentley find the collar."

Rondo shot me a look, but he put on his nicest big brother voice. "Okay," he said. "We want to help, too."

El lifted her head a centimeter.

"For real?" she asked. "You'll help? No matter what?"

"No matter what." Rondo patted her foot. This time she didn't shake him off. She sat up a little straighter and turned her watery eyes to me. Her face was wet and splotchy. I hated to see her like this. Shivery. Sad. Terrified.

"Epic? You'll help, too? Swear?"

"I swear, El," I said. "That's what we've been trying to do."

Elvis wiped some snot away from her nose. "Okay, good." Her shoulders relaxed, and she shot us a brief, grateful smile. "I thought she'd find it on her own, but we might have to lead her to it. Like you said. With some tricks."

Rondo and I leaned in.

"What are you talking about, El?" I asked.

"Do you think we could use some of those treats Madeleine has?" she asked. "Those work really well. We could make a trail for her to follow."

My heart may have stopped beating for the ten seconds it took for that to sink in.

"Elvis. You know where the collar is?"

El's face was wet, and she used a corner of her T-shirt to dry the tears off.

"Of course," she said. "I'm the one who hid it."

ENDLESS SUMMER
RETURNS

A loud horn honked like an alarm, and all three of us
flinched. More than flinched. Elvis screamed, and Rondo
almost fell off the dock. The synapses in my brain went berserk and gave me an instant headache. I thought I might lose
consciousness and the police would have to scrape me up off
the dock before they threw us all in jail. It was only my fear of
losing Pico again that kept me alert enough to grip his leash
until it dug into my palm.

Of course it wasn't the police. A few yards away, the *Endless Summer* made its way toward the dock. Miyon held up
a fish she'd caught, and her dad waved at us through the
haze. When I saw her, a mix of relief, dread, happiness, and
absolute terror churned in my stomach like a nightmarish
Tail-Wagger Smoothie. On the one hand, Miyon didn't have
anything to do with Bentley's collar. Which meant she was
hanging out with us because she *wanted* to. Because she was

actually my friend. On the other hand, my sister was a jewel thief.

"That's grand larceny, Elvis," I said while waving back. "What were you thinking? Mom and Dad are going to freak."

"You can't tell them."

"We *have* to tell them."

Elvis glared at me. "Not until Sir Bentley finds the collar. You *promised*."

I kept my eye on the approaching boat and tried to act like everything was fine. Great. Dandy.

"Promised what?" I asked through my teeth.

"To help. With the publicity stunt. So Sir Bentley can go back on the upswing. Like Declan said."

"Publicity stunt?" I looked to Rondo for help, but he sat there, stunned. And I could tell he was impressed, which made me mad. My siblings were out of control, and somehow I kept letting them drag me into their vortex. I'd gotten completely sucked in to Rondo's "detective agency." We weren't detectives. We were a bunch of annoying kids ruining things for everyone else. I was old enough to know better. I was the one who was supposed to have some kind of grip on reality.

"Elvis," I whispered. Miyon and her dad were almost at the dock. "You stole *half a million dollars* from a guest!"

"You promised." Her tears were back, and she said it in her baby voice. *Pwomised*.

"I didn't promise to be accomplice to—"

"You *promised*!" Elvis shrieked. She wasn't curled up in

a ball anymore. She was on her feet, with her arms flailing out in full tantrum mode. Pico started to howl as the dock swayed. The *Endless Summer* bumped up against the buoys.

"Everything okay here?" Miyon's dad asked.

Miyon didn't wait for anyone to answer. She dropped her fish in a bucket, scooped up Layne, and used the pup to lure Elvis onto the boat and down the stairs to the cabin.

"Is she okay? Do you want me to call your parents or anything?" Miyon's dad asked as he tied up the boat.

"It's okay," Rondo said. "She'll calm down."

"She's under a lot of stress," I said.

"Yeah, I saw it on the news."

"We're on the news?" Rondo asked.

Miyon's dad nodded. He picked up two buckets of fish. "You sure she's all right? I've got to bring these over to Bob, but if you need anything, I'm right there." He pointed to the marina office.

"Thanks."

Pico and I followed Rondo down the stairs. Miyon had set Elvis up on the couch with a blanket, a cookie, and a soft, snuggly puppy. While I was glad to see Elvis smile, I wasn't sure she deserved all the comfort.

Rondo immediately turned on the TV and flipped channels until a photo of our family standing outside the Perro del Mar flashed onto the screen. It was the picture from our brochure, and it was a few years old. Elvis was almost five, sucking her thumb. Rondo was six, with short hair that poked up on all sides—probably the last haircut he ever had.

I must have been nine. I was the only one not looking at the camera. Instead, I was looking at my siblings, and I remember why. Ten minutes before the photo shoot, Mom and Dad were busy with the photographer, and I was supposed to watch Rondo and Elvis. They talked me into making them ice cream cones. Chocolate. Which they got all over everything. The kitchen. Their clothes. Elvis even had some in her hair. I still remember the panic I felt trying to clean up their mess before we ruined the whole family photograph.

Some things never change.

"You guys are so cute," Miyon said.

We listened while a news anchor interviewed Luis about the investigation.

"We have a few leads and key suspects," he said. "I can't give details at this time, but we have reason to believe this was a professional job. Highly professional."

I suddenly realized how tired I was. Dead tired. Elvis-on-the-stairs tired. I would have given every cent of my birthday money to go home, climb in bed, and pretend the whole thing never happened.

"Did that detective come to your house?" Miyon asked. "Who do you think did it?"

I don't know if it was the exhaustion or the stress or the weird smirk that crossed my sister's face. All at once, the ridiculousness of everything that had happened zapped me like an electric shock. A celebrity Saint Bernard checking into the Perro. FiFi and her obnoxiously cute labradoodles. The giant crowd at Yappy Hour and the tiny Pomeranian flying through the air. My dad's explicit language going viral. Elvis going viral. My mom painting her "natural" furniture and Rondo sneaking into guest rooms and taking notes like a nine-year-old Sherlock Holmes. Me playing hooky and organizing a sting operation. At a canine salon.

My eight-year-old sister stealing a half-a-million-dollar dog collar.

For a publicity stunt.

To help a *dog's* acting career.

"Well?" Miyon said. "He said 'professional.' What if it was the Silk Bandit?"

Rondo snorted, and something small and gooey shot out of his nose. That was all it took. I started laughing, and I couldn't stop. I laughed so hard that my stomach muscles started to ache, and I *wanted* to stop, but the pain made me laugh even harder. I fell over on the floor, and Pico pawed at my belly, his rhinestone tattoo staring me in the face. Rhinestones on a skull and crossbones. On Pico's butt. I *actually* did that: I put a sparkly tattoo on Pico's butt. Tears rolled down my cheeks. There was nothing I could do but ride it out.

My laughing made Rondo crack up, and Elvis, too. Miyon was laughing, but she had no idea. She thought it was all about Rondo and his disgusting snot. She didn't know that everything was an absurd disaster. A full-on idiotic mess.

Maybe it wasn't as bad as I was making it out to be. Maybe when Mom and Dad found out, they would laugh, too. Madeleine would definitely be glad that the jewels were found. Luis would be relieved to have the mystery off his plate. Who knew? The Boones might even like the stupid tattoo. Eventually, the Dog-Friendly Town Award Ceremony would happen, and then everyone would leave. Madeleine would go on her trip to the Cayman Islands. Delphi and Melissa could go back to their stairless apartment in Los Angeles. FiFi, POO, Asha, and the film crew and music stars—they'd all disappear and life could go back to normal. Back to the way it was before anyone had ever heard of Carmelito or the Perro del Mar.

The terrible thing was, underneath all the laughing was the truth. A gnawing feeling in my gut that explaining away grand larceny wasn't that easy. That we were going to be in serious trouble. That we needed to get home as soon as possible and return the jewels before everything got much, much worse.

Elvis pushed Layne toward Miyon and stood up to do her signature hip wiggle. Her hair was sticking up all over the place from writhing on the couch, and her face was flushed from all the crying and laughing.

"They think I'm a *professional*!" she shouted. "Miyon thinks I'm the Silk Bandit!"

Rondo lost it all over again, and Miyon could barely hold

on to Layne as she gasped for air. But as suddenly as it had started, my laughter was gone. None of this was funny anymore. Miyon caught my eye.

"Wait. What?" She sat up and glued her eyes on Elvis.

"It's okay," I said. "We're going to fix it. Right now."

RANSACKED

My genius plan was to sneak quietly into the Perro, use the spare master key to enter Sir Bentley's room, and leave the collar someplace obvious, but not too obvious. So Madeleine Devine could find it and believe she'd misplaced it. It had been there all along.

It wasn't actually genius. It was the only thing I could come up with that didn't involve Elvis getting sent off to a juvenile detention center.

"The bathroom?" I asked.

Elvis scowled. She didn't like the plan.

"The bathroom's a good idea," Miyon said. She'd listened to our whole story—from spying on Delphi all the way back to leaving Elvis on the Ghost Stair—without saying much. I'd figured she was waiting for the right moment to ask us to get off her boat and stay far, far, away. Instead she said, "Let's do that. I bet they never checked in there. I mean, it's a *dog's* bathroom, right?"

"That's not a good plan." Elvis glared at me. "We're supposed to be doing a publicity stunt."

"Elvis." Miyon looked into my sister's eyes and squeezed her hand. "This is the right thing to do."

El rolled her eyes, but said, "Fine."

"Seriously?" I asked. "One word from her, and it's fine? What about everything I've been saying for the last twenty minutes?"

Rondo kicked me. "Just take it."

Miyon went into the bedroom and came back with her cracked Walkman and a blank cassette.

"In case you need it," she said to Rondo, "We should still put this in your book safe. Delphi didn't steal the collar, but the owner of the Pendleton Triplets is up to something. I think you guys are right that we need a confession, don't you?"

Miyon left her dad a note, and we let Pico and his rhinestone tattoo lead us home.

I still didn't think it made sense. That someone like Miyon, who was pretty and fun and could surf like a pro, would want to be friends with us. Especially now—after she had proof that we were criminal, snot-blowing weirdos. But it was a nice silver lining to the whole mess. Besides, I had bigger equations to solve. Like whether Dad would be in the kitchen or out in the garden. Either way, he'd see us if we tried to go in the back door. The main entrance could be safer, unless Mom was doing paperwork at the front desk.

We didn't get to decide. Half a block from the Perro, Mrs. Boone ran toward us full speed.

"You *found* him!" she sobbed.

She scooped him up and threw her arms around me, covering both of us with a mix of tears and sloppy kisses. I wriggled out of her arms as fast as I could, but she grabbed my wrist and practically dragged me the rest of the way to the Perro.

"It's been horrible!" she said. "I thought Clive had him, so I went to the store, but Clive was napping. In the kitchen, of all places."

"I'm sorry—" I started, but Mrs. Boone talked right over me.

"You won't even *believe* what our little Iggy did. He went bananas. Absolutely bananas. I have no *idea* how he got out."

"I forgot to—"

"Wait. Is this . . . a tattoo?"

I held my breath while Mrs. Boone examined Pico's rhinestone skull and crossbones.

"I picked the best one!" Elvis said with a bounce. "And he loves it."

"It's removable," Miyon said quickly. She'd seen the panic on my face. "And super cutting edge. Did you see the one Trixie got after *Dogs of War*? It's a purple heart."

"That dog won a Pawscar," Rondo added.

I could have hugged them all. Instead of flipping out, Mrs. Boone actually looked impressed. She even gave me a short nod of approval before turning her attention back to Pico.

"My *baby*! You wait until your daddy sees you. We wuv you so, so much. Even if you are a bad, bad boy."

She eyed the tattoo one more time, then smothered Pico with more kisses, and we followed her through the door of the Perro del Mar, up the guest stairs, and into Room 1.

Where absolutely everyone was assembled.

Luis. Mr. Boone. Mom and Dad. Delphi, Melissa, and Morrissey. Asha, Madeleine, Sir Bentley. Even Thomas Scott was back from Los Angeles, patting his sweaty forehead with a handkerchief. I could see why: It was a thousand degrees in the Boones' suite.

Room 1 was a disaster. Not a getting-Pico-ready-for-Puppy-Picnic-Week disaster. The couch cushions looked like a T. rex had chewed them open and vomited the stuffing all over the room. The bedsheets were crumpled in a pile on the ground, and the organic down pillows had apparently exploded. Tiny white and brown feathers dotted the carpet. Underneath the feathers were dozens of small, muddy paw prints. Iggy-sized.

"It's okay, everyone!" Mrs. Boone announced. "We can call the search party off. Epic saved the day!"

Luis sighed. "Come on, Clive. I rushed over because you said it was an emergency."

"It *was* an emergency!" Mr. Boone's voice boomed angrily, causing several people to flinch. He looked instantly sorry for losing his cool and added in a kinder tone, "Thank you all for coming to help."

Mrs. Boone set Pico down, and he headed straight for his dog bed. It was covered in feathers and fluff, but Pico climbed in anyway. He took a long look at all the people invading his space, covered his nose with his paws, and shut his eyes tight like he couldn't stand to see what he'd done.

I knew Pico had been really stressed out. When I'd been trying to wake up the Boones, I'd heard him pacing and whimpering. He'd torn up the note I slipped under the door, but could he seriously have done all this?

All the adults started to talk at once.

"How did you find him?"

"How do you think he got out?"

"Did you make sure to close the door, Epic? When you dropped him off before art camp?"

"I didn't . . ." *Drop him off . . . or go to art camp* is what I was going to say, but no one let me finish.

"Pico's never done anything like this. I don't know what came over him."

"He clearly needs better training. Why is this space heater on? It's eighty degrees in here."

"Because *someone* keeps turning up the air-conditioning. No wonder Pico went bananas. He's been freezing all week."

"I've told you, Sir Bentley needs cool temperatures. Don't you think she's been through enough?"

"Oh, please. Don't start that again. It's tedious."

"Is it? And the fact that you tried to turn my assistant against me? Is *that* tedious?"

"We didn't—"

Thomas Scott cleared his throat. "Can we focus on the real crime here? Bentley's collar?" His voice was getting louder with each word. "The one I paid *dearly* for?"

I gritted my teeth. The last time I'd seen Thomas Scott, he'd been in a great mood, laughing and making smoochy faces, offering us rides in his Tesla. Now he was super stressed out. Which was understandable. He'd spent a half a million dollars on a collar for his girlfriend's dog. And as far as he knew, it was long gone.

I nodded at Miyon and my siblings. It wasn't going to be easy, but it was now or never. I hadn't thought about exactly what to say or how to phrase it. While I was thinking, Miyon took Elvis's hand and squeezed it. My sister gave a little nod and stepped farther into the room.

"I know who took it," she said.

Thomas looked at her like he was going to pop an eyeball. "I left important business in Los Angeles to be here," he said. "Can we please. Not. Waste. Time."

"Thomas, calm down," Madeleine said.

Thomas took a breath and tried to smile. He lowered his voice almost to a whisper. "We could have left for the islands a week ago like I planned," he said through his teeth, "but you insisted on this . . . *circus for an overstuffed fur ball.*"

He said the last bit under his breath, but we all heard it.

And we all saw his foot twitch like he might want to give the Saint Bernard a swift kick in the rear. Instead, he mopped the sweat off his face. His shoulders slouched.

"Babe, I didn't mean that . . ."

Madeleine put her hands on her hips.

Elvis calmly stepped between Thomas and Sir Bentley, shoulders back, jaw set, and chin jut out. She didn't suck her thumb or use her annoying baby-talk voice. She was furious. And ready to take her punishment like a third grader.

Elvis stared Thomas Scott straight in the eye.

"It was me. I took Bentley's collar."

CONFESSION

The adults were speechless. They stood there in the disaster area and looked at Elvis like she was speaking Hungarian. And as strong as she was being, I saw my sister's chin quiver. Just a hair.

"It wasn't her fault," I blurted, and the adults swiveled their heads toward me. "I talked her into it. We were trying to help. Blame me."

It came out of my mouth before I could even think about it. All I knew was I couldn't let Elvis go down alone.

"Trying to help?" Dad asked.

"No he—" Elvis started, but Rondo interrupted her.

"We wanted Bentley to keep his show," he said. Miyon raised her eyebrows at us, and my brother shrugged. Like he didn't have anything else to do today, so he might as well throw himself under the bus with the rest of us.

Elvis kept her head held high, but her eyes got a little teary.

Madeleine's did, too. "That is the sweetest—"

"You *stole* from our guests?" Mom asked.

Luis shook his head. "This isn't a game, you guys."

Dad's eyes were getting watery, too. "Think of all the suffering you caused."

Thomas Scott was silent, but a tendon in his neck had started to twitch. Delphi couldn't help it. She started to giggle. Melissa shushed her and elbowed her in the ribs.

Mrs. Boone clucked her tongue. "Some kids turn bad early," she said. "When I was a girl, Chauncey Stewart stole a dress from—"

"I would never STEAL!" Elvis put her hands on her hips and stared them all down. "It was a PUBLICITY STUNT!"

Everyone shut up again.

"I'm TRYING to help Sir Bentley solve a real-life CRIME!" Elvis shouted. "So she will start TRENDING! And her show won't be CANCELED!" Her voice cracked. She was losing steam. "But it's not working out very well."

Mom looked horrified. "That's the most ridiculous—"

Madeleine took a protective step toward Elvis. "Now, now," Madeleine said, her eyes shining. "We can sort this out. For the record, I think she's a brave girl."

"But not very smart," Mom said. She held out her hand. "This ends now. Cough it up. Where's the collar?"

GHOST STAIR

"I used to be afraid of the Ghost Stair," Elvis said, like she was talking about ancient history, not three and a half days ago.

Even though we were in huge trouble, she was milking it. Making the most out of her rapt audience. With Rondo and me on either side of her like bodyguards, she led the whole crew out of Room 1, down the stairs, and across the lobby to the family wing. Only Elvis walked backward, talking and waving her hands like someone giving a tour.

"And then I realized it wasn't creaking because it was haunted. It creaked because one of the slats wasn't nailed down right! It was easy to lift up. So . . . obviously, that was the best place to put it. Don't worry, I set up an alarm system to keep it safe." She started to hum "Hound Dog" to herself.

I rolled my eyes at Rondo. It was incredible how much Elvis loved being the center of attention. Even now, when we were about to be grounded for life and have every privilege known to man stripped from our existence, she was still playing to the crowd.

Behind us, Luis was talking to Thomas Scott about whether or not he'd press charges. *Press charges.* Like, sue our family? Or send us to prison? If Elvis started to sing, I was going to throttle her.

"No, no," Thomas said. He'd calmed down and smoothed out his hair. He was even smiling again, relieved. "We have the collar back, no harm done. Let's pretend the whole thing never happened."

"Okay," Luis said. "We'll go straight to the station. I'll have my guy examine the jewels to make sure nothing got damaged. And obviously, I'll need to get a statement from you and Madeleine."

"You don't have to waste your time on that." Thomas gave Luis a friendly slap on the shoulder. "I'm happy. You're happy. We're all happy."

"It's routine," Luis said. "It won't take long."

I breathed a little easier. Thomas and Madeleine could have decided to make life miserable for everyone in my family. But it was all going to be fine. It was kind of amazing. Thomas was happy. Madeleine was happy. Elvis was *certainly* happy.

We passed the front desk, and my sister paused at the bottom of the family stairs for dramatic effect. Everyone bunched up around her, peering into the dim stairwell.

"And now . . . ladies and gentlemen—"

"Cut the theatrics, Elvis," Dad warned. Maybe not *everyone* was happy.

"Fine." Elvis started up the stairs.

"Wait! Don't go anywhere!" Madeleine and Sir Bentley came forward.

"I think we should film the stunt," Madeleine said.

"What?" I swear I saw Mom's eye twitch.

"The publicity stunt," she repeated. Like she'd suggested we make some peanut butter toast. "I think these kids were onto something. Asha can film it. Elvis, let's brush your hair. You can costar with Bentley."

Thomas nodded. "We'd need time to get some things ready."

"*We?*" Madeleine gave him an icy stare. "Don't you have 'important business' to do? I wouldn't want my overstuffed fur ball to hold you back."

"Babe, I didn't mean it. I was upset."

Madeleine ignored him and turned to Asha. "What do we need? Lighting. Wardrobe. Do you think we need audio?"

"No," Asha said. She already had her notebook out and was scribbling on the page. "Let's keep it short and do it like a silent film. That'll be more likely to trend internationally."

"Okay," Dad said. "If there's anything we can do to help—"

"Marc!" Mom snapped. "Haven't you done enough?"

"Me? I offered to *help*."

Mom's eyes were wild. She looked exactly like Elvis gearing up for a tantrum. "Look at what's happened. We're forgetting who we *are*. Our *kids* are forgetting who we are!" She actually stamped her foot. "I don't know *how* we got sucked into all this . . . petty . . . fame-grubbing . . . NONSENSE."

She was flipping out, but she wasn't wrong. I knew exactly what she meant. Things had gotten out of control. It was like we'd gotten swept up by a wave too big for any of us to handle. It was impossible to keep your balance and make rational decisions. Even Mom had gotten carried away, changing her furniture for a chance to get on the cover of some dog magazine. My brain was on another pendulum swing. I half wanted to join her, stamp my foot, and kick every single one of them out of our house. But I got what Dad was trying to do, too: Ride it out. They'd be gone soon. We didn't need to make any more trouble.

"Elly, Elly, calm down." Dad gave Madeleine an awkward smile and ushered Mom toward the kitchen door. "Let's step away for a minute."

"Step away?" Mom said in her grown-up Elvis-tantrum voice. "You want me to step AWAY? They turned my children into *criminals*. I let them PAINT my TABLE!"

Dad pulled Mom into the kitchen and left the rest of us standing at the stairs. The muffled sounds of Mom ranting and Dad soothing came through the doorway.

"Here's the plan," said Madeleine, like nothing had happened. "Asha, you do Elvis's and Bentley's hair. Delphi, you and Melissa can deal with lighting. This stairwell is too dim. We need something warm that will bring out Bentley's eyes.

Oh, don't look at me like that. I know you know I know you can do lighting."

Miyon leaned toward me and Rondo. "What kind of light brings out a dog's eyes?"

"You three!" Madeleine said. "Go find Elvis some decent clothes."

"She looks fine," I said.

"Bring me my rainbow skirt and my red tights!" Elvis said. She was practically glowing with happiness. Her Outlandish Idea was suddenly working out better than she'd planned— for her. She'd put us all through twenty-four hours of chaos and misery, and Mom was having a meltdown in the kitchen, but no big deal. Elvis was about to star in a video with her favorite celebrity. And people say crime doesn't pay.

"So I still need you to . . ." Luis tapped on his notebook.

Madeleine waved her hand at him like she was shooing a fly. "You can go," she said. "Or try to calm down *that* business." She nodded toward the kitchen, then added, "Thank you for your service."

"Hm," Luis said. He frowned, but moved toward the kitchen.

"Okay, everyone. Break! Meet back here in fifteen minutes." Madeleine paused and glared at Thomas. "Not you," she said. "I don't want to see you right now."

RONDO'S THEORY

"That was weird."

"Which part?"

"All of it."

Rondo dropped his backpack on the floor and flopped into his beanbag. I opened Elvis's sock drawer and dug around for a pair of red tights.

"Nice room," Miyon said. "It's huge."

"I guess." I'd always thought our room was tiny and cramped because there's barely any space to move around. But looking around at my bed, Elvis's and Rondo's messy bunks, three dressers, two bookshelves, my project desk, all Elvis's art supplies, it was probably more stuff than you could fit into the entire cabin of Miyon's boat.

"This is cool." She wandered over to the Beast and turned the handle that cranked the gears. Two metal ears lifted up. "What is it?"

"A work in progress," I said. "When I was little, Dad and I found these old bike gears on the beach, and I started making a creature out of them. I add stuff I find or build. It's mostly junk." As I said it, I realized I hadn't built anything in days. Not since Sir Bentley arrived.

"Have you thought about adding a tail?" Miyon said. "You'd need to make it wag. Maybe you could use an unbalanced motor. Or a—"

"Pull string!" I practically shouted it, totally expecting her to say the same thing at the same time. Mind meld, like Dec and I always had. I even lifted my hand, ready for a high five.

Miyon laughed at my sudden enthusiasm. "Sure," she said, slapping my hand. "I was going to suggest a pendulum."

"Oh. That's actually . . . a better idea."

"Pull the tongue," Rondo said, looking up from his tiny spy notebook.

Miyon pulled the tab I'd made, and a slow, deep voice sang, "Who . . . let . . . the . . . dogs . . . out?"

She pushed it back in. "Creepy."

"The battery's dying," I said. "Elvis wouldn't stop pulling it."

"I found the rainbow skirt." Rondo leaned over the beanbag and pulled a crumpled skirt out from a pile under Elvis's bunk. He tossed it in the middle of the room and went back to his notebook.

"What are you writing?" Miyon sat on the floor next to his beanbag.

Rondo tugged at his hair. "Something's not right. I'm trying to figure it out."

"Like?"

"For one, if Delphi and Melissa didn't take the collar, what was FiFi paying them for?"

"Rondo, don't start detecting again. We were wrong. Let it go." What I didn't say was that I agreed with him. Sparks were going off in my brain, but I was trying my best to ignore them. I was tired. Follow Your Curiosity didn't seem like great advice anymore. We'd miscalculated *everything* so far. We'd caused enough problems. Maybe it was better to go with the flow: Clap when people told you to clap and eat the elephant one bite at a time. It would be a lot less trouble.

Rondo squinted at me. "You *know* Pico didn't ransack that room."

"He didn't?" Miyon asked.

I shook my head. "No. Mrs. Boone was asleep when Mr. Boone tried to take Pico out for a walk. After that, *we* had him all day. If Pico made that mess, he would have had to have done it before he came downstairs."

"So someone broke in and tried to blame it on Pico? Poor Pico!" Miyon said.

"It was a shoddy job, too," Rondo said. "Did you see those lame footprints?"

"Pico would rather die than step in mud," I explained to Miyon. "But why would anyone trash the Boones' room?"

"To find the collar," Miyon said. "Ransacking happens all the time in detective novels."

"That doesn't make sense either," I said. "Luis wouldn't

ransack anyone's room. He'd investigate it, maybe, but not like that."

"The Silk Bandit might," Rondo said. He tapped his pencil on his notebook.

"Right." I laughed.

"Seriously."

"The Silk Bandit's in Los Angeles," I said. "Not Carmelito."

"The Bandit was in Los Angeles *last night*," Rondo said. "Stealing diamonds from Shaunté Stevens. But they could be anywhere today."

Music drifted up from downstairs, a weird, slow, vaguely familiar tune.

"What do you think Dad's listening to?" I asked, trying to change the subject before my brother really went off the deep end, and to distract myself from doing the math. How long would it take to break into Shaunté Stevens's house, then drive from LA to Carmelito? I pushed the question away.

"I don't know, Leonard Cohen or something," Rondo said. The music shut off. Mom can't stand Leonard Cohen. "Anyway, did you notice how sweaty Thomas Scott was?"

"Yes," Miyon said. "And he had a silk handkerchief!"

"He *always* has a silk handkerchief," Rondo said. "In the pocket of those dopey vests he wears."

Miyon leaned closer. "He said he was in Los Angeles last night. For *business*."

Again, the gears in my brain started to turn. Sparks tried to ignite, but I resisted. I was not going to get sucked into this again.

"He's not the Silk Bandit," I said. "He's some rich dude who bought a half-a-million-dollar dog collar. And someone stole it from *him*. Not the other way around."

"Trust me," Rondo said. "If I'm right, I bet the collar's worth a lot more than that."

"We're ready, we're ready, we're ready!" Elvis burst into the room. Her hair was in a ridiculous pair of curly, high pigtails with red sparkly ribbons in them.

"Is that *makeup*?" I asked. "Mom is going to kill you."

"She'll have to go through Sir Bentley first," Elvis said. Pure joy. "Where's my skirt?"

PUBLICITY STUNT

"Okay, everybody," Madeleine waved us all into a huddle. "This is a rehearsal run. We need to teach Bentley where her mark is. What's the better angle, Asha? Should we film from the bottom or the top of the stairs?"

"Both," Asha said. "Then we have choices."

"Good. Let's start at the top."

Delphi and Melissa each held rectangular boxes that looked like miniature versions of the film lights the Animal Universe crew had used at Yappy Hour. They moved up and down the stairs, finding the right angle to make both Bentley's fur and Elvis's eyes shine.

"There. That's it. Don't move." Asha stood at the top of the stairs and glared down at Delphi and Melissa. "And don't you dare ruin this for us."

Melissa's face got red, but Delphi smiled sweetly and said, "I make zero promises."

Madeleine clapped her hands. "Everyone ready?"

The narrow staircase was crowded. Madeleine stood

on an upper stair, and I crouched between Delphi and Melissa, ready to lift the Ghost Stair on Madeleine's cue. I looked down at the small crowd of people and dogs hanging around outside the kitchen door. Mom stood next to the Boones with her arms crossed, pretending she couldn't hear whatever Dad was saying to her. Mr. Boone was snapping photos on his phone, and Mrs. Boone was all revved up, bouncing on her toes and beaming like we were at an actual taping of *Bentley Knows*. I felt like a traitor participating after Mom's meltdown. No one was taking her side.

Next to Dad, Miyon patted Layne's head and gave me a thumbs-up. Morrissey lounged on the floor at her feet, eyes fixed on Sir Bentley. Luis and Thomas Scott were the only people not paying attention to the rehearsal. Thomas hung back by the dining room, looking hurt and upset because Madeleine had thrown out the flowers he'd picked for her from our garden. Luis was totally spaced out, staring at the polka dots on Thomas's vest like he'd been hypnotized by the multicolored fashion statement.

Madeleine asked Rondo to stand at the bottom of the stairs and give Bentley the signal to start the trick. Elvis prepped the Saint Bernard by showing her a treat, letting her smell it, and placing it on the first stair. When Rondo raised his arm, Bentley lumbered forward. Madeleine made a hand gesture and the dog lifted her chin, then tilted her head to the side. She actually looked like she was thinking.

Madeleine nodded at Elvis, who placed a second treat one step down from the Ghost Stair.

Sir Bentley, following Madeleine's cues, sniffed around and pawed her way, one step at a time, toward the center stair. She scrunched up her furry forehead so folds of skin furrowed around her eyes. You could practically see her trying to solve the crime. Even without music, it felt suspenseful.

Elvis was bursting with pride. I had to admit, the dog was a good actor. And this was only the rehearsal.

Madeleine held out her hand, and Sir Bentley paused at the Ghost Stair. "Asha, what's better here? Do we want her to lift the stair with her paw or her nose?"

"Paw!" Elvis said.

"Nose," Asha said.

They stared each other down.

"It's Elvis's stunt," Madeleine said. "Paw."

My sister fist-pumped the air.

"Epic." Madeleine nodded at me. "I'll give the signal, and you pull up the board when you see her paw lift. Asha's going to step down to get a slow close-up here, so stay to the left, and no one will see you."

"Sure," I said.

"Three, two, one . . ."

Madeleine's hand went down, Bentley's paw came up, and I lifted the top of the Ghost Stair.

An eerie, slow-motion version of "Happy Birthday" played inside the stair.

Madeleine shrieked.

"Your dad wasn't playing Leonard Cohen," Miyon said.

Even in the bright lights, Madeleine's face was gray. She looked like she'd seen a ghost.

"Don't worry," Elvis said from behind Sir Bentley's giant rump. "That's my alarm system. I used it a lot, though, so it's running out of battery power."

Elvis couldn't see that the birthday song wasn't what Madeleine was gasping about. She was gasping because when I'd lifted the broken step and Bentley's wise brown eyes gazed triumphantly into the secret vault where a devious jewel thief had hidden the stash . . .

There *was* no stash. Not a single jewel. Just an old used-up birthday card taped to a creaky board.

"The collar's not here," I said.

THURSDAY

6:00 A.M.

You Can't Teach an Old Dog New Tricks
posted by @pooperscooper1

Here we are, folks. A mere twenty-four hours until the Dog-Friendly celebration of the decade! Can't make it out to Carmelito, California, in time? No problem. Our Dog Dish pooper-scoopers will have live cams stationed at Paradiso Park so you won't miss one minute of the action. Keep your eye out for:

- Red carpet glitz and glamor! Carmelito's family-style Puppy Picnic just got a *major* pupgrade. Dog Elegance™ has announced their theme for the daylong event: All Dogs Go to Hollywood! There'll be champagne, caviar, and an honest-to-goodness red carpet where visiting dogs and their humans will get VIP treatment and photo shoots to boot. Formal wear is encouraged, obvs.

- Sharon Henderson and Newt!! The duo returns to Carmelito for a duet performance with vocal SUPERSTAR Misty LaVa! Will the fur fly when Newt and Sir Bentley meet again?

- Sneak Preview of The Pendleton Trilogy!!! Remember when we met George Lucas's personal assistant at Yips & Sips? Yep. He leaked three unedited clips of dogalicious audition videos for the film. During tomorrow's gala, we'll post one at a time. When? You'll have to stay glued to this page to find out!

- Up-to-the-minute pupdates on Sir Bentley's missing bling!!!! The manhunt continues despite a recent red herring. We admit, there was a moment when even your trusted pooper-scoopers thought Sir Bentley might *actually* solve the crime. <u>Check out this exclusive video</u> of the detective hot on the trail . . . then cue the "game over" music. Of *course* that old slobber factory got it wrong. What were we thinking? Either we're gullible or we have to admit that the Saint Bernard has some decent acting chops now and then.

- And yes, the pigtailed perfection costarring in that Sir Bentley flop is indeed the hip-swiveling sensation from our favorite viral video of the week. Go ahead, <u>click here</u> to watch her sing it again. It'll tide you over until the Dog Elegance™ event we've all been waiting for. See you on the red carpet!

#dogfriendlytown #poopscoop #olddognotricks

Sponsored by: Digger's Dentistry & Doggy Clinic, Houndstooth Haberdashery, Dog Elegance™, Lucasfilms Canine Division

DOG GOSSIP

I honestly didn't think Dec was going to show up for our morning walk. After the things we'd said to each other, I figured there was a 90 percent chance I wouldn't hear from him all summer. But when I walked downstairs and opened the front door, Dec and Frank were waiting in front of the Perro del Mar, as usual.

"You showed up," I said, relieved.

"Of course I did. Where's Pico?"

Frank's fluffy tail was flopping out of control, he was so excited to start the walk.

"Actually, I came to see if you were here, but I can't walk today. We're kind of on lockdown," I said.

"That stinks."

"I also wanted, I mean, I feel . . ." I had a lot of words I wanted to say, but I could only come up with two of them.

"I'm sorry."

Dec grinned. We'd said it at exactly the same time. Mind-meld.

"You were right," I added. "I've been closed-minded and selfish. You're better at trying new things than I am."

"For the record, I'm going to miss Sunny Day, too," Dec said. "But I think Carmelito Middle is going to be great. New school, new adventures. Right?"

"If you say so," I said. "I'm glad you're going to be there at least."

"We're going to shake that place up. Questioning Humans Unite!"

Dec did a weird half–fist explosion, half–flourishy-jazz-hands thing in the air.

I made a face.

"I don't know," he said. "It's a friendship signal. I'm working on it. Anyway," he took his phone out of his pocket. "Did you know your sister's on the Hollywood Dog Dish again?"

For a second, I'd been feeling good. Dec and I were solid. Life was going to be okay. But when he handed his phone over and I skimmed through the gossip about pop stars and the Pendleton Triplets, it reminded me that everything else was still a horrible mess. It had been an awful night at the Perro. Mom and Dad basically locked us in our room except for chores and dinner, which meant I had to spend hours listening to Elvis cry and Rondo spout ridiculous theories about the Silk Bandit and the Hollywood Heists. Which, I kept reminding him, had nothing to do with Sir Bentley or the Perro.

Not that I had any watertight theories. Whoever had taken

Bentley's collar from the Ghost Stair was clearly in the room when Elvis explained where she'd hidden it. Which eliminated FiFi, but her accomplices were definitely there.

Rondo kept telling me I wasn't looking at it from the right angles. "You're thinking inside the box, bro. Think like there *is* no box!"

But now I stared at Dec's phone and groaned. I'd scrolled down to the part about Elvis. If Elvis's video went viral again, Mom was going to spontaneously combust.

"How do they get this stuff?" I started to hand Dec's phone back, but my eye caught a sentence in the beginning of the article that I'd skipped over . . . *live cams stationed at Paradiso Park so you won't miss one minute of the action.*

Live cams. Live cameras.

A brain spark flickered. Anyone could have filmed the video of Elvis singing at Yappy Hour. There were a ton of people at the Perro that night. But Sir Bentley looking for the jewels in the Ghost Stair? We'd only rehearsed it. We never actually filmed it. Unless Asha recorded the rehearsal without telling anyone. Or the lighting department had their live cams on.

"What other videos have they posted on this site?"

"You saw the one of your dad swearing, right?"

"Unfortunately."

"Well, there are a lot of Sir Bentley blooper videos . . . more stuff from Yappy Hour . . . Oh, there's a hilarious video of a bulldog trying to go up a set of stairs." He reached for his phone. "Want me to find it? It's ridonkulous."

"It's okay," I said, holding on to the phone so I could read the article again. "I've seen it."

Maybe Delphi and Melissa had nothing to do with jewels. Maybe they were gossip bloggers who were ruining my family's lives. It was plausible. They wore cameras as a fashion accessory, and they were on their phones all the time. They took money from FiFi Khan, but maybe that didn't mean she was a criminal mastermind. Maybe she hired them to . . . write gossip? Was that a thing people did? It was bizarre, but less sinister than grand larceny.

I stopped myself. If I was going to let myself go down the Rondo path and make deductions, I needed to be objective. Unbiased. I had to compile all the data points, no matter how unlikely. Besides Delphi, Melissa, and Asha, the only other person who'd had a camera out while Sir Bentley rehearsed was Mr. Boone. I thought it through. Mrs. Boone had been taking notes when Morrissey was climbing the stairs that first night at the Perro. Did she also take a video? The Boones *did* love celebrities. And dogs. They'd been super chummy with Asha at Yips & Sips, bragging about how they saw George Lucas's assistant. *Asha spotted him. She knows everybody.* But no matter how objective I tried to be, the thought of Mr. and Mrs. Boone as celebrity dog bloggers made me laugh. It didn't add up. Asha, though—

"Epic. You okay?"

Dec waved his hand in front of my face. I was still staring at his phone, but the screen had gone black.

"Not really," I said. "I gotta go. I'm supposed to stay in our room until art camp."

"Brutal."

"In so many ways," I said.

POTENTIAL ENERGY

Mom walked us to the door of the Kleenex Box and promised that if we weren't there waiting when she got back to walk us home at twelve thirty, we would live to regret it for the rest of our lives. She included all of us when she said it. Like she'd forgotten that I didn't have to be there. I was only going to art camp to get El and Rondo out of her hair. Why I'd agreed in the first place was a mystery to me now.

In reality, it turned out to be a decent distraction. Mrs. Doughty was home sick, so the seventh-grade science teacher was there instead. She had us do a kinetic art project where we arranged Popsicle sticks into complex patterns that exploded when you released them. It was pretty ingenious. We wove the sticks under and over one another so each one was slightly bowed and ready to spring. But none of the sticks could move because they were wedged in place. Barely.

"You see how the pattern is filled with tension?" the teacher asked. "The whole thing is itching to spring apart? That's called potential energy." She held a colorful Popsicle stick triangle at arm's length, aiming the point toward the ground. "When we release that tension, we generate *kinetic energy*—energy created by movement. Watch out. It has more force that you'd expect."

She let go of the triangle, and the minute it hit the floor, it exploded. Red, blue, yellow, and green Popsicle sticks flew in every direction. Kids jumped and ducked, screaming and laughing.

Despite wanting to be anywhere but inside the Kleenex box, I grinned. The only thing I felt like doing right now was building some stuff and then blowing it up.

For three hours, we worked on kinetic art, building a long cobra pattern that snaked around the room. It felt great not to worry about dogs and celebrities and stolen jewels. All that mattered was the build-out. One stick on top of the other. With a concrete plan and a concrete goal. A question I already knew the answer to.

In the end, our cobra didn't work. It started to. When we pulled out the first stick, the snake began to unravel as planned. The force of the unleashed kinetic energy lifted the sticks off the ground in unison and flung them apart. Like it was unzipping an explosive zipper. Or toppling a row of dominoes on a sugar high. Letting go. Releasing the tension and catapulting the sticks into the air.

The class cheered. But ten inches before the end, the snake stopped. One of the Popsicle sticks was wedged too tightly to come apart. It held firm, holding the rest of the snake in place. When we unwedged it, the final sticks disengaged in an unimpressive flop.

The whole thing left me feeling more deflated than I should have. There was something about spending all that time working on the project and not being able to see it through to the very end. The heavy feeling stayed with me the whole drive home. And when we got back to the Perro, I felt even worse. Mom's after-camp plan was for us to eat lunch and go straight to our room. We weren't supposed to look at, talk to, or step within five feet of a guest. When I'd told Dec we were on lockdown, I wasn't making it up.

But when we walked into the kitchen, it was full of people. Even Mom couldn't keep Elvis from running to Sir Bentley and practically squeezing the life out of her.

There were two arguments going on. Madeleine and the Boones were at each other's throats, and Thomas was nice-fighting with Luis. Dad stood at the coffee bar, stuck in the middle, looking stressed.

Luis and Thomas were talking about the investigation and whether Thomas and Madeleine were really going to leave for the Cayman Islands after the Puppy Picnic tomorrow. Thomas didn't care about the jewels anymore. They were too much hassle. He told Luis he'd let his worry and stress about the collar come between him and Madeleine and all he wanted now was to leave it behind and relax on an island with the woman he loved. *Gross*.

"This whole thing has reminded me to put life in

perspective," Thomas was saying. "Value what's *really* important, you know?"

"But if you stay a couple days . . ." Luis started.

"We'll leave tomorrow."

"I'd feel a lot better if you got on that plane *with* your jewels. And a signed statement in our office."

Thomas forced a smile. "If that's what you want," he said, all nicey-pie. "I think you need to step up your investigation. Because we prefer to leave in twenty-four hours. With or without the collar." He glanced over at me and Rondo, then leaned closer to Luis and lowered his voice. "I've got a few ideas for you, but it's best if we take it out in the hall."

Luis followed Thomas out of the kitchen just as Mr. Boone's voice reached shouting volume.

"For the fifth time, we are not poaching Asha!" Mr. Boone said.

"Oh, really?" Madeleine seethed. "You didn't offer her another 'opportunity'?"

Mom sighed loudly and walked deliberately in between Madeleine and Mr. Boone to hand me a bunch of kale to wash. I turned on the sink, and Mom made a show of getting out plates, slamming them on the counter harder than she needed to. She was being super obvious about the fact that we were getting ready for *family* lunch and they should all take a hike, but the Boones didn't get the hint. They kept arguing while I rinsed the kale.

"Asha gave us some tips," Mrs. Boone said. "She was very helpful."

"*Tips?*" Madeleine asked. "What kind of tips?"

My brain knew that the Boones weren't tech-savvy enough to be bloggers, but they *had* been acting strange. Meeting with Asha, making scrapbooks from celebrity magazines, writing down every word Madeleine said.

Mr. Boone gave Madeleine a stern look. "You don't value her enough. If you ask me, she's the magic behind *Bentley Knows*. Talent like that could skyrocket our career. We *would* poach her if we could. We offered her a much higher salary than what you're paying."

Madeleine sucked in her breath, and the kitchen went silent. I was confused. Skyrocket their career? What career? Mom rolled her eyes at me as she pulled leaves off the kale stems I'd washed. She looked like she wanted to rip apart more than leafy greens.

"Don't worry," Mrs. Boone said. "She didn't take it. She won't leave Sir Bentley unless she has to. She's devoted to that dog."

"She said that?" Madeleine asked.

Mr. Boone was ready to continue his lecture, but Madeleine held up her hand. She seemed to think for a second, then shot a glare in the direction of the lobby.

"I *have* been distracted," she said. "Maybe I haven't been taking care of the people who *really* love Bentley." She nodded at Mr. Boone. "You're right. I'll make it up to her. A raise—"

"And a producer credit," Mr. Boone said.

Mrs. Boone cleared her throat and adjusted the collar and tie around Pico's neck. "With all this publicity, the Save *Bentley Knows* movement is gaining momentum," she said. "If the show gets renewed, we'd be available . . . if there was a part."

Madeleine squinted her eyes at Pico. "I won't say he doesn't have a certain star quality," she said. "If you're into the whole small dog thing. Well. What are you doing now? You want to grab coffee? I'll call my agent."

I almost dropped my knife. The Boones weren't pumping Asha for celebrity gossip, they were trying to break Pico into show business. They wanted Pico to be on TV.

Mom had had enough. She pried Elvis off Bentley, handed Rondo the stack of plates to bring to the table, and physically pushed the Boones and Madeleine out to the lobby. When we finally had the kitchen to ourselves, I served up apple kale salad in a daze. Elvis blabbered on about kinetic art and cobra patterns, but I couldn't concentrate. All I could imagine was Pico getting lugged around to movie sets with lights and moving cameras and strangers everywhere. Nothing in the world made sense anymore, but at least I now knew one thing without a doubt: Delphi and Melissa were the bloggers, not Asha, and definitely not the Boones.

We'd barely finished eating when Dad and Luis came back to the kitchen. Luis sat down at the table with us, and Dad put his arm around Mom. She let out a heavy sigh.

"What now?" she asked.

Luis had a duffel bag on his lap. "Rondo," he said. His voice sounded heavy and tired. Like the last thing he wanted to do was say the next sentence. "Can I show you some things we found upstairs?"

RONDO

"You were in our room?" I asked.

Luis looked pained. Whatever he was going to say, he was not happy about it.

"You can't do that," Elvis said. "Not without our permission."

"I gave him permission," Dad said.

"Why?" Mom asked. "What's this about?"

"Thomas has . . . a theory . . . that Rondo's mixed up with the missing collar," Luis said.

Even Elvis was at a loss for words.

"It doesn't hold water, but he called my boss. So now, Lieutenant Phalin wants me to ask some questions." He muttered, "*I* think this is bigger than the Perro. I'm asking questions in the wrong room."

Rondo didn't say a word. His hair had fallen over one eye, and he didn't bother to push it away. Just stared at Luis from behind it.

Luis pulled a book out of his bag. He set it on the table.

"*The Right Way to Do Wrong?*"

Rondo didn't respond.

"That's the kind of book he likes to read," I said. "Criminal theory. From the eighteen hundreds."

Mom opened the book and ran her finger down the table of contents. "'Professional Burglary' . . . 'Thieves and Their Tricks' . . . 'Pickpockets at Work.' Seriously, Rondo? Is this what you're reading?"

She looked at Dad. He pulled at his mustache until Luis handed him Rondo's mint tin. My brother flinched as Dad opened it and laid everything out on the table. Mirror, mini flashlight, bobby pins. Everything except the spy notebook. I'd seen Rondo writing in it on our way to camp. He must have brought it with him and left the tin behind.

Mom held up a bobby pin that had been bent in half. "Are these for . . . picking locks?"

Rondo shrugged.

"Have you ever picked a lock with it?"

Rondo shrugged again.

"I'll take that as a yes." Mom's voice was getting tense. Luis reached over and put his hand on her arm.

"It might not be what it seems," he said.

Mom frowned. "We've been trying to let the kids follow their interests, but maybe we should have . . . kept a closer eye . . ."

Dad's shoulders drooped, and he looked at Luis, waiting.

"There's one more thing," Luis said to Rondo. "Can you

tell me about something that went down with stolen money at camp?"

Dad sighed. Mom made a strangled sound and dropped her face into her hands.

Rondo barely even blinked. He might as well have been stone.

My foot wouldn't stop tapping the floor, and I had a twisted-up feeling in my stomach. Most of this *was* ridiculous. So what if Rondo read books about crime? They were ancient. It was like reading a history book. And sure, he liked to try his "skills"—seeing around corners, picking pockets, picking locks—but that was like a puzzle or a difficult math equation. Something he wanted to test out and see if he could do. He'd never taken anything he hadn't given back.

I knew for a fact Rondo wouldn't *steal* the collar, but the mention of art camp put a small kernel of doubt in my brain. What if he did it as a test? To see if he could? Or to prove a point? Like with Eugene at camp.

"He didn't steal anything!" Elvis said. She'd hopped out of her chair and was doing Sun Salutations. She moved to Warrior Two pose, held her arms out, and glared, pointing the fingertips of her right hand straight at Luis. "Rondo's. Not. A. Thief!"

"Elvis," Dad said. "No one's calling anyone a thief."

"He is." Elvis locked her Warrior gaze on Luis.

"I don't think I can take any more," Mom said. "Can we wrap this up?"

Luis leaned forward in his chair. "Look, Rondo. Real talk,

bro. I doubt you had anything to do with this. Thomas and my boss disagree. So if you know anything—"

Mom jumped in with a firmer line. "Think hard, Rondo," she said. "If there's something you want to tell us, you'd better—" Her voice cracked, and Dad reached out a hand to rub her back. He looked like he might cry.

"Okay, guys. Let's give Rondo some space," Luis said. "Do you have any questions before I go?"

"Yeah." Rondo let his hair fall farther into his face, and his words came from somewhere way in the back of his throat. "What were you talking to Thomas Scott about?"

Luis perked up, interested. "Travel plans," he said.

"And?"

"He's going to the Caymans tomorrow."

"Even though yesterday he threw a fit about not going anywhere until he found the collar?"

Luis studied Rondo with the same look he used when he was sizing up a good wave. "Exactly," he said.

"That's what I thought," Rondo said.

There was a knock on the kitchen door, and Melissa peeked her head in.

"Excuse me," she said quietly. "I know the brochure says High Tea begins at two o'clock, but some guests have already arrived. More than some. A crowd."

She looked around at all the frowning faces in the room. Mom. Dad. Luis in his police uniform. Her eyes fell on the collection of Rondo's objects on the table.

"It might not be a good time, but they want to get their picture taken with—"

"Go knock on Madeleine's door," Mom snapped at Melissa. "It's *not* a good time. And I'm not in charge of Sir Bentley's photo ops."

"Not Bentley," Melissa said. "They're here for Elvis."

HOUND DOG

Mom had Luis escort us upstairs while she and Dad dealt with the crowd of people and dogs gathering in the lobby for High Tea. When we'd walked out of the kitchen, they'd all started talking at once, rushing toward Elvis and holding up their phones.

Dad held them back, and my sister smiled and waved like this was the kind of thing that happened to her all the time.

"Hey, guys!" Delphi and Melissa waved from the breakfast bar. "How was art camp?"

They were wearing their matching dragon pins. Acting like the crowd had nothing to do with them. Waiting for my family to do something else stupid so they could post it for the whole world to see—like Rondo getting pinned with grand larceny.

I purposely looked in the other direction and helped Luis push my siblings toward the stairs.

"Don't answer. Keep walking," I said to Rondo and Elvis.

"That was rude," Elvis said when we got to the stairs. "What did Delphi and Melissa ever do to you?"

"He's a rule follower, El," Rondo said. "Mom said he's not supposed to talk to guests. So what do you expect?"

He grinned at me. For someone who'd been accused of being a jewel thief, he was suddenly acting pretty chipper. His smile grated on me. Rondo could be in serious trouble. This was *not* an okay time to joke around.

"I don't want to talk to Delphi," I said.

"Why?"

"I'll tell you later."

Behind us, Luis's shoe hit the Ghost Stair. The loud creak shot a current of relief through my spine. Instantly, I realized that even though things were bad, they weren't as bad as they *could* be.

I turned toward Luis, but I didn't say a word until Rondo and Elvis had galloped up the rest of the stairs and into our bedroom.

"What's up?" Luis asked. He leaned on the wall of the stairwell, looking frayed at the edges.

"Rondo didn't take the collar," I said. Without a doubt. One hundred percent true.

Luis rubbed the back of his neck. "I'm with you," he said. "But Thomas got the lieutenant involved, and now we have to go through the process. I'll do everything I can to help, but—"

"No. The Ghost Stair reminded me. Elvis put a birthday card in there as an alarm system."

"Yeah, I remember." Luis said. "Worked real well."

"Actually, it kind of did. We heard it go off. Me, Rondo, and Miyon. When we were in our room getting Elvis's outfit."

Luis got out his notebook and clicked his pen. "*Before* the rehearsal?"

"Right. We didn't know what it was at the time, but obviously, it was someone taking the collar. And it wasn't Rondo because he was with us."

Luis looked relieved, too.

"Thanks, dude. I'll get a statement from Miyon."

He turned, and I realized there was one more thing I needed to say.

"Delphi and Melissa are gossip bloggers."

Luis groaned. "I know all about that."

"They're taking photos and videos of everything and posting it online."

"Trust me, Asha already filled us in. She wants us to put them in jail or something, but there's not much we can do."

"I mean, maybe you could use it."

Luis clicked his pen. "Like?"

"Like maybe they caught something on camera without realizing it. A clue. Something that could help with the investigation?"

"Epic!" Luis broke out into a full-on grin, scribbled something in his notebook, and held out his fist. I bumped it with my own, feeling a little lighter. Luis was going to take care of it. He'd fix everything.

"I've got this. Keep your brother out of trouble, okay? And calm *that* down." He nodded toward the bedroom door. Elvis was belting out "Hound Dog" at the top of her lungs for everyone downstairs to hear.

"I will," I said.

But his words knocked a bit of the lightness out of my step. Keeping Elvis calm and Rondo out of trouble? That had become a NASA-level operation. For some reason, Mom, Dad, and all the other adults seemed to think I was qualified to make it happen. I used to think I was, too. Except now it felt like we were all on a Vomit Comet, hurtling through the atmosphere at 550 miles per hour. Up and down, high and low. Even with the knowledge that my brother was in the clear, that Luis was on the case, I still had a sinking feeling that it was too late. That everything had already spiraled too far out of control. I could practically feel the zero gravity kicking in, and the solid ground slipping away underneath my feet.

SHORT CIRCUIT

Calming Elvis was not going to happen. I got her to stop singing, but she was literally bouncing around the room like a
rabbit.

"I'm a celebrity!" she said. "Did you see all those people
who wanted my picture?"

Rondo was in his own zone of hyperactivity, sitting in his
beanbag chair and flipping through his notebook like a sci-
entist about to cure cancer.

"I'm right," he said. "You know it. I know it. Thomas Scott
is the Silk Bandit."

"I don't know anything," I said. "Especially not that."

"He took the collar for sure."

"It's *his* collar," I said. "Why would he take it?"

"It might be his collar, but trust me, they're not his
jewels."

I couldn't even. "Of *course* they're his jewels."

"It's really smart, actually," Rondo said. "Think about it.

He steals the jewels from Hollywood celebrities, but then what? It's not like you can go cash them in at the bank."

"Right!" Elvis said, giggling. She put on a nasally voice and pretended to hop up to a bank teller. "I'd like to trade these diamonds for a gazillion dollars, please."

"Remember Miyon said Grand Cayman Island is where all the crooks go to hide their money?"

"In *detective novels*," I said. "This isn't a detective novel."

"Mom says most authors take pieces of reality and turn them into fiction," Elvis said midhop. "So it could be true."

"But how would you smuggle the jewels to the island? That's the genius part." Rondo's eyes were shining. "I can't believe he came up with that. Who would think to put the jewels on a dog collar?"

"Nobody," I said. "Nobody would think of that. Only you."

"Wait!" Elvis stopped jumping. She was out of breath. "Thomas is using Sir Bentley to smuggle jewels?"

"No," I said. But somewhere in the back of my mind, I remembered a few comments Thomas had made. *Everyone changes the rules for celebrities. She could get away with anything.*

"Epic. It's obvious. Before Elvis took the collar, Thomas told Madeleine to make sure Bentley wore the jewels on the plane. You heard him, right?"

"Yes, but he's that kind of guy. Fancy."

"Listen." Rondo checked his notes, and ticked off several items with his pencil as he talked. "Yesterday, when the collar was missing, he went on a rampage and said they couldn't leave until the jewels were found. Then Elvis confessed and he was all happy. But he wasn't so happy when Luis said they'd inspect the collar at the station. So he agreed to try the publicity stunt. Why do you think that was?"

"I don't care." I was starting to feel hot. Like the time I was building out the Beast's eyes and I chose the wrong resistor for the circuit. It let too much electricity run through to the LED lights. The wires got warm and then hot, and before I knew it, the bulbs made a fritzing sound and the whole thing shorted out.

"To buy time and get the collar back without having to go through a police inspection! Then today, when Luis asked him to stay until the collar is found—"

"He said he doesn't care about the collar and still wants to go!" Elvis sucked air in through her teeth. "To hide his jewels on the Grand Cayman Island! The *criminal*!"

"Well, not like bury them or anything," Rondo said. "More like sell them on the black market and put the money in an offshore account that's outside the law. It's pretty brilliant."

The thing about shorting out an LED circuit is that before the bulb breaks, it gets brighter. I don't know how Rondo does it. He's so earnest and excited when he spouts his theories, you can't help getting caught up in his enthusiasm vortex. I could feel myself lighting up, turning the ideas around in my brain, and taking them to the next logical move—nabbing the thief. What would it take to get a confession? Or better yet, catch him red-handed? The Dog Dish article Dec had shown me said that Misty LaVa was performing at the award cere-mony tomorrow. Wasn't she the person Rondo thought was next on the Silk Bandit's list? What if we could catch Thomas Scott in the act of trying to steal her jewels?

"Madeleine won't leave without Bentley's collar, though," I said. "Unless you think she's in on it. So what's he going to do, pretend to find it in the bathroom accidentally?" I paused. The whole bathroom thing was the plan I'd come up with the last time Elvis and Rondo sucked me in to one of their schemes. My hands started to sweat. I was not falling for this again.

Rondo tapped his pencil on his knee. "I'm telling you. The Silk Bandit will find a way. He's a total genius."

"I wish you wouldn't say stuff like that."

"Like what?"

I felt woozy. It was too much. "Why do you think Dad and Luis gave you the third degree? You're constantly talking about criminals. Like the Silk Bandit is your hero."

"Being interested in something doesn't make you a crim-inal."

"It's not normal. Why can't you act like a normal person once in a while?"

"Leave him alone, Epic," Elvis said. "That's not very nice."

She said it in her baby voice—*weave 'im awone*—and it made the fritzing sound go off in my skull. I felt like Pico. Like I'd been keeping it together and keeping it together while every-thing else around me was falling apart. My brother could be in serious trouble, and El and Rondo were treating it like a game. Couldn't they see I was trying to protect them? To keep them safe?

I short-circuited.

"Why do you talk like that?" I blurted. "You're not five. You're eight. And you're smart! Use your normal voice! Is it that hard to use a normal voice?"

Elvis's eyes filled with tears. Rondo stepped protectively to her side.

"Like you're a real expert," he said. "Why don't you teach us your normal ways, Epic? Since you're smarter than everybody else."

"I don't think I'm smarter than everybody else."

"Yes you do. Every time something goes wrong, it's our fault. Every decision that's not yours is stupid."

"That's not true."

Elvis nodded. "Even Declan. You think he's silly because he's excited about public school."

"I never said that."

"Let Dec be how he wants to be," Rondo said. "And lighten up. If it wasn't for us, you wouldn't have the guts to do anything fun."

"I would."

"You'd never have talked to Miyon," Elvis said. "You'd never have gone on her boat."

That was true.

But it wasn't the point.

"How do you think you're going to survive next year when I'm at middle school? You can't even go to art camp without a built-in babysitter. That's messed up."

Elvis was mad for real now. She put her hands on her hips and spat out every word. "We went to art camp to help *you*!"

"No, you didn't."

"Yes. We. Did."

I shook my head. "I made that up so you'd go."

"*What?*" Rondo looked at me like I'd shot him with a harpoon.

I wished I hadn't said it, but now that it was out of my mouth, I couldn't stop myself from doubling down. "You were stressing Mom and Dad out. They would have done anything to get you out of the house. You stress everyone out. Especially me!"

My siblings didn't say anything. Rondo picked up a book and let his hair fall in front of his face, and Elvis went to her secret drawer and pulled out her picture of our old dog, Yoda. She climbed into bed with it and sucked her thumb, silent and still, tears dripping down her cheeks.

We ignored each other the rest of the afternoon. Rondo read and Elvis painted a portrait of Yoda and Sir Bentley drinking from the same canine fountain. I tried to tinker with the Beast, but my mind kept wandering. Why had I been so hard on them? I liked that my family wasn't normal. They were interesting and smart. Fun to be around. Which was better than normal. The whole reason I didn't like that Dec was happy about leaving Sunny Day was because I was afraid public school would *turn* him normal. I didn't want him to change. *I* didn't want to change. But it didn't seem like I had much choice about it.

I picked through a mess of resistors I'd let pile up on my desk and sorted them by their color bands. Rondo and Elvis weren't the problem. The problem was me. Trying to hold back the current so it didn't blow the whole system was burning *me* out. And it wasn't even working. I wasn't helping anybody. I was only making my siblings feel bad.

I tried out a new question: What would happen if I didn't hold back the current? If I did nothing? I didn't *have* to care that Rondo thought Thomas Scott was the Silk Bandit. I didn't *have* to manage it. I could sit back and let Rondo be Rondo. Either he was right or he wasn't. Nothing I did was going to change that. Maybe it would be easier on everyone if I rode this one out.

Before dinner, Mom let us out of our room to do chores. I weeded the garden while Rondo and Elvis helped Dad in the kitchen. When Mom and I came in with handfuls of cilantro and mint for a Thai salad, only El and Dad were chopping vegetables.

"Where's Rondo?" Mom asked.

"In the lobby," Dad said. "Thomas asked him to help box up the rest of those *Bentley Knows* books."

Terrible idea! I thought. *He's going to try to sleuth all over the place—*And then I stopped myself. Let them be in charge. Let Rondo be Rondo. Ride it out.

"Do you think we went too far?" Mom asked Dad. "Letting him read anything he wanted?"

Dad tugged at his mustache. "I don't think he did anything wrong." But he frowned like he wasn't completely convinced.

When Rondo came back to the kitchen, he was still mad at me. Maybe even madder. He glared at his food, and after dinner, he went straight to his bunk and wouldn't talk to anybody.

I lay awake counting most of the night. Again. With Elvis's snores, Rondo's tossing and turning, and the growing guilt I felt for everything I'd said to them, it was almost morning by the time I fell asleep. I promised myself that when my siblings woke up, I would apologize first thing. Tell them they were going to be fine without me next year. That I was the one who was going to miss *them*. But when my alarm went off, Rondo was already up and out of the room. I heard dishes clinking in the kitchen downstairs. And voices.

I bolted out of bed.

Realistically, there was no logical reason for the full-on, 100-percent gut-punch feeling in my belly. No one had screamed in the middle of the night. I hadn't had one of

Elvis's outer space nightmares. But Rondo's bed was perfectly made. The sheets were tucked in, and the pillow was propped up at the perfect bed-and-breakfast angle Mom was always preaching about. It was the precision that tipped me off: my plan to ride it out had backfired. Rondo's bed was a cry for help.

"Epic, what's wrong?" Elvis sat up in the bottom bunk, her bedhead sticking out in a thousand directions at once.

"I don't know," I said. "I think Rondo's in trouble. Big trouble."

FRIDAY

5:45 A.M.

CONFESSION #2

Mom and Dad weren't in their room, so we headed downstairs. Elvis stomped right on the Ghost Stair, and the creak didn't make her freak out at all. At least one good thing had come out of the whole Dog-Friendly Town week.

"Is it Woofy Waffle day?" Elvis asked, pushing open the kitchen door. "If it is, I'm going to ask Dad to . . ." Her voice trailed off as we entered the kitchen.

It was five forty-five in the morning, but Sir Bentley, Madeleine, and Thomas Scott were at the kitchen table with Rondo and Mom. Dad was making coffee. No one seemed to notice we'd walked in.

Mom was in a hoodie and pajama pants, and her bedhead was almost as impressive as El's. "Okay, Rondo." She rubbed her temples. "What's the emergency?"

My brother stared at the table, his jaw set, hands in the front pocket of his sweatshirt.

Thomas leaned forward so he was practically breathing

down Rondo's neck. "It's okay, buddy. We're listening. What's on your mind?"

Rondo stiffened. He inched his head away from Thomas. Then he pulled a hand out of his pocket and placed a glittery, jeweled dog collar on the table.

Dad dropped his second coffeepot of the week.

Elvis yelped and grabbed my hand as it shattered. Sir Bentley scrambled to her feet, looking around for someone to save, and Madeleine threw her arms around the dog to keep her from running toward the glass.

I caught Rondo's eye as Madeleine, Dad, and Mom started talking at once.

"What is going on? Where did you find it? I'm so confused."

"Seriously, Rondo? Why?"

"Elrond! Explain yourself! Now."

My brother and I stared at each other. I knew he hadn't taken the collar from the Ghost Stair. He'd been upstairs with me and Miyon when my sister's birthday card alarm went off. So how did the jewels end up in his sweatshirt pocket? And why did he look so scared?

"I wanted to see if I could pull it off," Rondo mumbled. But he didn't take his eyes off me. He jutted his chin toward the collar that Thomas was already refastening around Bentley's neck. I pulled El closer to get a better view. The jewels were tightly packed against each other, but they were all different shapes and sizes. I had no idea what a set of jewels was *supposed* to look like. Maybe it was normal for the stones to be mismatched, but I had a vague feeling that the collar seemed different than the first time I'd seen it. Was it bigger? Even more sparkly?

Something wasn't right. While Dad swept up the glass, Mom interrogated Rondo, but he wasn't answering any of her questions. My brother stared straight at me and Elvis, his face blank. Like he was concentrating extra hard on something. He closed his eyes for a second, opened them, and closed them again. Then he blinked fast three times in a row.

At first I thought maybe he was trying not to cry. I wouldn't have blamed him. It had been a rough week, and I had no idea how he'd ended up at the kitchen table confessing to a crime I knew he didn't commit. Then I noticed his blinking had a pattern. Short and long blinks. And the sequence had started over.

Three fast blinks in a row.
Three long blinks.
Blink. Blink. Blink. Extra fast.
S.O.S.

Elvis sucked in her breath and squeezed my hand. I squeezed back a few short and long pulses. *WT. Wait.* It wasn't going to help Rondo if Elvis jumped into a panic or started shouting something dramatic in his defense. First we had to figure out what was happening, and then we had to find a way to help.

"I should call Luis," Dad said, but Thomas shook his head.

"It's too early to bother him now. I'll catch him up at the Puppy Picnic. He'll be there for the setup, isn't that right, babe?" Thomas didn't wait for Madeleine to answer. "We're just grateful the collar is safe and sound. Right on time for our trip." He paused and gave Rondo a pointed look. "You did the right thing coming clean, Rondo. Trust me, you don't want to be a criminal. It's a messy business."

It wasn't even six in the morning, but Thomas had his hair all slicked up, and he was wearing a vest with palm trees on it. He pulled a silk handkerchief out of his breast pocket, cleaned his glasses with it, then tucked it back in, adjusting and poofing the fabric until it stuck out at the right jaunty angle.

Suddenly, all Rondo's far-fetched theories swirled in my brain and I knew. They were true. The jewels on the dog collar were mismatched because they were *other people's jewels.* Chloe Cosmo's, for one. And all the celebrities from the Hollywood Heists. Thomas had been in Los Angeles the night Shaunté Stevens's jewels went missing, and now Bentley's collar had even more glitter than before. I never thought I'd believe it, but Rondo was right.

Thomas Scott was the Silk Bandit.

SHERLOCK HOLMES

"There *is* something you could do for us," Thomas said, pushing his chair back. He was all smiles. I tried to imagine him breaking into Shaunté Stevens's bedroom. Did he wear a black cat burglar suit? How did he know where she kept her jewelry?

"Anything. Anything you need." Mom and Dad were falling all over themselves, apologizing and promising to make sure Rondo got the punishment he deserved.

Thomas waved them off. "I made a few missteps of my own when I was a kid. In fact, I want to help Rondo out."

Mom looked worried. "Meaning?"

"Do you know what restorative justice is?"

"A little," Dad said.

"It's been proven that it's therapeutic for a criminal to spend time with his victims. If he can see his actions have an effect on real people's lives, he'll be much less likely to become a repeat offender."

I could tell the word *criminal* cut Mom to the heart. And

repeat offender made Dad twist a dish towel into a tight, thin rope. But none of these words had anything to do with my brother. *Thomas* was the one who'd stolen the jewels from the Ghost Stair so Luis wouldn't inspect them. He needed Rondo to confess so he could smuggle the jewels out in plain sight. No one would suspect a celebrity Saint Bernard of carting around twenty million dollars' worth of loot.

Thomas told my parents that he wanted Rondo to spend the morning helping him and Madeleine get ready for the Puppy Picnic. Set up the swag table. Help with the sound check. Now that I was clued in to what was happening, it all seemed so obvious. Thomas wasn't going to let Rondo out of his sight until he was safely off to the Cayman Islands. How could my parents possibly buy any of this? He was smiling at them like they were all BFFs, and my parents were so grateful he wasn't mad that they were smiling back. But I could see it clearly now: Thomas Scott's smile was an absolute fake.

"He can make up for some of the pain and suffering he caused my poor snookums." Thomas tried to make a smoochy face at Madeleine, but she curled her lip like the word *snookums* made her want to vomit. The whole Thomas-almost-kicking-Sir-Bentley thing had reduced the overall schmoop level in the house by almost 100 percent. Which made me 75 percent certain Madeleine had no idea what was really going on. She gave him the evil eye, but she didn't disagree with his plan.

"Make sure you put enough of Bentley's books on display," she said to Rondo. "I don't want them anywhere near those awful *Pendleton Triplet Diaries*."

Elvis had my hand in a death grip. I'd expected to have to hold her back, but she'd been watching Thomas and Rondo, quiet as a mouse. El was terrified. I looked at Mom and Dad for help, but Dad was offering to cook an early breakfast for Thomas and Madeleine, and Mom was making arrangements to meet up at Paradiso Park after all the other guests had been served. Both of them seemed equal parts embarrassed and sad.

"I could help set up, too," I said.

I couldn't decide if it was a good idea or not, but it was better than nothing. We *had* to help. Riding it out wasn't an option anymore.

"That's sweet, but Rondo needs some time to reflect on his actions. Alone." Thomas clapped his hand onto Rondo's shoulder and kept it there. "Don't worry. I won't let him out of my sight. Seems like a fair deal to me. Seeing that we're not *pressing charges*."

He was acting all kindness-and-generosity, but to me, it sounded like a threat.

"Do you want to bring a book?" I asked Rondo. What I *wanted* to say was, *Run for your life! He's a crook!* But it was clear none of the adults were going to take that seriously. And who knew what would happen if Thomas found out we were on to him? I had no idea how dangerous he was. Better to lay low and play it safe until we came up with a plan. "I can go grab *Sherlock Holmes* for you."

"Epic," Dad said, "he's going to help, not read."

But Rondo looked relieved and Thomas shrugged. "Why not? Madeleine's got interviews to do, so there may be times when we need him to keep quiet."

It was not my imagination—the words *keep quiet* came out louder than the rest.

I ran upstairs, got the book, and made sure there were fresh batteries in Miyon's tape recorder. It wasn't much, but it was the best we could arm him with for now. Maybe he could record a confession while Elvis and I convinced Mom, Dad, and Luis to rescue him.

When I got back downstairs, Thomas was grinning happily at Rondo. Like he was our long-lost uncle, finally getting to spend some time with his favorite nephew. "Let's go set up some swag!"

Rondo tucked *Sherlock Holmes* under his arm, and followed Thomas and Madeleine to the lobby. When the kitchen door swung shut behind them, Mom put her head in her hands.

"Rondo," she groaned.

"They're being super nice about it," Dad said. "That could have gone badly."

I checked the door to make sure the lobby was empty. Then I rushed back to Mom and Dad.

"He's the criminal," I said. El had started crying.

"You *think*?" Mom asked. "He *told* us so."

"Not Rondo. Thomas Scott! We need Luis. Dad, where's your cell phone?"

"Epic!"

"We need to call him right now!"

Mom threw her hands in the air. "You have *got* to stop. These ridiculous theories are making it worse."

"They're not ridiculous," Elvis said through her tears.

Mom clenched her jaw. "Yes. They. Are." Her own eyes got watery, and a tear slipped down her cheek. "This is all my fault. I wanted my kids to be Questioning Humans and think for themselves. I didn't expect it would turn out like . . . *this*."

"Hey, hey!" Dad rushed to her side. "It's going to be okay, Elly."

He rubbed her back and turned to me and Elvis.

"Guys, I know this is really hard. Your brother has a problem, and we have to figure out how to help him. But the detective game needs to stop."

"It's not a game," I said. "We're serious."

Dad sighed. "Could you go be serious somewhere else for a while and let me and your mom figure some things out?"

"Like *where*?" Elvis said. Her tears had dried up. She was getting mad.

I tugged on her sleeve. Sass was not going to help us. And neither, apparently, were our parents. We didn't have time to convince them. Rondo needed us. And we needed the police. Now.

I checked my watch: 5:57 A.M.

"Can we go walk Pico?" I asked. By which I meant *Can we use Pico as an excuse to go find Luis and help him catch a criminal mastermind?* "I know we're on lockdown and we're not supposed to—"

Mom and Dad might as well have been robot kids from Mrs. Doughty's art class. They spoke in perfect unison.

"Go!"

PARADISO PARK

"Salutations!" Dec said, and Frank wiggled his husky-side ear at us. I'd completely forgotten they'd be waiting outside for our walk. "I checked our schedule. We've got three leash swaps today. One at—"

"Change of plans," I said. But before I could explain, Elvis got her old self back.

"We have to save Rondo!" she blurted. "Thomas Scott is the Silk Bandit and Bentley's collar is full of stolen jewels and he forced Rondo to be a criminal and they're at Paradiso Park with *Sherlock Holmes* setting up swag. We have go there *now!*"

She started running down Main Street. Pico and Frank strained at their leashes, desperate to chase after her.

"Just jog," I said to Dec. "I'll explain."

Going to Paradiso Park wasn't a bad idea. We could make sure Rondo was there and that he was safe. And on our way, we'd stop at Luis's apartment. Or the police station. Because, as I explained the situation to Dec, that's what the ultimate plan had to be. We had to find Luis. We had to let him take

care of it. My brother might be able to come up with elaborate methods for exposing a jewel thief, but I couldn't.

Except Luis wasn't home. We checked the beach, but we
found Miyon instead, toweling off after surfing Dawn Patrol
with her dad. Elvis stood on the bike path and jumped up
and down yelling, "Mayday! Mayday!" until Miyon scooped
up Layne and ran to join us, leaving her surfboard for her
dad to carry home.

We ran straight from the beach to the police station,
but the lights were off and the sign on the door said HOURS:
8:30 A.M.–4:30 P.M.

"Shouldn't the police station be open longer than Dogma
Cafe?" Miyon complained.

"I told you!" Elvis said, already running toward Paradiso
Drive. "We have to get Rondo ourselves."

Paradiso Park looked like it belonged in some other town.
Hollywood, not Carmelito. There was a giant billboard at
the park's entrance that had the words DOG ELEGANCE™
PRESENTS: ALL DOGS GO TO HOLLYWOOD! in giant, person-
sized letters, and below that, in small type you could only see
up close, CARMELITO: AMERICA'S #1 DOG-FRIENDLY TOWN. All the
farmers' market booths had been pushed back to the edges
of the grass and decked out with white balloons with the Dog
Elegance logo. The gazebo was covered in white streamers.

A giant stage—ten times the size of the Perro's Yappy Hour
stage—was set up at the far end of the park with a Star Wars
backdrop featuring three fluffy Pendletons. Closer to us,

near the street, a crew was setting up a gigantic wooden cut-out of Penelope. Or was it Olivia? Oleander? Some monster-sized labradoodle. I scanned the park and scanned it again, but I couldn't find Rondo.

"Whoa. Is that a *Tesla*?" Dec pointed toward the workers struggling to assemble a second Godzilla-sized labra-doodle cutout. Behind the plywood labradoodle, Thomas Scott leaned against the hood of his convertible, checking his phone. In the passenger seat sat a small kid with long hair bent over a book.

"Wait. Rondo's in the *Tesla*?" Dec asked.

I grabbed his elbow, and we headed toward the convert-ible.

GLITZ

"That's a first-generation Roadster!" Dec said as we slowed to a walk.

"I know."

"From 2008? Version one point five?"

"Yep."

Miyon gave me a funny look. "You guys know a lot about cars?"

"Just this one," I said.

"We did a school project on the Roadster." Dec was typing something into his phone. "And 2008 was when they had the battery pack in the trunk. Remember? In the next model, they moved all that to the front of the car."

"Dec," I said. "Focus."

Elvis was getting all teary-eyed again. "Is Thomas going to kidnap Rondo?"

Miyon shook her head. "I'll get a picture of his license plate, though," she said. "Just in case."

I fiddled with Pico's leash and tried to come up with a plan. *What would Rondo do?* Probably the exact opposite of whatever I decided.

"Dec, can you hang out at your mom's booth and keep an eye out?" I asked. "Call my mom if anything happens. Anything. Like if they leave your sight for a second. Elvis and I will try to spring Rondo and bring him home. Then we'll get Dad to find Luis."

"I'll come with you," Miyon said. "I bet if Layne gets worried, Elvis could calm her down."

We all knew she meant the opposite. Even Elvis.

"Thanks, Miyon," she said.

Pico sniffed at Frank like they were making their own plans.

"Dec!" I said. "You're our Hound of Hades, okay? Be a guard. Keep an eye out."

"I've *got* you." Dec nodded, but he was still scrolling with his thumb as he led Frank toward Flo's Floral Essences. Even though I'd decided to support his new curiosities, I still wanted to throw his phone in the ocean.

Elvis, Miyon, and I walked toward the car. There were two wooden labradoodles standing in front of it now and a third being assembled, almost as tall as a house.

"Remember," Miyon said. "We're taking a walk, and your brother's helping out a guest. In the passenger seat of his car. It's no big deal."

"Right. Act normal," I said. Thomas had no idea we knew his secret. Why would he? Still, my mouth was dry, and I had to convince my feet to move forward.

Thomas looked up as we neared the Tesla. He smiled.

"Walking Pico?" he asked. As if that wasn't obvious. "Beautiful day for it!"

Behind him, Rondo sat in the passenger seat of the sports car, pretending to read *Sherlock Holmes*, even though there were only ten real pages in the whole book. He held the edges tightly, but seemed relieved when he saw me. Like he had a get-out-of-jail-free card. Except I wasn't sure how to spring him.

"Yeah, dog walking," I said weakly. "It's part of the Perro's Canine Comfort Guarantee."

I moved toward Rondo's side of the convertible, but Thomas managed to keep himself between me and the car. My brother looked small, locked into the seat belt like a scared little kid—or a prisoner. Not hurt, just stuck.

"I was wondering if Rondo could maybe . . . walk with us a little. Just since . . . he's not really doing anything right now."

Pico's ears lifted into helicopter mode, and he pawed at me. Like even he knew I was messing it up.

"Nah, swag table's going to arrive any minute," Thomas said.

"I could come back as soon as it gets here." Rondo closed his book and looked hopefully at Thomas.

I inched toward the passenger door. Maybe I could simply open it and yell, *Run, Rondo! Run!* The Roadster had a touch pad you had to press instead of a regular door handle, and I was almost within striking distance when Thomas nudged me out of the way.

He reached over the side of the convertible and patted my brother's shoulder. Extra hard.

"You remember our chat last night, right, Rondo?"

Rondo nodded and gave me a sideways glance. He lifted *Sherlock Holmes* up closer to his chest, and I held my breath. Elvis reached out to hold Miyon's hand. This was it. Our chance to get a confession.

Rondo spoke up loud and clear. "I remember it. You said I had to help you, otherwise . . ."

Thomas frowned and cut him off. "*Otherwise* you would miss the opportunity to learn a valuable lesson. You don't want to *miss* that opportunity, do you, Rondo?"

Rondo lowered the book and shook his head. I exhaled. Thomas wasn't an idiot. He wasn't going to say anything incriminating, even to a bunch of kids. He put on a bright smile.

"Looks like my partner in crime isn't going anywhere," Thomas said. "So. We'll see you all later."

He turned his back to Rondo, leaned his butt against the Tesla, and scrolled on his phone. Springing Rondo wasn't going to happen. I needed a brain spark, but I had nothing.

"Okay." I picked up Pico for good luck and tried to choose my next words carefully. "Rondo, Dec's over at Flo's booth if you need him, and we're heading home to *help out*. Want anything?"

"No, I'm good." Rondo faked a yawn and stretched his arm, grazing a folded magazine on the dashboard with his fingertips. It was the magazine from Sir Bentley's room. Still open to the page with Chloe Cosmo, Shaunté Stevens, and Misty LaVa.

Miyon let out a girly squeal that was totally unlike her. "You have a copy of *Glitz*? I've been dying to read this issue. The dresses are so pretty. Could I borrow it? I'll bring it back when the picnic starts."

She reached right past Thomas Scott and swiped the magazine off the dashboard. Thomas barely glanced up from his phone.

"Never seen it before," he said. "Must be Madeleine's. Go ahead and keep it."

Even though we hadn't rescued him, Rondo looked a little lighter. Less scared out of his wits.

On the way home, we checked the police station and Luis's apartment again, in case he'd gone into work early or come home. But after all that, we found Luis's cop car parked outside the Perro. We raced inside, but he wasn't in the kitchen talking to Mom and Dad.

"Where's Luis?" I asked.

Mom shook her head. "We agreed to call him *after* the Puppy Picnic. He's got enough on his plate today."

"His car is here," I said. "Is he upstairs?"

"Why would he be—"

Elvis was already out the kitchen door, sprinting for the guest stairs. "Luis!" she yelled. "Luis! WE NEED YOU!"

BRAIN SPARK

Elvis practically beat down the door of Room 5 with her tiny fists.

Luis was sitting on Delphi and Melissa's bed with three laptop computers open in front of him.

"Sorry, Luis," I huffed. I was out of breath after chasing Elvis up the stairs with Pico in my arms. Miyon and Layne were right behind me, and Mom and Dad not far behind them. "I know you're busy, but we really need—"

"Rondo didn't take the collar!" Elvis yelled, red-faced. "He said he did, but he DIDN'T!"

"What are you talking about?" Luis asked. "Where *is* Rondo?"

"At Paradiso Park," I said. "In Thomas Scott's Tesla."

Luis stood up.

"It's okay," Dad said. "He's doing community service. Sort of. To smooth things over."

"What is all this stuff?" Mom asked, but Luis held up his hand.

"I need quiet for a sec," he said, and walked out into the hall, talking code into his police radio. "Ten forty-nine Paradiso Park, ten eighteen . . ." He closed the door behind him, shutting us all in the tiny room.

Elvis looked exasperated. "*No one* will listen to us," she said.

Next to the computers, Delphi had several photographs spread out on the bed. Close-ups of Sir Bentley, mostly. Some shots of Thomas and Madeleine, candids from Yappy Hour, and a few celebrity photos. I recognized Chloe Cosmo from the magazine in Miyon's hand. Where Luis had been sitting, there were two photos side by side. One was a fuzzy blown-up shot of Bentley in her collar. The other was a publicity photo of Chloe Cosmo in her bling.

Mom blinked at Delphi and Melissa. "*What* do you do again? Behavioral science?"

"Partly." Delphi said. "Mel goes to night school, but—cat's out of the bag—most of the time, we work for a dog gossip blog. We're supposed to be on the down-low, but . . ."

Dad shook his head. "Dog gossip?"

"Hollywood Dog Dish," I said. "I'll explain later. I need to tell Luis that Thomas Scott's the Silk Bandit."

"What's a silk bandit?" Mom asked.

"Why is Luis working on dog gossip?"

My parents were not keeping up. Even Elvis and Miyon were getting off track.

"They're pooper-scoopers!" Miyon said. "OMG, I read

your column every day. They posted your video, Elvis. And the thing with your dad screaming. That was hilarious."

Mom took a step toward Delphi and Melissa. "*You* posted Elvis singing?"

"Wasn't that a cute one?" Melissa asked. "You guys got so much publicity from that. That was one of the highest click-through rates we've had all year."

Mom's eyes narrowed.

"It's not their fault," I said. I needed to rein this in. Now. "FiFi paid them to do it, but it *doesn't matter*." I hugged Pico extra-hard, and he wiggled until I loosened my grip. "I need Luis—"

"Technically, Dog Elegance paid us to do it," Delphi said. "FiFi is sort of . . . an under-the-table cosponsor. We met her through our friend Misty LaVa. We're not really supposed to talk about it."

"*Dog Elegance?*" Mom took another step forward, but Dad put his hand on her arm.

"I know, right? Dog Elegance is a big deal," Melissa said. "I'm sure we only got the assignment because Del's photos are so good."

"Aw, Mel," Delphi said. "It's your stories that sell it. That Newt thing was genius."

"*You* posted about Bentley and Newt?" Elvis asked. "That *lie*?"

"I wouldn't call it a *lie*," Melissa said. "Brands pay us to make things . . . more interesting. Besides, Sir Bentley would never have gotten all that publicity without us."

Delphi chimed in. "You're lucky we ended up at your bed and breakfast. You got way more press than anyone else."

"Lucky?" Mom had the wild Elvis-tantrum look in her eyes again. "LUCKY?"

Pico flinched when she raised her voice. Elvis was getting ready to burst into tears.

"Forget about the dog blog!" I said, and Pico cringed again. Where was Luis? I tried to leave the room, but when I opened the door, Mr. and Mrs. Boone were right there, blocking my way.

It was barely seven in the morning, and neither of them were in their pajamas. Mrs. Boone's hair was perfectly done, and Mr. Boone was wearing his best Hawaiian shirt. "Mind if we collect Pico? Asha's going to do his hair and makeup."

"Hair and *makeup*?" I wasn't sure if I should hand Pico over. He stuck his cold, wet nose in my ear. Like that was going to calm either of us down.

"Madeleine set up a meeting with her agent!" Mrs. Boone said. "So we've got to take him down to Dunham's and get headshots. Isn't this exciting?"

She scooped Pico out of my arms. Mr. Boone leaned toward Melissa.

"Nicole and I couldn't help overhearing," he said. "We're

interested in partnering. We've got a . . . let's call it *healthy* budget."

"I can get you set up this morning," Melissa said. "We'll be taking photos and reporting from the red carpet, so swing by and I'll run some ideas by you. Delphi got a great shot of Pico in his leather—"

I lost it. "Photo shoots?" I yelled. "Dog blogs? My brother is in a getaway car with a criminal mastermind! WHAT IS *WRONG* WITH YOU PEOPLE?"

The Boones looked offended and left the room, but my outburst accomplished two things: 1) Everyone else shut up, and 2) Luis poked his head back in from the hall.

"Everything okay in here? I sent some undercover guys over to keep an eye on Thomas," he said to Mom and Dad. "Now I need you two to go to Paradiso Park and stick to Rondo like glue until I can get there."

"Because of . . . the Silk Bandit?" Dad let out a nervous laugh, like he was desperate for all of this to be a joke. But Luis's face was so serious that Mom and Dad straightened up and went into full-on panic mode.

"Is Rondo okay? What's happening? *Why* are your guys watching Thomas?"

"Look, I think Epic's onto something, but I don't have proof," Luis said. "This guy's slippery. He's gotten past the Los Angeles Police Department fifteen times."

"Sixteen," I said, remembering one of Rondo's favorite rants. "If you count the house in Malibu."

Luis nodded, surprised. "Dude. That's right."

Mom took Dad's hand. "You . . . think Thomas is a . . . bandit?"

"Just go!" Luis said. "Don't let Rondo out of your sight. And it's important—*don't* let Thomas know we know. I don't want to spook him until I've got something concrete. These photos aren't going to cut it."

Mom and Dad took off, and I let out a deep breath. I'd promised myself that once I got Luis on board, I'd back off and let him do his job. This was too important to mess up. Rondo could get hurt.

But Luis turned to me. "Any bright ideas?"

"You're asking *me*?"

"Depends on the idea," Luis said. "I've learned my lesson. I'll at least listen this time."

I studied the photos on the bed. Chloe Cosmo. Shaunté Stevens.

The magazine from Thomas's car was still in Miyon's hand, open to Misty LaVa's permasmile. A day-old brain spark flickered in my skull. I'd tried to shut it down, but it kept resurfacing: the idea that we *might* be able to catch a criminal in the act. Red-handed.

If Rondo's theories were right, then Thomas Scott stole Chloe Cosmo's jewels the day before he checked in to the Perro del Mar. On Tuesday, he went back to LA for the Shaunté Stevens heist. If Misty LaVa's jewels happened to show up at the Puppy Picnic, what would Thomas do? I had a hunch the Silk Bandit wouldn't be able to resist adding them to his collection.

I turned to Delphi. "You said Misty LaVa is your friend. Do you know her well enough to ask a favor?"

It was like building a circuit. I needed to connect each component in the right order, calculate how much electricity should flow through and make sure the wires were distributing the electrons in the right direction. If we could convince Misty LaVa to use her jewels as a decoy, we could lure Thomas Scott into stealing them and capture the whole thing on one of Delphi and Melissa's dragon cams. Luis and his undercover cops would be watching on standby, ready to make the arrest.

It was easy to get Misty on board. She and Delphi had worked at an animal shelter together, back before she was famous and Delphi became a sneaky dog blogger. They called it Shelter Solidarity. She agreed to bring the jewels from the *Glitz Magazine* article and plant them in plain sight of Melissa's dragon cam.

"We need the other camera on the red carpet," Delphi said. "If we don't live-stream at least part of this event, we'll never get another gig in Hollywood."

"It's okay," I said. "One camera is all we need."

Melissa reprogrammed her live cam, restricting the video feed to a small, private group. Only Luis, Mom and Dad, Delphi, Melissa, and Miyon would be able to follow the action on their phones. The trick was, we had to play it cool. Act like it was any old Puppy Picnic. Hold back, resistor-style, so Thomas would think *he* was in charge. And then, when he least expected it, we'd strike.

At Sunny Day, it was the kind of brain spark we'd put on the Outlandish Idea Board. Absurd or world-changing, time would tell.

Puppy Love!
posted by @pooperscooper1

All. Dogs. Go. To. HOLLYWOOD!!! Dog Elegance™ has
truly outdone themselves for their 10th Anniversary Dog-
Friendly Town celebration. The DE fairy godmothers have
transformed Carmelito's Paradiso Park into an outdoor
Hollywood ballroom, complete with a Pawscar-worthy red
carpet. It's even *better* than Tinseltown because *this* walk
of fame is flanked by 12-foot Pendleton Triplets. We'll have
one of our exclusive live cams posted at the red carpet all
morning, so you won't miss any of the glitz and glamor.

So far, we've spotted Chippy Chihuahua looking dapper in
a plaid bow tie, Newt sporting a striped KhanArts jacket
with faux-fur fringe, and two of Misty LaVa's latest rescue
dogs—a Lhasa apso with elegantly braided locks, and an
adorable beagle pup. Keep your eye on Misty today, folks.
Not only is she a longtime friend of the Hollywood Dog
Dish, but we've heard she's going to put on a showstopping
performance you won't forget.

Even the locals are getting into the game. Our favorite so
far is a certain Mr. Tough Guy, decked out in a black leather
jacket, hip shades, and a skull-and-crossbones rhinestone
tattoo. Is local Iggy, Pico Boone, a star in the making? Your
pooper-scoopers think so. Trust us, Pico's one to watch.

And because we love you, <u>here's the first</u> of our three
surprise Pendleton Trilogy previews sponsored by
Lucasfilms Canine Division and everyone's favorite doggy

lifestyle corporation, Dog Elegance™. May the paws be with you!

#dogfriendlytown #poopscoop #heavenlyhounds #bentleybling

Sponsored by: Dog Elegance™, KhanArts Boutique, BooneyTunes Incorporated, Lucasfilms Canine Division

RED CARPET

Miyon and I stood in the back of the red-carpet line, waiting to get Layne's picture taken under the giant labradoodle cutouts. It was ten in the morning, and there were already dozens of people and dogs in fancy outfits in front of us waiting for the photo op. Music was pumping out of speakers planted all over Paradiso Park, and everywhere you looked, there were groups setting up picnic blankets, playing Frisbee, and dancing on the grass.

"Feel a little underdressed, Layne?" Miyon asked.

Layne was busy sniffing at a cocker spaniel in fairy wings. The spaniel's owner was wearing a gown made of silver sequins. Waiters walked around offering people champagne and fish eggs. At the Puppy Picnic. For breakfast. It made zero sense.

"What do you think is taking so long?" I asked.

We checked her phone again. Nothing. It was the same live video of grass we'd been watching for the last ten minutes.

Ahead of us, Delphi and Melissa had set up a tripod and laptop at the end of the red carpet, and Morrissey was sacked out at their feet wearing Melissa's black beret and Delphi's scarf, like an exhausted French film director. To anyone else, it looked like they were offering complimentary family photos. Of course, they were also writing dog gossip and using Delphi's dragon pin to secretly upload live video of everyone who walked by to Hollywood Dog Dish.

The second dragon pin was on Elvis.

"Look," I said. "She's with Sir Bentley. They're on the move."

A glossy, white-tipped tail flicked into view on Miyon's screen, and Elvis's feet started to move forward on the grass.

It was my sister's job to charm her way into the Green Room—a roped-off area next to the stage exclusively for performers. We'd decided Elvis was the only one who could rub elbows with the celebrities without getting kicked out or raising suspicion. Once inside the ropes, she'd plant the dragon pin camera with a clear view of Misty LaVa's purse. All Misty had to do was take off her jewels when Thomas was watching, place them in her purse, and walk away.

"I can't believe we're doing a sting operation with Misty LaVa!" Miyon said. "And I thought this summer was going to be boring."

For the seventh time, I scanned the park for Declan. I hadn't seen him anywhere, even though he'd promised to keep an eye on Rondo. My parents and Thomas were at the swag table, sticking to my brother like Velcro. Mom and Dad had kicked into super-parent mode, handing out T-shirts and key chains to people passing by, while keeping Rondo between them like their lives depended on it. It had taken them long enough to get on board, but at least once they did, they were all in. It was a small relief, but all the standing around was making the circuits in my brain churn on overdrive.

Even if we did catch Thomas on video, it wasn't a guarantee we'd be able to nab him. He'd gotten away from the LA police sixteen times. What made us think we were better than that? And if he got away, what would he do to make sure Rondo didn't talk? We didn't have any idea what the Silk Bandit was capable of. I hadn't thought that through. What if he shoved Rondo in the trunk of his Tesla and drove away to Alaska or the tip of South America? It was possible that I'd put my brother in even more danger than he was already in.

My fingers were starting to twitch. I had to think about something else. Put my brain on autopilot. I rummaged in my bag and pulled out a Brushbot for Layne.

"That's cool," Miyon said. "What is it?"

"A mini bot," I said, handing it to her. "I made it with one of Dad's old electric razor motors. It doesn't do much but roam around, but Pico likes them."

"Nice." She touched the piece of foam I'd taped to the motor's shaft. "You unbalanced the motor so it'll vibrate."

"Yeah," I said, but all I could think about was Thomas Scott driving away in his Roadster getaway car.

"What's this for?" Miyon asked. She handed the Brushbot back to me and pointed to the electrical tape that I'd placed around one of the wires.

"I didn't have an on/off switch," I said. "So I rigged the tape to keep it from going off in my bag."

I removed the tape from the disconnected wire and froze.

"You look weird," Miyon said.

"The Tesla's an electric car. It has a safety disconnect!"

"A what?"

"It's a way to disconnect the auxiliary power. So you don't get electrocuted if you're helping someone in a crash."

The people in line shifted, jostling us, but they weren't moving forward. They were craning their necks toward the stage, trying to get a better view.

"I've got to find Dec," I said.

"Hold on!" Miyon picked up Layne and nodded toward the Green Room. Behind the velvet ropes, Misty LaVa had arrived with a crew of people. Her black hair was braided to match her Lhasa apso's, and her bright-orange dress had a built-in pocket for her beagle pup. His nose poked out and everyone within a hundred yards said, "Awww!"

Despite high-voltage currents of anxiety and adrenaline shooting through my veins, I managed to smile back at Miyon.

"Showtime," she said.

SAFETY DISCONNECT

Delphi had said the Green Room was supposed to be a place the performers could relax in private, but there was nothing private about it. We could all see Sharon Henderson and Newt hugging Misty while FiFi Khan's labradoodles and the Lhasa apso sniffed at each other. By the time Madeleine and Sir Bentley showed up with Elvis glued to Bentley's side, the whole park was watching the celebrities lounge on patio furniture like it was part of the show.

I don't know how my sister did it, but after less than two minutes of being the center of attention, hugging all the dogs, and doing windmill arms for Misty LaVa, the video feed on Miyon's phone stopped moving around. Elvis had planted the camera perfectly. Suddenly, we were looking at an inside view of the Green Room. Celebrities chatting, dogs sitting on cushions, and—front and center on the screen—Misty LaVa's purse on a glass table next to a vase of flowers.

Miyon and I huddled over her phone and watched as

Misty LaVa reached behind her neck and unlatched the most elaborate diamond necklace I've ever seen. Even on the tiny screen, I could see it glistening in the light. The sun practically made a *cha-ching* sound as it bounced off the jewels. And then, right on cue, the necklace disappeared into Misty's purse.

"Is he watching?" I asked.

Our whole plan hinged on Thomas Scott seeing Misty's display, but the line of people in front of us had shifted, and I couldn't see the swag booth anymore.

Miyon stood on her tiptoes. "Can't tell. But I think everyone's watching."

The line shifted a little more, and in the gap between two of the Pendleton cutouts, I could see Thomas Scott's Tesla, still parked behind one of the wooden labradoodles. Dec was letting Frank drink at a nearby canine fountain and scrolling on his phone.

"Be right back," I said.

Dec looked relieved to see me. "That Tesla's a 2008 for sure," he said. "I found the owner's manual online. The battery's in the trunk, and behind the battery is the . . ."

We said it at the same time: "Safety disconnect."

Dec grinned. "Mind-meld!"

It took about seven seconds before I realized our fatal flaw.

"How are we supposed to open the trunk?"

Dec smirked. "That guy loves to show off his Tesla. When you left, I asked him to give me the tour. He even popped the trunk so I could see the battery, and that's"—Dec put on a goofy grin—"when I *socked* it to him."

"*What?*" Dec might be braver than me, but he didn't have it in him to hit *anyone*, let alone a known criminal.

Dec waggled his eyebrows and pointed to his feet. He had both of his shoes on, but only one sock. I looked at the Tesla. A tiny piece of white fabric peeked out from the back of the trunk.

"It's not locked," Dec said. "I snuck my sock in there before he could close the trunk all the way. Get it? I *socked* it to him? Like, my sock?" As if I hadn't put the pieces together.

"Yeah, I get it," I said.

"Anyway, that's not the problem." Dec said. "It's the safety disconnect cable. I know how to find it, but I don't know how we're going to cut it."

I shifted my messenger bag and dug past the dog toys, Brushbots, extra motors, wires, and batteries until I found a pair of wire cutters. Dec's grin came back, full blast, until we argued about who was going to cut the cable.

"It won't take more than twenty-five seconds," Dec said. "You can do anything for twenty-five seconds."

I rolled my eyes. "That worked real well with Pico."

In fact, I knew exactly what Pico must feel like when his flight initiation response kicks in: like you're light-years away from safety; like you've got to get out of there. Fast. But it was *my* brother and *my* outlandish plan. It was up to me to take the risk.

"Now or never," Dec said. "I've got your back."

My legs felt like Jell-O as we walked slowly toward the convertible. Dec lifted the trunk and shoved his dangling sock in his pocket. The safety disconnect was behind the battery pack, near the passenger side wheel well.

"You're good," Dec said, keeping a lookout.

I took a breath and put my brain on autopilot. *Black 0, Brown 1, Red 2, Orange 3.* My hands shook as I slid the jaws of the wire-cutter around the cable. *Yellow 4, Green 5, Blue 6.* It was harder to get my muscles to work than I'd hoped. I used both my hands and squeezed as hard as I could. *Violet 7, Gray 8, White 9.*

The wires snapped. I could barely breathe. Dec helped me close the trunk as quietly as possible, then he picked up Frank and we sprinted toward the red carpet, feeling like astronauts who'd just landed on the moon.

When we caught up with Miyon and Layne, they were at the front of the line. Melissa led them toward a backdrop with a massive Dog Elegance logo. When she saw me, Dec, and Frank, she pulled us onto the red carpet and made us pose next to Miyon and her pup.

"I think we're good," Melissa whispered. "He's over there like Pooh Bear looking for honey. Boys, why are you so sweaty?"

Before we could answer, Mrs. Boone emerged from the crowd and ran toward us, hurling Pico into my arms. He was wearing a tuxedo shirt with a black bow tie. I had to admit, he looked pretty great.

"Get Pico in the photo!" Mrs. Boone said. "Epic, isn't this so FUN? Now, don't move, I'm going to go get Clive."

She rushed off into the crowd. In the half hour we'd stood in line, Paradiso Park had filled with more people and dogs than I'd ever seen in Carmelito.

Melissa adjusted Pico's bow tie, turned Frank's face toward the camera, and fluffed Layne's fur.

"Say cheese!" Delphi said, and snapped the photo. We started to move, but Miyon grabbed my arm.

"Um, guys . . ." She held up her phone. The screen was dark.

"Your phone died?" I asked. "Do you have a charger?"

Melissa checked the video feed on her laptop. "Mine's dark, too," she said. "There must be something wrong with the camera. You'd better go find Elvis."

Pico's ears lifted, and he wiggled in my arms.

"I'll tell Nicole you've got Pico," Delphi said. "Be cool over there. Act like you don't care about any of it. That always works."

We found a patch of grass near the Green Room where we could sit down and try to act cool. Like we were only there to watch Layne, Pico, and Frank sniff at each other. Elvis got the signal and barreled over to us, a satisfied grin on her face.

"Didn't I do great?" Elvis whispered. "Declan, did you see what a great job I did?"

"Where'd you put the camera, El?" I asked.

"The best spot! Right?"

"But where?"

Elvis rubbed Layne's belly and grinned. "It was easy peasy. There was a shawl hanging on a coatrack. In the exact perfect spot! No one even saw me . . . What?"

Miyon shook her head and nodded toward the Green Room.

"Is the shawl still there?" I asked.

Elvis stood up, and her smile disappeared.

RECONNAISSANCE

"Okay, Thomas!" Madeleine Devine stood up and hollered to him from her side of the Green Room. Louder than she needed to. "I've decided I want to talk to you."

Thomas glanced at a bouncer, who was guarding the velvet rope to the Green Room like he was a Secret Service agent protecting the leader of the free world, but Madeleine said, "Not *inside* the rope. You can walk around!"

Thomas Scott sighed but faked a cheery smile. He put his arm around Rondo's shoulder and pulled him away from the swag table. Mom and Dad tried their best to follow, but they were mobbed by people grabbing Sir Bentley and Pendleton Triplet merchandise as fast as they could hand it out.

Thomas practically tripped over Miyon as he and my brother walked toward the Green Room. Rondo locked eyes with me, and I shook my head. I couldn't eyeball-Morse-Code the fact that the camera was missing and if we couldn't catch

Thomas on video, our entire plan was dead in the water. Pico scrambled into my lap to get out of Thomas's way.

"What are you kids sitting here for?" Thomas muttered. "Go . . . do something useful."

"He's right," I said after he walked by. "We've got to do something."

"Reconnaissance," Dec said. "Sweep the area for the shawl."

I had to give it to Dec. He was focused. Once we'd filled him in on the details of the Misty LaVa sting operation, he hadn't checked his phone once.

"Let's walk around the Green Room," I said. "Maybe it fell. Elvis can go . . . I don't know . . . pet Bentley or something, and hang it back up."

We must have looked ridiculous: four kids and three dogs walking in slow motion past Thomas, Rondo, and Madeleine, trying to act like we could care less about anything around us. FiFi was sitting next to the coatrack, pretending to check her phone, but her eyes were on the velvet rope between Thomas and Madeleine. The Pendleton Triplets were asleep in a heap on a satin couch at her side. There was nothing on the coatrack. No shawl on the ground.

"Come on, baby," Thomas was saying in his schmoopy voice. "We've been planning this for ages. Think about it—tropical beaches, sunset swimming—I can't go without you."

"It's not a good time," Madeleine said. "I've got a meeting with the network, and to tell you the truth, I don't want to go to Cayman Island with you."

Rondo jerked his head around to catch my eye, and Dec kicked me in the shin. As if I hadn't heard.

"We'll change the ticket, sweet thing," Thomas said. "Where do you want to go? Switzerland? Switzerland would work for me."

"Thomas, you're not listening. I don't want to go with *you*."

FiFi put down her phone. She wasn't even pretending not to stare now. None of us were. Even the bouncer had lifted his sunglasses to the top of his head and was soaking it all in like it was his favorite soap opera. Thomas set his jaw, but kept up his *sugar-pie*, *honey-bunch* pleading.

"It's Asha," Elvis whispered. "She's wearing it."

I tore my attention away from Thomas Scott and turned toward Asha. She was on a lounge chair watching Madeleine. Her blood-red spike heels were propped up on the table next to Misty LaVa's purse. As usual, she looked like a movie star. With a thick pink shawl tossed around her neck and shoulders.

"I'll get it," I said. There wasn't much choice. Elvis's charms were powerless against Asha.

I picked up Pico, and he pressed his cold nose to my neck. "Come on, buddy," I said. "We've got this."

I'd managed to disable the Tesla, and I hadn't felt prepared for *that*, but somehow, Asha's lipsticked pout and spike heels seemed even more intimidating. Pico's ears perked up as we made our way past the distracted bouncer and ducked under the rope toward the back corner of the Green Room. *How badly could it go?*

GREEN ROOM

When I crossed under the velvet rope, I was exactly two steps from where I'd been standing before, but it felt like I'd entered a swanky living room.

"Hon, you're not supposed to be in here," Asha said as I stepped onto the bamboo floor. "Can I help you?"

"Well, yes. I was just . . . I mean, I hope if you . . . " I scratched Pico's ear to calm myself down. I had to pull it together. "My sister's pin," I said. "I think it got hooked to your shawl."

Asha lifted an eyebrow, but she set her phone on the table, stood up, and stretched. The shawl was draped around her like an elaborate cape, and as she started the process of unwrapping herself, I caught a glimpse of the dragon, hidden in one of the folds.

"There it is," I said. I shifted Pico onto my hip and rushed forward to unhook the pin.

That's when FiFi stood up and stamped her foot on the

Green Room floor so hard that the Pendleton Triplets woke up and tried to untangle themselves from each other. Pico whimpered, and I flinched, almost dropping the dragon pin.

"No means *no*, Thomas!" FiFi stepped past the Triplets and stood protectively next to Madeleine Devine. "You're not *listening* to her!"

Asha leaned toward me, an odd look on her face. She bent so close that I could smell her strong, fruity perfume.

"Let me see that."

Pico shoved his head into the crook of my elbow as she grabbed the pin from my hand.

"This isn't your sister's. This is one of Delphi's."

Asha held the pin closer, and her perfect, supermodel lips formed a perfect, supermodel O. *"I know what this is!"*

Before I could do anything about it, Asha threw the dragon camera on the bamboo floor and smashed it with her spike heel. She had incredible aim, splintering the camera into bits on the first try, but she stomped on it five extra times for good measure.

"Those. Girls. Almost. Ruined. Bentley."

FiFi, Madeleine, and Thomas stopped fighting. The bouncer dropped his sunglasses back onto his face and turned his attention toward me. Elvis, Dec, and Miyon rushed to the velvet rope, and all the dogs sat up, awake and ears alert.

"Asha!" Madeleine said. "What on earth?"

Asha was furious. She glared at me and waved her hands in the air. "They're all in cahoots!" she said. "They've been *filming* everything! And *lying* about Bentley on their blasted blog!"

Thomas Scott and I locked eyes, and I could feel Pico's heart thumping against my chest. Or maybe that was *my* heart. The stare was practically electrical. I got the distinct feeling that if he could zap me with a bolt of lightning, he would. Then Thomas swiveled his head toward the swag tent. Mom and Dad had left their post. The table was unattended, and people were stuffing their bags with handfuls of key-chains, T-shirts, and mugs.

Thomas's gaze went back to the crushed camera, the Green Room bouncer, and to Miyon, Dec, and Elvis, who were shooting me terrified looks. He scanned the rest of the park, and I did, too. There were two cops hanging out at Barker Bisson's, and a third checking his phone next to the stage. Mom, Dad, and Luis were on the other end of the park, leaving Flo's booth and heading our way.

"Okay, I get it," Thomas said, sadly. His voice was all sweet, and he gave Madeleine a kissy pout. "If you don't want to come, you don't want to come. Asha, you want help cleaning that up?"

He grabbed my brother by the arm, ducked under the velvet rope, and stepped past Madeleine and FiFi toward the mess. Rondo was still gripping his *Sherlock Holmes* book, and almost took a header as Thomas dragged him across the Green Room.

"Oh, poor Bentley." Thomas leaned over Sir Bentley's couch. His voice was dripping with kindness. "She got a scratch, but I've got first aid in my car. Come on, pal. We'll get you fixed up."

"I'll take care of that," Madeleine said, but Thomas looked heartbroken.

"Let me do *one* nice thing before I go," he said, reaching for Sir Bentley's leash. He sounded so sad and genuine I almost felt sorry for him. Except that his grip on Rondo's wrist was making my brother grimace, and there wasn't a single scratch on that dog. Thomas had a Plan B. He was going to take Sir Bentley to the airport himself. Was he planning to take Rondo, too?

"No!" Elvis ducked under the rope and rushed to Sir Bentley's side, but Thomas's foot got in her way, and she tripped, sprawling headfirst onto the bamboo floor.

Thomas let go of Rondo's wrist and reached down to help her up. "Sweetie," he said, all concerned. "You could have gotten *seriously hurt*. Let the grown-ups take care of things, okay?"

He hovered over Elvis, one hand wrapped around Sir Bentley's leash, the other reaching toward my sister. As I stepped close to help her, Pico let out a low, angry growl. I could barely hang on to him as he stretched out his neck, shook his propeller ears, and sunk his teeth into the back of Thomas Scott's hand.

Thomas yelped and let go of my sister so he could take a swing at Pico. I hugged Pico close and tried to dodge out of the way, but a small, fluffy labradoodle was behind my left foot. The next five seconds were like that moment when you're losing your balance on a surfboard. You can feel the wave throwing you down and the water crashing in on all sides. All you can do is flail your arms and try to figure out which way is up.

Pico and I fell backward as Elvis screamed. Or maybe that was *my* scream.

SILK BANDIT

I managed to hang on to Pico until I hit the ground. But when my butt slammed onto the bamboo floor, scattering pieces of what was left of Delphi's pin, I could feel the Iggy slide out of my arms. Before I had time to grab his leash, it disappeared from view.

"We'll catch him, Epic!" Miyon yelled. She and Dec ran after Pico with Layne and Frank in tow.

Rondo and El were at my side, and the Green Room bouncer was standing over me, frowning at all of us.

"I'm going to have to ask all y'all to leave," he said, flexing his gigantic bodybuilder muscles. "And I don't know what you think you're doing, sir, but I'd stop that right now." He took a threatening step toward Thomas, who was unhooking Sir Bentley's jeweled collar. Madeleine waved him off.

"It's his collar," she said. "Let him have it. As long as he leaves, I don't care."

"Whatever you say, ma'am." The bouncer gave Thomas

another long look, but let him slip the collar into his vest pocket.

"They're not his jewels—" Elvis started, but a man's voice boomed through the speakers above our heads.

"Testing. Testing. One, two, three."

Asha almost jumped out of her spiky heels.

"They're doing the sound check! That's our cue," she said to FiFi and Madeleine. "The show's going to start in five minutes!"

I stood up and adjusted my messenger bag. The show? Who cared about the show? But Asha started brushing Sir Bentley's fur like her life depended on it. Madeleine whipped out a stick of lipstick and ran toward the mirror hanging on the side of the stage.

I craned my neck, searching the park for Luis and my parents, but I couldn't see them through the thick crowd that was gathering in front of the stage. People pressed in on one another, vying for the best view of Misty LaVa and her rescue dogs.

The crowd closest to the Green Room was laughing and pointing in our direction. If they'd noticed any of the drama, they seemed to think it was normal celebrity behavior. Besides, every one of them was distracted by puppies. The labradoodles had scattered to three different corners, and one of them had managed to get its head stuck under a throw rug.

FiFi grabbed the bouncer by his thick forearm.

"Forget about this loser," she said. "I need your help rounding up the Triplets."

"You sure?" the bouncer asked Madeleine, who barely glanced away from the mirror.

"That's fine," she said, blotting her lips with a tissue. "Goodbye, Thomas. Good luck living your best life."

Rondo and El looked at me. I hoped Miyon and Dec had caught Pico and were getting help. Because none of the adults had a clue. They were going to let Thomas Scott walk away. Free to go. He patted his pocket and smirked as the bouncer and the women gathered the celebrity dogs and ushered them backstage.

The crowd who'd been watching POO shifted their attention to the stage, where an announcer was talking about bathrooms and sponsors. Everyone was waiting for the dogs to come on.

I stared as the last tail disappeared behind a black curtain. They left us. Alone.

"*You three.*" Thomas whispered it, and smiled for any onlookers who might be watching us instead of the show, but his voice was so angry it felt like a slap in the face. "Sit. Down."

He motioned toward a silk-cushioned couch and stepped toward us until we sat, side by side. El's eyes got watery, and Rondo clutched his book to his chest. I sat on the edge of my seat, ready to yell my head off if Thomas tried anything on either of them. The thought of him tripping my sister and getting ready to kidnap my brother gave me a power boost I didn't know I was capable of. I felt like suddenly I was paddling out to the big waves full-speed ahead and I didn't care how hard I might get pummeled.

"We know everything!" I said. "About Chloe Cosmo, and . . . that . . . other actress . . ."

"Shaunté Stevens." Rondo's voice trembled. Thomas's glare was so intense I could tell he wanted to stomp us into bits. I didn't care. I kept talking.

"We know you forced Rondo to confess to a crime he didn't commit!" I said.

A tear slipped down Elvis's cheek.

"If you think"—Thomas leaned close so we could hear every word—"that I am going to let three brats stop me after I've outwitted the best detectives in Los Angeles . . ." He paused to chuckle. "Well, it's not worth wasting my breath on."

He turned to Rondo and pierced him with his eyes. "I meant what I said last night," he hissed. "If you care about your family—your smart-aleck brother and your insipid little sister—you are going to do exactly as I say. You're going to sit here until I am out of this park. And you are going to forget I exist. Because I will *never* forget about you. Got that?"

Rondo winced, but he nodded.

"I'd like to hear that in the affirmative," Thomas said.

"Yes, sir." I'd never heard my brother's voice sound so small.

Then Thomas stood up to his full height. He smoothed out his tropical-patterned vest and adjusted a button.

"Also," he said, "thanks for the parting gift. It's the perfect addition to my collection."

Thomas turned, walked slowly out of the Green Room, and disappeared into the crowd.

The minute he was out of sight, I jumped up and grabbed Misty LaVa's purse off the table. The bag felt light. Empty, even.

Which made sense, because when I opened it, the only thing inside was a silk handkerchief.

KINETIC ART

"Come on," I said, taking El by the hand. Tears streaked her face.

"We can't go anywhere," she said. "You heard him. If we leave, he's going to . . . We don't even *know* what he's going to do."

"It's okay, El," I said. I showed her Misty LaVa's purse. "This is evidence. We've got to bring it to Luis."

"And this," Rondo said. He opened up *Sherlock Holmes* and pressed the stop button on Miyon's Walkman.

"You got it?" El asked. "You got the confession?"

Rondo pushed his hair out of his face and acted like he'd never been scared. Like he'd had it all under control the whole time.

"Of course I did," he said. "I started recording the minute he tripped El. That was dogged up. That dude's going to *jail*."

Elvis sniffed and cracked a smile. "Dogged up," she said. "This whole week was doggy."

We ducked under the velvet rope and pushed our way through the mass of people and dogs. As we got farther from the stage, the crowd thinned and we could see the red carpet lined with the three giant Pendleton cutouts and the Tesla convertible parked behind it. Thomas was trying to open the driver's side door with the touch pad.

Rondo sucked in his breath.

"Don't worry," I said. "The car's not going anywhere."

Thomas tried the door a few more times, and when he couldn't get it open, he jumped right over the side of the convertible, landing in the seat like he'd been training his whole life to be a stunt man in an action film. Only, instead of peeling out for a high-speed car chase scene, Thomas didn't go anywhere. He sat in the Roadster and tapped furiously on the control panel.

"There's Luis!" Elvis said.

Luis, Mom, and Dad were approaching the Tesla with two other cops behind them. A third cop was stationed at the canine water fountain. Delphi was at his side taking photos while Melissa scribbled furiously into a notebook.

We caught up to them just as Luis was asking Thomas to get out of the car. Thomas Scott shot them all a flashy smile and honestly looked like he was glad to see everyone.

"We've got the confession!" Elvis yelled. "And Epic has the evidence!"

Thomas chuckled and winked at Mom. "You've sure got

imaginative kids," he said. "Not surprising, with a talented artist like you in the house. My friend Calla is going to *love* to meet you."

The Silk Bandit was slick. Calm and happy. Relaxed. He was so good at lying, I almost doubted I was holding Misty LaVa's empty purse in my hand.

He turned his charm on Luis. "Thanks again for your help this week, Sergeant. I'm glad it was all a mix-up. Probably the most exciting crime that's ever happened in your little town, don't you think?"

He laughed again, but his smile faded as a cop car pulled off of Paradiso Parkway and screeched to a halt behind the Tesla. The sound of the rubber wheels sliding on the pavement sounded exactly like the Screambot I'd made for Pico. Somewhere nearby, I heard an Italian greyhound howl.

Two more policemen got out of the cruiser. Thomas tried his ignition again, but when the Roadster wouldn't start, he slammed his hand on the steering wheel and looked around for another escape. I looked around, too. Something odd was happening. All around us, the park was dissolving into chaos. Pico's howl had set off a chain reaction, and every dog in Paradiso Park began to howl, bark, yap, and growl.

I spotted Dec and Miyon running toward the giant labradoodle cutouts. Miyon had Pico tucked into the crook of her arm and they were chasing Frank, who'd gotten free from his leash. He was going berserk, jumping over the beams that propped up the wooden Pendletons. I sucked in my breath. The beams looked like giant Popsicle sticks. Filled with potential energy.

With everyone distracted, no one was watching Thomas Scott. Out of the corner of my eye, I saw him slide to the passenger seat of the Tesla. He reached for the door handle, ready to make a break for it. I thought of the sixteen other times he'd escaped the police.

Not today.

"Miyon! Dec!" I yelled, and ran toward the closest wooden labradoodle. Pico caught my eye and instantly howled his heart out, looking all classy in his tuxedo and bow tie.

As soon as I got behind the cutout and threw my weight into it, Miyon and Dec did the same. A messy-haired kid with a brown Lab—Dec's soccer friend—slammed his shoulder hard into the wood next to me, and the gigantic Pendleton looming over our heads started to sway. We scattered as all three Godzilla labradoodles creaked, buckled, and fell away from the red carpet like the world's largest dominoes. Thomas barely had time to duck down before the first plywood puppy landed squarely on the convertible, slammed down like a lid, and locked him inside.

For a nanosecond, the entire park was silent.

Dogs stopped barking.

People stopped shouting.

Everyone stood still and looked at the fallen labradoodles, without a clue that there was a Silk Bandit trapped under one of them.

Even Elvis brought her voice down to a whisper. "That was *great* kinetic art," she said.

But a nanosecond isn't very long.

"Hello, everybody!"

A microphone screeched onstage, Asha flashed her superstar smile at the crowd, and the whole audience swiveled their heads back toward her. Madeleine and FiFi stood on either side of Asha, with DJ Doggone, Misty LaVa, Sharon Henderson, and a whole band behind them.

Newt balanced happily on Sharon's guitar as if nothing bad had ever come of that plan.

Sir Bentley was front and center, picture-perfect, posing like a pro.

And, of course, the Pendleton Triplets, extra fluffy, stood at adorable attention.

Which meant almost nobody watched as Luis and his guys pulled the Silk Bandit out of his Tesla trap and cuffed his hands behind his back. Nobody saw Rondo hand over the confession tape, or Mom and Dad hugging us all like they thought they'd never see us again.

Instead, everyone watched DJ Doggone throw his fist in the air. The band started to play, and Sharon Henderson and Misty LaVa began singing their next multiplatinum hit: a dance version of "Hound Dog."

Even Elvis pried her eyes away from Thomas Scott angrily getting loaded into the back seat of a police car.

"That's my song!" she said, and kicked in a massive series of windmill arms.

Onstage, Asha leaned over the mic and yelled over the thumping drums.

"Let's give it up . . . for America's Number One Dog-Friendly Town!"

The crowd went wild.

FUREVER FRIENDS

"I can't believe Pico's letting you walk him," I said. "We calculated it was going to take us all summer to get him ready for strangers."

Miyon grinned as Pico let her lead him down Main Street with me, my siblings, Dec, and Carlos following behind.

"Did you factor in the coefficient of how awesome I am?" she asked.

I rolled my eyes. "No. But maybe I was overthinking it." Not maybe. Definitely. To be honest, I'd been kind of sad when Delphi had an easy time walking Pico—like he was going to forget me or learn to like someone else better. But now I was just glad he wasn't stressed out. He seemed happy and chill.

"Maybe Pico's growing up," El said. "Or maybe it's because I picked the perfect tattoo for him!"

She was still dancing, and she blew an air-kiss in Pico's direction.

During El's song, the police car had driven away with

Thomas, and we'd told Luis everything we knew. Then Mom and Dad started filling out a ton of paperwork, and even Rondo agreed that the adults could handle the Silk Bandit from there. I was exhausted. Light-headed. My lack of sleep and the stress of the whole week were starting to sink in like an aftershock. All I wanted to do was get some sand under my feet, play Screambot with Pico, and run around in the waves. So we'd stopped by the Perro to pick up swimsuits, and our whole crew headed for the beach.

It was strange how quiet and deserted Main Street felt after all the chaos in Paradiso Park. We didn't pass a single person or dog on the sidewalk. For a while, none of us said a word, not even Elvis. We walked and listened to DJ Doggone's beats grow fainter in the background.

"I can't believe we had a criminal in our house," I said, breaking the silence.

"Yeah, but we caught the Silk Bandit," Rondo said. "Do you realize how huge this is?"

"It's ginormous!" Elvis gave a little hop and started to hiccup. "We're going to be celebrities. Celebrity—*hic*—detectives! Everyone's going to want to—*hic*—hire us. And Mom and Dad are so proud! They'll—*hic*—HAVE to get me a new dog! I'm going to name her—*hic*—Yoda Two!"

Rondo and El high-fived and skipped ahead, talking about what they would say in news interviews about how Rondo narrowly escaped death with the help of his crack detective team.

When the dogs stopped to drink at a canine water fountain, I closed my eyes and splashed some of the water on my face. It almost didn't seem real. Like maybe none of it had really happened. Any minute now, I'd wake up and everything—the Silk Bandit, the celebrity dogs, Dec's soccer career, even the fact that the girl in the green swimsuit was hanging out with us—would turn out to be one long ridiculous dream.

But when I opened my eyes, Miyon was still standing next to me, and Dec and Carlos were taking a selfie with Frank.

"So," Miyon said. "Week one is over . . . What are we going to do for the *rest* of the summer?"

"Dec said you guys like Stratego?" Carlos asked. He actually seemed nice. His hair looked like he'd just rolled out of bed, and I respected that. "I've got a four-player board at home, but my brothers won't play with me anymore. Apparently, high school makes you too cool for games."

Dec and I grinned. I knew we were both thinking of all the new, complex strategies you'd get to develop if *four* players were involved. We looked at Miyon.

"Sure, I'm in," she said. "Also, there's the Central California Surf Dog championship. Want to help me train Layne?"

I grinned again. Maybe this was what life was going to be like now: dog surfing; four-person strategy games; fighting crime.

"Yes," I said. "And we could build some stuff. I want to

make a solar-powered bot with the components from Dad's old garden lights."

"I've got a remote control," Miyon said. "We could make the bot wireless!"

"You guys should join our robotics team at school," Carlos said. "We could use a few new people."

Dec waggled his eyebrows at me. Like he was telepathically sending me his lecture about *new opportunities.* Maybe he had a point. A robotics team was definitely something we didn't have at Sunny Day.

Rondo and El had paused outside the window of Furever Friends, where they were arguing over which shirts had the funniest dog puns. Rondo liked the wiener dog lounging inside a bun with the speech bubble HOLD THE RELISH. And El liked LIFE IS RUFF, but I'm pretty sure it was only because the shirt featured a Saint Bernard puppy.

"I like this one," Miyon said, pointing to a yellow tee that read LIFE GOAL: PET ALL THE PUPPIES.

Everyone had an opinion, and as the debate raged on, I reached down and picked up Pico. He was so happy to be held that he wriggled his tail and stuck his propeller ears straight out. His tuxedo was rumpled, and his rhinestone tattoo was wearing off. But he was calm. As calm as an Iggy gets, anyway.

I rubbed Pico's ear and tried to telepathically send him some messages. Who knew? Maybe he'd like animal acting.

Just because it was new didn't mean it wasn't going to be interesting—or fun, even. I tried to tell him to be brave and trust his instincts. Even if some things had to change, he knew how to make sure the important parts of the equation would always stay the same. Friends. Family. Loyalty. Love.

"I like the store logo best," I said. "Furever Friends."

"Yeah," Dec said. "That's a good one."

"Dog race to the water?" Miyon asked. She let out Layne's lead and drew an invisible line on the sidewalk with her toe.

Pico's tail wag went into overdrive as I set him on the starting line next to Frank and Carlos's dog, Comet.

Rondo held his towel in the air like a starting flag.

"Okay, crew!" Elvis yelled. "On your marks . . . get set . . ."

Pico pulled at his leash, and I got up on my toes. With my friends and my siblings at my side, I actually felt ready. To rocket forward. Toward new adventures, challenges, and world-changing responsibilities.

"GO!"

TWO MONTHS LATER

Big Heroes in Small Packages
posted by @pooperscooper1

Good morning, good readers. We're writing to you today from a top secret location in a land far, far away. We can't reveal exactly where on *Earth* we are, but we can tell you that our view looks an awful lot like a pup-populated Tatooine.

That's right, folks, we are fully embedded *ON LOCATION* with The Pendleton Trilogy. The first day of shooting starts tomorrow and, oh-my-mother, these Pendleton cuties are killing it in rehearsal. For real. Olivia took down a storm trooper with her bare paws twenty minutes ago.

Speaking of killing it, do you remember the pint-sized hero of that Carmelito Caper back in June? Trust us. Every dog has its day, but this is *not* the last you are going to hear of Pico Boone. Reliable sources have confirmed that the irresistible Iggy has signed a two-year contract with Houndstooth Haberdashery to headline their new advertising campaign for small dogs. They've even named their new line of diminutive headwear Pico for Pups.

This is a big get for a little dog from Carmelito, and it's only the tip of the tail. You've all heard the rumors of a *Bentley Knows* reboot, right? Well. We're not saying it's happening, but could a plucky Pico-sized sidekick be exactly the shot in the arm that tired show needs? All we're saying is, you heard it here first!

One last note:

Ever since we broke the story about Pico and that sly dog Thomas Scott (aka Silk Bandit aka smarmy Fake CEO of Chow Chow Enterprises), we've been getting bucketloads of fan mail from our dear readers. We'd like to say thank you and give a piece of advice to those of you who have expressed interest in learning to write, blog, and investigate canine-related fashion, culture, and crime. Our advice is simple:

Follow your curiosity. We double-dog dare you.

#dogdish #pendletontrilogy #picoforpresident

Sponsored by: Houndstooth Haberdashery, Lucasfilms Canine Division, AAA Animal Acting Agency, BooneyTunes Incorporated

ACKNOWLEDGMENTS

I had the brain spark for *A Dog-Friendly Town* when Aunt Joey and Uncle Jim told me that Carmel, California, had won *Dog Fancy Magazine*'s coveted Dog Town USA award. And when I learned that Carmel's famous dog-friendly Cypress Inn was co-owned by Doris Day (a movie star, singer, and animal activist I adored), the spark grew into a full-blown Outlandish Idea!

I wrote this book mainly to make my husband, Kevin, laugh, and to give him some dogs to hang out with since we can't have one in the house. He named Pico and helped me tinker with plot details small and large. He watched episodes of *Dogs With Jobs* with me, speculated about Pawscar nominations, and helped this Wisconsin girl understand what it was like to grow up in sunny California. I am so grateful for his deep sense of story structure and his goofy sense of humor. Kevin's influence is everywhere in this book.

Like Epic, I am super lucky to have siblings who always have my back. While writing this book, each one of my five sibs lent their invaluable help and expertise. Steph made sure I had beautiful, comfy places to write. Ali gave me feedback on the logistics of Dog Elegance event planning and publicity. Alan gave me tinkering ideas, tested out cobra stick bombs, and helped me come up with countless ways to find circuit components around the house. (Need a button cell battery? Try a singing birthday card! A 9-volt motor? Take apart an old electric razor!) Getting real-time texts from him while he read the manuscript was one of the highlights of my year (happy fortieth, bro!). Anna read unfinished drafts with absurd, bullet-point endings and helped me work through key plot points. Bethye coordinated an online coworking room to keep us all motivated, then entertained us with pawfully perfect dog puns in our chat room breaks. Clearly, writing a book is a family affair!

Special thanks to: "Lieutenant" Danyon Phalin for always being on call for missing-dog-collar police procedure questions; Kerry Ann Collins for veterinary advice (even though the clinic scene got cut in the end); Carol Martin, Ann Braden, Reba Richardson, and Saya Chu-Shore for reading; and Michele, Jim, Jennifer, and Rick for helping me celebrate every step of the journey. Resources I consulted constantly: *Bark Magazine, Make Magazine, The Right Way to Do Wrong* by Harry Houdini, and *Animal Stars: Behind the Scenes of Your Favorite Animal Actors* by Robin Ganzert with Allen and Linda Anderson.

An enthusiastic tail wag to my agent, John Cusick, and editor, Grace Kendall. Their insights, support, and encouragement helped me keep digging even when I didn't think it could be done. Thank you to the smart, enthusiastic teams at Folio Jr. and FSG/Macmillan who worked hard to bring *A Dog-Friendly Town* into the world, especially: Elizabeth Lee, Brittany Pearlman, Melissa Zar, Shivani Annirood, Cassie Gonzales, and Hayley Jozwiak. And to Xindi Yan for bringing dogalicious joy and energy to the illustrations and cover art!

Lastly, a shout-out to my childhood dog, Trixie, who truly was a kid's best friend. She was always there to cheer me up when I had a bad day, at my side for every forest adventure, and kept me in snuggles and good company on the gazillion days when I was home with bronchitis (which, as it turns out, was often triggered by my allergies to cats and dogs . . . Who knew?). Of all the dogs I've ever known, real and imaginary, Trixie is still #1.